VICIOUS OATH
IVANOV CRIME FAMILY, BOOK TWO

ZOE BLAKE

Poison Ink Publications

CONTENTS

Chapter 1	1
Chapter 2	10
Chapter 3	20
Chapter 4	31
Chapter 5	38
Chapter 6	48
Chapter 7	62
Chapter 8	72
Chapter 9	79
Chapter 10	90
Chapter 11	99
Chapter 12	104
Chapter 13	107
Chapter 14	117
Chapter 15	123
Chapter 16	134
Chapter 17	141
Chapter 18	145
Chapter 19	147
Chapter 20	156
Chapter 21	165
Chapter 22	175
Chapter 23	186
Chapter 24	191
Chapter 25	201
Chapter 26	206
Chapter 27	214
Chapter 28	225
Chapter 29	233
Chapter 30	240
Chapter 31	251

Chapter 32	260
Chapter 33	270
Chapter 34	277
Chapter 35	282
Chapter 36	285
Chapter 37	293
Chapter 38	299
Epilogue	307
About Zoe Blake	309
Also by Zoe Blake	311

Copyright © 2021 by Zoe Blake

All rights reserved.

No part of this book may be reproduced in any form or by any electronic or mechanical means, including information storage and retrieval systems, without written permission from the author, except for the use of brief quotations in a book review.

Cover Design by Dark City Designs
Photographer: James Critchley

CHAPTER 1

Damien
Washington, D.C.

SHE KNEW I was watching her.

Like an innocent creature in the woods who sensed danger nearby, her body reacted to the force of my gaze. Only the trained eye of a hunter could pick up the signs. There was the slight tensing of her shoulders. The way her head tilted in my direction but didn't fully turn. Her hand self-consciously rose to cover her heart as if her palm could smother the sudden rapid beating.

She angled her head a little further as she swept a thick golden curl behind her ear. I could just see the high curve of her flushed cheek as she trained her gaze downward, no doubt trying to catch a secretive glimpse of me from under her soot-black lashes. Her pink tongue flicked out to lick her lips. The champagne light from the chandelier suspended above picked up on the faint shimmer left behind.

Balls of ice clattered then settled in my glass as I tipped the smooth, amber liquid past my lips. The Macallan Rare single-malt scotch might as well have been rotgut whiskey for all I tasted it. The smoky vanilla and clove tones of the liquor did nothing to soothe my anger or cool my rising lust. Placing the now empty glass on the silver tray of a passing catering server, I crossed my arms over my chest as I leaned against the doorjamb.

The little minx was now doing her best to ignore me.

Her head was thrown back, and even over the annoying din of the surrounding party guests, the sound of her laughter reached me. It was too high-pitched and hollow as if she were forcing the sound past stiff, nervous lips. Some asshole in a cheap off-the-rack suit grabbed her hand and pulled her onto the makeshift dance floor set up in my parents' spacious living room.

I didn't recognize him but then I didn't know many of the guests. I suspected neither did my little sister, Nadia, despite it being her eighteenth birthday party. Many would be high-profile businessmen with their wives as well as the occasional politician or policy maker. These were the people my family associated with in the light of day to help keep up the veneer of legitimacy.

My job in the Ivanov family was to associate with the types who only crawled out of their holes in the dead of night. I kept to the corners of fine society. Dark corners for doing dark deeds. It was how I had earned the moniker Demon Damien. If I showed up on someone's doorstep, there were no more second chances. It was game over.

I nodded a greeting to my brother Gregor. He stopped a server and gave them some quick instruction before approaching. Despite being separated by several years, we were thick as thieves, always had been. We stood silently surveying the crowd. The same server approached with an old-fashioned glass filled with clear liquid, only one small cube of ice. No doubt Stoli Elit, his favorite vodka. Although Russian to my very core, I never developed a taste for the stuff, preferring the rich malty flavor of scotch instead.

Gregor nodded toward the server. "You need another?"

I trained my gaze back on *her*.

The DJ was playing *I'm on Fire* by Bruce Springsteen.

Hey little girl is your daddy home; did he go and leave you all alone...

Ignoring her dance partner, her body swayed to the soft, somnolent beat. Each curve hugged by crushed pink velvet, the dress slinking all the way down to her ankles. No doubt a designer dress she'd stolen from some boutique. She turned her back on me and shifted her hips from side to side. The velvet fabric caught snatches of light, illuminating the gentle swell of her ass. Her slender arms rose and slipped under her thick curtain of hair, raising the long length to expose the vulnerable pale skin of her neck. I could just make out the image of a small pink heart tattooed in the center. Irrational anger twisted in my stomach at the thought of another man touching her in such an intimate place, even if it was only with a tattoo needle.

Fuck.

I shifted my stance, trying to ease the increasingly pleasurable pain below my belt.

The little minx was toying with me. Foolishly thinking this crowded house full of guests would protect her.

She played with fire.

Knowing I had better at least be mostly sober for the fight that was brewing between me and her, I shook my head and waved the server away.

The man she was dancing with placed his hand on her hip, and I stiffened. Fortunately — for both of them — she swayed in the opposite direction, dislodging his grasp. She did it so effortlessly there wasn't a doubt in my mind she had had plenty of practice dodging unwanted grabs. My jaw clenched so hard I swore my back teeth cracked. I took a deep breath through my nose, forcing myself to remain calm.

"His name is Pavel Rasskovich," offered Gregor. I didn't even bother to pretend to not know what he was talking about. "A low-level thug for the Novikoffs. He's here as a bodyguard for one of the useless brothers."

If he touched her again, he was a dead man.

I had no right to feel so possessive toward her. No right at all.

In fact, it was practically criminal. The girl was barely eighteen to my twenty-seven years.

Yelena Nikitina, my little sister's best friend… and the very definition of trouble.

Stubborn and untamed, her father had let her run wild

since her mother's death with virtually no supervision or discipline.

There was the time eight years ago I'd caught her stealing a few silly makeup items from a local store. I had been home from college for the weekend. Her mother had just died, if I recall. She fought me like a wildcat when I snatched her by the arm after witnessing her pocketing the stolen loot. Her arm was so thin, I was worried I would break a bone if I squeezed too hard. She looked so small and vulnerable, but those big blue eyes still shone bright with defiance. Ignoring her protests, I had dragged her to the McDonald's next door and bought her a Happy Meal.

She ate every bite as if it were her last meal. Or more accurately… her first.

It had made me sick to think that may have been the only half-way decent meal she had had in days. I'd made a mental note to have my parents speak with her father. He was a low-life hanger-on who occasionally did small jobs for my family. The sort of stuff we wouldn't dirty our hands with. True to her nature, she'd stared me down the entire time, refusing to utter even a single word. She did, however, slip the small Hello Kitty toy that came with the meal into her pocket when she thought I wasn't looking.

As I came back to the present, the same sick feeling twisted in my gut, but this time it was guilt. I'd spoken with my mother about Yelena's welfare but that was as far as I'd taken it. Shortly after, Gregor got into that mess at his college and was shipped off to St. Petersburg. My life became more complicated with him gone. It was no excuse; simply the hard truth.

Still, I should have made sure my parents took an interest and looked after her.

I wasn't technically responsible for her welfare but that wasn't how I saw it.

I had let her down, abandoned her to the sloppy care of that piece of shit she called a father.

And now that little girl with the big blue eyes had grown into a woman — a young, still naive one — but nevertheless a woman.

And now she was in trouble — real trouble.

This time, I wouldn't be able to pay off a simple shopkeeper and threaten him not to call the police.

She had gotten herself in deep with some ruthless people so dirty even *my* family refused to work with them.

Her only hope was for me to do what I should have done years ago.

I would let it be known she was under my protection.

I wasn't sure even that would be enough to save her, but I'd be damned if I'd let her down again.

I would get her out of this mess and then send her far away. I'd lock her up in some European college where she would be safe from her own mistakes.

And from me.

There was no denying it. I wanted her, badly. My gaze hardened as I watched her body sway to the next song. Jealous of every undeserving man in the room who was witnessing her display. A display I was certain was done purely to antagonize me. I couldn't say why. It wasn't like I had spoken a word to her or even seen her in years. Just somehow, I knew she was as aware of me as I was of her. I could feel it, even across this distracting sea of chattering guests. A primal clash of wills.

Her soft hair fell in waves down her back. I itched to wrap the long locks around my fist as I claimed those full lips. I could practically feel the warmth of her skin and ached to inhale her scent as I crushed her to my chest. I needed to know if her eyes changed color when she was aroused. Would they become a deeper sapphire blue?

Clearing my throat, I forced myself to look away.

Christ.

She was my little sister's friend and barely an adult.

This was wrong.

If I was truly going to save her, then it had to also be from myself. While I might be a better man than her father, it was only by a few degrees.

My life revolved around blood money. Selling arms to the highest bidder with no thought to who or what that man or country may be and not having the slightest care regarding their intentions. I wasn't the one pulling the trigger, so I didn't give a damn what they did with the guns I sold them. I never had a choice about entering the family business so there was no point in being morally judgmental about it. It was better to accept it and move on; after all, family was family, and they came first.

I didn't have a choice, but I would make sure Yelena did.

She wasn't like us. Her family didn't have an empire to protect. She could escape this life if she chose. And even if she didn't choose, I was choosing for her. She deserved better. I had the money to buy her a decent life... one away from me and all this violence and bullshit.

Glancing at my brother, I asked, "Have you seen Samara yet?"

He shook his head.

Speaking of family bullshit, my brother was being forced into an arranged marriage with our little sister's other close friend, Samara Federova. Unlike Yelena, Samara's family did have an empire. *One they sold her to protect.* It wasn't my brother's idea. It had been our father's dying wish, one Gregor would see through no matter his feelings on the subject. His unenviable responsibility as the eldest son. Family was family. The millions Samara's father demanded for her hand in marriage was paltry compared to the business and diplomatic connections we would receive once the Ivanov family was joined in marriage to the Federovs.

Gregor reached into his pocket and pulled out a Regius Double Corona cigar. They were the finest cigars in the world. Like me, he always demanded the best. It was part of the golden handcuffs which kept us tethered to this lifestyle. The luxury our ill-gotten gains afforded us had a rather seductive pull.

"I'm going to escape out the back and have a smoke. You coming?"

I shook my head.

Gregor followed my gaze as I once more watched Yelena on the dance floor. "When are you going to take care of that little situation we learned about today?"

Gregor was of course aware of the trouble Yelena had caused a few days ago. He had planned to handle the situation himself, but I insisted on taking ownership of the problem.

Just because I was forcing myself not to touch her — to claim her for my own — didn't mean she wasn't mine. In some strange way, I felt responsible for her. Her problems were my problems. "Soon."

Gregor nodded as he took another sip of his drink. Laying it on a nearby tray, he nodded to me again and slipped through the crowd.

I returned my attention to Yelena.

Another man in a cheap suit had grabbed her from behind, wrapping his fat arms around her slim middle.

All my previous good intentions were gone.

Forgotten.

Fuck my good intentions.

Someone with my black soul had no business having good intentions anyway.

Yelena was mine and right now that asshole was touching her, which meant he had to die.

I stormed toward the dance floor... and her.

CHAPTER 2

Yelena

IN HORROR, I watched Damien Ivanov as he shoved through the crowd, barreling toward me. The look in his dark eyes would surely have burned me to ashes. Choking on my panicked indrawn breath, I turned to run but the unwanted arms around my waist held tight.

"Let go!"

The man slurred something in Russian I didn't understand.

The only thing Russian about me was my name. My mother had married some Russian thug after my father split while she was pregnant with me. The only thing my stepfather had ever given me was his surname. *Oh, and plenty of bruises.*

Digging my nails into the backs of his hands, I tried to claw my way free. The man only held me tighter as he continued to drunkenly babble. The pressure on my ribcage increased, cutting off my air. His stale beer and sauerkraut breath made me want to retch. I could feel the disgusting press of his heavy gut, and something else, against my lower back. Technically, I wasn't in any real danger, except for possibly vomiting all over the Miu Miu designer dress I had taken great pains to steal just for this party. We were on a crowded dance floor; all I had to do was cry out and I'd be rescued, but I was loathe to draw that much attention to myself.

Shoving my hair away from my face, I looked up but could no longer see Damien.

Maybe I had been wrong. Well, I knew I had been wrong about a lot of things, but maybe I needed to add Damien's sudden interest to the pile.

I could have sworn he had been watching me earlier.

I hadn't seen him in years, and even before that, I'd avoided coming over to Nadia's house like the plague after *that* day. When he was home from college and had caught me stealing. It was too humiliating seeing the anger in my best friend's cute older brother's gaze turn to pity. I didn't want his pity. I didn't want anyone's pity. I had taken care of myself since even before my mother's death and didn't need anyone's help.

The fact that I had kept the silly Hello Kitty figurine and actually added to my collection of Happy Meal toys had nothing to do with memories of him and the meal he'd bought me, and definitely had nothing to do with the protective tone he'd taken when he'd asked if everything was okay.

I brazenly lied that day.

I lied to anyone who asked, including his mother.

Everything wasn't okay.

Nothing had been okay for a very long time.

But it soon would be.

The day I graduated, I was skipping town. I finally had enough money to escape and never be found. When I caught Damien staring at me earlier, I thought he had learned of what I had done a few days ago. It was silly, of course. Just me being paranoid. There was no way he could have learned about what I had done. No one knew. I had gotten away with it. I was sure of it.

It had been a risk to taunt and secretly flirt with Damien. He wasn't some immature high school boy who tripped over his words and feet. I guess I'd thought I was safe because deep down I didn't really think it was me he was watching.

After all, he was a man.

A very large man.

A very large man with lots of scary tattoos.

Unfortunately, he was also sexy as hell. Tall with black hair and eyes so dark blue they were almost black. His sharp facial features and dark brow gave him that charismatic brooding look like Heathcliff from *Wuthering Heights*.

Everything about him was darkly sensual. Everything about him screamed danger — keep away.

Tamping down my irrational disappointment that

Damien actually hadn't been watching me earlier, I turned my attention back to the drunken arms that were slowly squeezing me to death. As I raised my knee, ready to drive my spiked heel straight into his toes, I jerked backwards as his grip was wrenched from around my middle.

Turning, I realized Damien had stormed up behind me and was now holding the inebriated man by the collar of his wrinkled cheap linen suit.

He kept his voice low. If I hadn't been standing so close, I wouldn't have even heard him over the music and laughter. Whatever he said in Russian, it had pierced through the fog of alcohol, because the man's eyes widened in stark fear. Sputtering an apology in English to me, the drunk scampered off the dance floor where he was quickly met by Nadia's family's scary head of security, Mikhail Volkov.

Damien captured my gaze.

Uh oh.

Frantically spinning about, I reached out for the hand of my earlier dance partner. His smile in greeting quickly faded when he saw the monster standing over my shoulder.

"Leave. Now." Damien's command was dark and forceful.

With an apologetic shrug to me, my dance partner hurried away.

I tried to inhale a shaky breath but my lungs seized. Even with my four-inch heels on, I could feel the immovable wall of towering strength that was Damien Ivanov looming over me. Stiffening my trembling limbs, I slid one foot forward in the hopes he would just let me walk away.

The warm restraining hand on my hip told me otherwise.

His body pressed close to mine from behind. His breath ruffled my hair as he leaned down to whisper in my ear. "May I have this dance?"

I licked my dry lips and tried to swallow before responding. "Do I have a choice?"

He chuckled. I felt the vibrations in his chest. The sound was strangely pleasant given the situation.

"No."

"You must be a Scorpio."

"A what?" he asked, eyebrow raised.

I was babbling; anything to stem the fear seizing me. "A Scorpio. They are a very intense sign. Very single-minded and… and aggressive," I finished weakly. I couldn't stop the rising tide of panic as it gripped my chest.

He turned me to face him. I kept my gaze carefully averted as his arm wrapped more securely around my waist.

Being this close to Damien was dangerous. Something told me he wasn't as easily fooled as the rest, that he would see my secret. See through the facade. My breathing came in fast pants, and I began to feel faint.

The opening strains of the next song filtered over the dance floor. Of course, it would be a slow song. The early haunting notes of the romantic lullaby *Everytime* by Britney Spears drifted over us. My stomach clenched.

This song reminded me of Damien and having to listen to it while standing inside the circle of his powerful embrace was just too much.

He smelled wonderful, like sandalwood and a crisp winter morning, as if someone had spritzed cologne onto a smoldering campfire.

He was impeccably dressed, damn him. One day, I hoped to work in the fashion industry, so I couldn't help but notice his Ralph Lauren cream cashmere sweater paired perfectly with grey Merino wool trousers. Looking down, I stared at the silver and black Rolex wrapped around his thick strong wrist. His skin looked richly tanned next to the ivory of his cuff. Everything about him screamed wealth and power — with all the arrogance that came with it.

His chest rumbled slightly as he spoke, his words for my ears only. "In the future, I expect you to dress and behave with more decorum." Each word was curt and sharp. There was no mistaking his anger.

What the hell?

I tried to jerk out of his embrace but he held firm. I raised my face to fire back at him but, remembering, I quickly lowered it and allowed my hair to fall over my cheek. He mustn't look at me too closely. If he did, he would see and then the pity would return to his eyes. I would take his anger over his pity any day.

I seethed through clenched teeth. "Are you trying to say that man's boorish behavior was my fault?"

"If you hadn't been putting yourself on display, it might not have happened."

My mouth gaped open in outrage. How dare he basically call my attempts at flirting whorish! After a second failed attempt to extract myself from his arms, I settled for stomping on his foot. My mouth twisted in wry satisfaction at his slightly pained groan. "Good, I hope I smudged your fancy Italian leather shoes. You deserved it."

Damien quipped back. "They're brushed suede actually."

"Well, I'll have you know this dress is a Miu Miu from their Fall collection."

I hazarded a glance up through my lashes in time to catch the sardonic raise of his eyebrow. He whistled softly. "Impressive. I wonder how a little girl in school could afford such a pretty, and expensive, dress."

My cheeks pinkened. I had walked right into that. I bristled at his tone and him calling me a little girl, which cut too close to the bone with how I felt whenever I was around him. Like some clumsy lost little girl to be pitied. I ignored his question and prayed for the song to be over.

Damien continued. "Spending your winnings so soon?"

Fuck. He knew.

My heart was beating so fast I worried I might actually pass out. So that was the real reason why he had been watching me like a hawk. It wasn't some schoolgirl crush realized. It was something far more dangerous. "I didn't do anything against the law."

Technically, that was true, but I was pretty sure the racetrack owners would disagree.

From the time I could walk, my sleazy stepfather had

dragged me to the racetrack and off-track betting sites. He was the worst kind of railbird, turning the sport of kings into something seedy and pathetic. Half my childhood was spent in dingy rooms filled with acrid cigarette smoke and floors littered with discarded ticket stubs. The places always smelled the same, reeking of horse shit, despair, and broken dreams.

A few years ago, he'd started messing with the horses and then recruited homeless people or people he found at the unemployment office to place bets on the fixed races for him. It helped if it wasn't the same person winning over and over again. The random recruit got a small cut and then was threatened to keep their mouth shut.

I'd noticed he would place the bets on random races for a long shot horse to win in first place which always seemed to pan out. When I was finally old enough to understand he was part of a scheme to fix races, I'd put a plan into place. Lucky for me, although I'd hated the subject, I was really good with math. Like really, *really* good.

So, I had come up with a math equation which took advantage of the parimutuel betting system at the tracks. In short, I'd come up with an algorithm to place bets, not on the prospective winner but on the second-place horse, which would have been the first-place horse, if the mafia hadn't fixed the race. By staying out of the first-place winner's circle, I'd figured I would fly under the radar.

And I had, until a few days ago.

That's when my stepfather hit me for what I'd determined would be the last time.

I'd known graduation was in two weeks so I had nothing to lose.

I'd started placing higher, riskier bets.

And they paid off — big.

Casting a quick glance at Damien from under my lashes, I asked, "How did you find out, anyway?"

Through clenched teeth, Damien said, "Placing three Pick Six bets in one week and winning every time. Did you really think no one would notice?"

By the stiffening of his arms, I could tell he was angry.

It was a stupid and rash mistake. A Pick Six was nearly impossible to hit. All a person's horses must win six consecutive races for it to pay out. It was a unicorn bet, and I had made it and won three times in a row. I had foolishly believed I would be long gone before anyone put two and two together.

As we were still on the dance floor and observed by the guests, Damien kept his voice low but it still had a harsh, biting edge. "Do you have any idea how much trouble you are in?"

I refused to answer. My mind scattered in a million directions. Had anyone found the money where I had stashed it? Had my stepfather? Were all my plans ruined?

Without warning, Damien grabbed me by the chin and forced my head back. "Yelena, I expect an answer."

My eyes widened.

Maybe he wouldn't notice.

His quick inhalation through his teeth told me otherwise. His dark gaze hardened to two diamond chips as he stared at my face and at *my black eye.*

It had happened days ago and was already fading. I had hoped my heavy eye makeup would cover it.

I guess not.

Without saying a word, Damien wrapped his hand around my upper arm and dragged me across the dance floor. Using his flattened palm, he shoved open the nearest French door and pulled me over the threshold into the pitch-black night.

CHAPTER 3

Yelena

"Let go!"

Yanking my arm did nothing to loosen his strong grasp.

"Damien, stop! Where are you taking me?"

He refused to answer.

In the darkness, I tripped over the rounded edge of the cement patio. The moment my open-toed high heels sank into the damp grass, I balked. "Are you crazy? These are satin and suede Sophia Websters! I'm not walking in the wet mud and grass in these!"

He turned so quickly I slammed into his chest. His face could have been carved in stone if it weren't for the tic high on his right cheek. His lips, thin and tight with anger, didn't move. Bending over, he pressed his shoulder into my middle and hauled me up high. My startled gasp was muted to a strangled puff of air as I absorbed the impact to my stomach.

Before I could even protest, his warm hand wrapped around my ankle. I was not prepared for the sensual shock of feeling his skin against my own. I had been so distracted on the dance floor with trying to hide my black eye while still arguing with him that the impact of his nearness hadn't really registered.

It certainly did now.

Especially since, for all intents and purposes, we were alone.

He pulled one high heel off, then the other. With an outraged cry, I threw out my arms, vainly trying to catch my shoes as he tossed them to the side onto the damp turf.

Planting my palms against his back, I leveraged myself up as high as I could and drew a deep breath into my lungs. "Do you have any idea what those shoes cost? Those are her iconic butterfly wing heels embellished with real crystal! You don't throw shoes like that into the mud!"

"I'll buy you another pair," Damien ground out.

"I don't want you to buy me anything. I want you to put me down!"

He pressed on, carrying me deeper into the wooded backyard. Past the soft glow from the lower windows of Nadia's house, which cast long slanted beams of light onto the lawn. The music and laughter receded till the guests were just shifting shadows inside.

I caught the glow from a cigar around the corner. I

momentarily considered crying out for help from the stranger but immediately thought better of it. I had no idea who that might be, and there was a very real chance that whoever it was would take one look at Damien's stormy expression and scurry away.

The hollow sound of wood planks beneath his feet told me he had stepped onto the dock, which stretched out over the Potomac River and ended in a large octagon gazebo. It was dizzying and disconcerting to look down and see the edge of the dock and then nothing but dark churning water.

I cried out and fisted large clumps of his sweater as his body dipped low to cross the gazebo entrance then straightened. Looking up, I could see the whitewashed rafters and the candy cane-striped life rings that hung on deep metal hooks along the edge. Our sudden appearance disturbed a nest of sparrows. Two of the small brown birds took flight, squawking their protests to the night sky.

Damien flipped me back and deposited me on one of the wide inlaid benches that lined the circular walls. Thankfully, each was covered with a thick cherry red cushion or the impact to my backside would have jarred every bone up my spine. I did not stay seated for long. Springing up, I raised an arm and pointed a finger at him. Immediately, I realized that without my four-inch heels, his already imposing height became impossibly tall and threatening. Without my fashionable shoes, the top of my head barely reached his shoulder.

Hating the disadvantage, I hiked up my dress skirt and stepped onto the bench. Feeling on more even footing, I placed my hands on my hips, raised my chin and prepared to do battle.

Damien gave a sharp inhale.

Even in the dim moonlight, I could see the hard glint in his eyes as he advanced, his arms raised. Startled, I stumbled backward, wrapping my hands around the post at my back to steady myself, and then followed his gaze.

Horrified, I realized the rounded neckline of my gown had pushed down when he'd lifted me onto his shoulder. The curves of my breasts were spilling over the top, and I could see the white lace edge of my bra. From my position on the bench, my chest was now practically at his eye level, completely on display.

"Christ, babygirl," Damien growled before lunging for me.

With a squeal, I dipped under his outstretched arm and scrambled in my bare feet along the bench to the other side of the gazebo. Keeping one steadying hand on the post, I yanked up the neckline of my dress.

Once again pointing a finger in his direction, I warned, "Don't you touch me!"

His mouth twisted in a grin. "We are long past that being an option, my malen'kiy padshiy angel."

Since he barely remembered to feed me as a child, my stepfather definitely never took the time to teach me his native tongue. I really only knew a few curse words and the phrase *useless brat* in Russian.

I narrowed my gaze. "What does *malen'kiy padshiy angel* mean?" I asked, sounding it out phonetically.

Reaching down, Damien pinched the hem of my dress

between his finger and thumb. He pulled on the pink velvet. "It means my little fallen angel."

My cheeks flushed at the implied intimacy of such a nickname, not to mention the sexy way he'd said it.

To be honest, I had never liked the sound of the Russian language. It had always sounded course and guttural to my untrained ears, like they were grinding rocks with their teeth as they spoke. It wasn't the same with Damien. When he spoke Russian, it was more like the low warning purr of a lion.

He twisted the excess fabric in his hand. The dress pulled tight around my hips. I resisted his tug as I clung to the post behind me. He twisted his fist again. This time the dress shifted down, once more exposing the top of my bra. Without thought, I let go of the post and flattened both palms protectively over my chest.

It gave him the perfect opportunity.

With a swift tug, he propelled my body forward, sending me crashing into his arms. It was like hitting a brick wall. Grasping his shoulders for purchase, I still couldn't stop the momentum and slid down until my knees hit the padded bench. Now all I had to do was tilt my head upwards for my mouth to be only inches from his....

Time stood still.

I cried out and tried to escape.

Damien leaned in close, his lips caressing my ear as he whispered in a low soothing voice, "Shhh... malyshka. I won't hurt you. Not if you give me what I want."

I started at the double-entendre of his words.

He slipped a finger under my chin and raised my head.

His eyes were such a dark blue they were practically black. They gave away nothing.

With his thumb, he caressed my lower lip. Smearing the clear shimmering gloss I had just put on. Keeping his focus on me, his hand slipped lower to the opening of my dress. He pulled on the neckline till one of the delicate buttons popped. With the dress gaping open, he could once more see the white lace of my bra.

His thumb swiped the upper curve of my right breast, then the left, marking them with a shimmering trail of glitter from my lipstick.

I bit my lip to keep from crying out, whether from misplaced desire or fear, I had no idea.

Damien ran his knuckle back and forth over the upper swell of my left breast. He observed darkly, "In my line of work, there are so many creative ways to make a person talk."

He pressed his hips against my body, and I could feel the push of his erect cock against my stomach. I inhaled sharply as if pulling away from a hot brand.

He leaned his head down and whispered against my open mouth. "So. Many. Creative. Ways."

My ears buzzed with the sound of the water lapping against the shore and my own hesitant breath. Beneath my hand, there was the steady drumbeat of his heart. My lips parted, and for a spare moment, we shared the same air.

He lifted his right arm and cradled my cheek. My skin, chilled by the night air, felt cool compared to the heat of his palm. The pad of his thumb caressed the outline of my cheekbone.

"Now tell me, who hurt you, babygirl?"

My heart skipped a beat. Part of me yearned to curl up in his arms and spill all my problems onto his big shoulders.

Twisting my head to the side, I lowered my gaze. "It's nothing."

Placing a finger under my chin, he forced me to turn back. "It's far from nothing. Someone hit you. That's not acceptable. You need to tell me who so I can deal with the matter."

My curiosity got the better of me. "Deal with the matter? What are you going to do?"

His jaw shifted as he inhaled deeply through his nose. "That is none of your concern. Just give me the name."

"None of *my* concern? You've got that backwards. I can't see how any of this is *your* concern."

Damien wrapped his free arm around my waist, placing his palm against my lower back and pulling me forward till his hips pressed into my stomach. He leaned down till his lips were barely a whisper from mine. "If you think that, then you haven't been paying attention."

His lips claimed mine.

It wasn't a kiss; it was a fierce possession.

His tongue pushed into my mouth and dueled with my own.

Tasting me.

Owning me.

His body was hard and unrelenting as it pressed close to mine. The hesitant, unskilled kisses from the boys at school had done nothing to prepare me for the feeling of complete domination by a man.

He controlled everything. His hand shifted from my cheek to the base of my skull where he grasped my curls, tilting my head and holding me still for the onslaught of his mouth. His arm held me tight as his tongue dueled with mine. Swirling and teasing before capturing the tip between his teeth and playfully biting.

Allowing me a fleeting breath of air, he whispered harshly against my lips. "Tell me, Yelena. I need to know." He punctuated his command with a tug on my hair, sending tiny stings of pleasurable pain over my scalp.

Feeling like the foolish girl I was, I loved the sound of my name on his lips.

Still, I refused to tell him. It wasn't out of any misplaced loyalty to my stepfather, he could rot in hell, but rather my pride. I didn't want Damien's pity or his help. I could take care of myself.

With a growl, he recaptured my lips. This time moving his hand over my hip to grasp my ass. His large hand spanned the underside curve. He gave it a squeeze which had me moaning against his mouth. Each of his hands flexed and tightened on my body at the sound. His lips traced a path across my cheek. Using the tip of his tongue, he flicked the soft curve of my earlobe before scraping the edge of his teeth along the shell of my ear. My fingers dug into his sweater as I tried to calm my racing heart.

Both his hands shifted to caress my hips before he slowly pushed up the velvet fabric of my dress. My slight groan of protest was swallowed by his mouth as his lips returned to mine.

Pressing a knee between my thighs, he bent forward. Supporting my back with his arm, he shifted above me, pushing me onto the thick softness of the bench cushion. The weight of his body followed, pinning me down. His hips wedged between my legs. His cock pressed through his wool slacks against my core. Placing his forearm near my head, he caged me in as his mouth lowered to the top curve of my breast, tracing the lace edge of my bra with his tongue. My hips surged upwards as I pushed my fingers into his hair.

He placed his fingertips between my breasts. His fingers scorched my skin as he reached inside the neckline to grasp my bra. Fisting it and the fabric of my dress, he pulled down so sharply that a seam tore. Both my breasts were exposed. Mesmerizing me with his intense sapphire gaze, he opened his mouth over one pert nipple. His tongue stretched and flicked the hard nub.

"Oh God," I breathed.

He flicked my nipple several more times, all the while holding my captured gaze. I knew what he wanted me to think just as surely as if he was whispering the illicit words in my ear. Looking down, I tried to clench my thighs in response to the surge of pleasure the sensual sight sent straight to my clit, but wound up pulling his hips in closer.

I had never been with a boy, let alone a man like Damien. I only knew pleasure from the tips of my own fingers but now, watching his tongue as it laved and played with my nipple, I practically howled to the night sky with an obsessive need to feel his tongue down *there*.

His warm breath against my skin was like a caress. "Be a good girl and tell me what I want to know."

Is he seriously still thinking about my stupid black eye? Now?

Clenching my fingers as much as I could in his shortly cropped dark hair, I tried to pull him back down to my breast. "No. It's fine. It's handled."

And I *had* handled it. I had gambled and won. Big. Now that I knew the Ivanovs were aware of my racetrack scheme, I would have to push up my plans and leave town even before graduation. My stepfather would never hit me ever again.

"Moya malen'kiy padshiy angel, ty ne mozhesh' skazat' mne net," he growled as his hand stroked the top of my thigh. His thumb caressed the inside curve only a few dangerous inches from my core.

I'd heard the term for fallen angel again, but something from his tone told me that whatever he'd said wasn't an endearment.

Before I could ask, he translated for me. "Angel, you are not allowed to tell me no."

Somehow it sounded better in Russian.

I wrapped my forearm over my exposed breasts. "Hold on. Just because I let you kiss me at a party doesn't mean you can suddenly waltz in and start dictating orders and take control of my life!"

He muttered something low and ominous in Russian before saying, "You are one very foolish little girl playing with fire if you think *this* is ending with a few simple kisses." He punctuated his threat with a thrust of his hips, grinding his hard shaft between my legs.

This was no longer some innocent flirtatious game I

had started on the dance floor with my best friend's older brother.

I was alone with Damien Ivanov.

Demon Damien Ivanov.

My whole body went cold with fear.

CHAPTER 4

Damien

I SHOVED myself off her and stood. "Cover yourself up," I crudely commanded as I paced a few steps away, willing my painfully erect cock under control.

Christ, there was nothing I wanted more than to just forget everything and sink deep inside her tight pussy. But this was Yelena. She wasn't some random woman I had met at a bar. She was my little sister's best friend. Whether she wanted to admit it or not, she needed my help. In more ways than one.

Glancing over my shoulder, I caught the look of confusion and fear on her face as she sat up and adjusted the neckline of her dress. She was too beautiful for her own good. She looked like one of those damn Disney princesses my sister used to like. Long hair the color of spun gold. Impossibly bright blue eyes. Creamy ivory skin

I just wanted to lick and full pink lips I wanted to bite. And her body. Christ, it would haunt my dreams. She was all soft curves and sleek long legs.

My perfect malen'kaya shalun'ya. My little minx.

It wasn't just her beauty, although I wouldn't deny that it was what had first drawn my eye when I'd seen her on the dance floor tonight. It was everything. The sound of her laughter. The mischievous glint in her gaze when she thought I wasn't looking. My grudging admiration for the scheme she'd pulled off at the racetrack a few days ago. It took guts and brains.

I still needed to learn all the details from her, but there was no denying she had pulled off something both the Italians and the Columbians had never managed to do. She had won eighteen races without actually fixing the horses. And by all accounts, she had won big—at least a high six figures. Both groups would be clamoring to get their hands on her to exploit her methods.

In short, Yelena Nikitina was the whole package. Beautiful and intelligent.

The problem was that package contained a bomb.

Neatly tied up with pretty pink ribbons but a bomb nonetheless.

And that was before I'd forced myself to remember her age. She was barely eighteen. A child.

What was I thinking bringing her out here?

She was like dangling a glass of cool, clean water before a man dying of thirst and telling him not to sip.

If I'd been really honest with myself, it wasn't just her drop-dead gorgeous looks and intelligence that drew me to her like a moth to a flame. It was her vulnerability.

She needed protection. Someone to step in and slay her demons. Someone to save her from her own reckless actions. A champion.

I wasn't usually that person — for anyone.

Even my little sister turned to Gregor, the eldest, first if she needed something.

The Ivanov family didn't hold power by playing nice in the sandbox. We ruled with an iron fist through cunning and intimidation. We only resorted to violence when we had to, but when we did, it was brutal and bloody. It sent a clear message that we were not a family to fuck with.

I was the demon in people's nightmares. The enforcer.

Never the knight in shining armor, but I could be… for her.

My whole life was about destruction, whether it was with my fists or the guns I sold. All I'd ever left in my wake was scorched earth. It would be nice, just this once, if I could create instead of destroy.

Yelena was headed down a dangerous dead-end path. I could turn that around for her. I would settle things with the Italians and the Columbians and then sneak her out of the country. I'd find some respectable college in Switzerland. *A girls-only college.* Where no one would think to look for her. She'd have a whole new identity.

The idea of having her locked away where only I'd know where she was appealed to the selfish bastard in me. Before tasting her lips, my intentions had been good.

Now they were, well, not *as* good.

She would be my very own Rapunzel, locked away in a tower where no one could touch her.

Completely under my protection and control.

Deep down, I knew she was still forbidden fruit for me, but that didn't mean I wanted anyone else to have her. My gut twisted at the idea of someone else even touching her.

It screamed mine, all mine.

Even if I had no right to even think it.

Yelena had pulled the hem of her dress down over her knees and had started to rise. I prowled back and caged her in. My fingers clenched around the wood railing behind her as I leaned down.

"No more games. I want the name of the man who hit you."

Yelena smoothed the wrinkled fabric of her dress over her lap. "What makes you think it was a man?" she hedged.

Ignoring her delay tactic, I demanded, "Is it a boyfriend? Is that why you're trying to protect him?"

The weather-aged wood creaked and groaned as my fingers dug into it. I tried to control my rage at the thought of her already belonging to another man. I hadn't gotten a chance to slip my fingers *or cock* into her sweet wet heat, but the idea that she had already been claimed made me want to tear the man's throat out.

"I'm *not* protecting him," she said softly.

I went down on my haunches. Her face was mostly shielded by a curtain of blonde curls. With the back of my hand, I brushed one side over her shoulder. Her head remained lowered. She looked so small and vulnerable. Placing a knuckle under her chin, I lifted her face to mine. Her eyes glistened with unshed tears.

"Tell me, baby."

"Why are you being so nice to me?"

I smiled. "Let's just say I have a weakness for a pretty malen'kiy padshiy angel with big blue eyes."

Her voice barely above a whisper, she finally answered, "It was my stepfather."

I had suspected as much, but it was still a gut punch to hear it. Her stepfather. The man I'd essentially sent her home to eight years ago after knowing she was unsupervised and half-starved. I really was a bastard.

Rising, my voice came out slow and controlled as I commanded, "Get up. We're leaving."

She popped up from her seat. Without those ridiculous high heels, she barely reached my shoulder. She looked like an angry little chipmunk as she placed her hands on her hips and challenged me. "Leaving? Where? They haven't even brought out the cake or pulled on Nadia's ears yet!"

"I'm taking you to a hotel."

She shook her head. "I'm not leaving Nadia's birthday party. Besides, who says I *want* to go to a hotel with you?"

I sighed. It was my fault she was making that assumption. I hadn't read many chivalrous books, but I was pretty sure the knight in shining armor was supposed to rescue the damsel *before* he tried to fuck her.

"You're not going *with* me. I'm getting you your own room."

"I don't need a room."

I placed my hands on either side of her face. "You can't go home tonight."

Her gaze lowered. "It's fine. It's not like it's the first time. I've got it handled."

Not the first time. Another kick to the gut.

It was time to spell things out. "Baby, things are going to get bloody, and I can't have you there."

Her eyes widened. "No. Damien. No! He's not worth it. *I'm* not worth it."

Unable to resist, I gave her a hard kiss on the mouth. "Don't ever let me hear you say you're not worth it again."

"What are you going to do to him?"

"Something I should have done a long time ago."

Before she could protest, I gathered her up into my arms and strode across the dock toward the lights of the house. Ignoring the warm vanilla scent of her hair and how she felt curled up in my arms, I set her on her feet on the smooth cement patio and went to retrieve her shoes.

As she leaned over to secure the thin patent leather straps around her heel, I once again caught a glimpse of her full breasts as they were hugged by the delicate white lace bra which seemed to barely contain her generous curves.

"You can stay for cake," I said gruffly, "but after that I'm taking you to a hotel. Understand?"

She straightened. Lifting her arms, she fluffed her hair and smoothed her cheeks before abruptly turning her back on me.

Before she could take one step, I snatched her around the waist and pulled her back against my front. "Otvet' mne."

She huffed. "I don't speak Russian."

"Answer me," I repeated.

She stubbornly stayed silent. I could practically hear the gears in her mind angrily spinning over my high-handedness.

"Answer me or I'll drag you over to that lounge chair and put you over my knee."

Fortunately, the muted sounds of the party still happening inside muffled her outraged shriek.

"You wouldn't dare!"

I splayed my hand over her flat stomach and pulled her back even tighter. Making sure she could feel every inch of my still-erect cock against her back. "Try me," I growled.

"Fine," she said through clenched teeth.

I was almost disappointed. There was definitely a part of me that wanted her to continue to defy me. I would have enjoyed seeing that cute ass of hers pink and rosy after a spanking.

"Tomorrow. After I've dealt with your stepfather, you and I are going to have a nice long chat about your little stunt at the racetrack."

She remained silent.

I released my grip on her waist, and she stormed inside without a backward glance.

I should have known she was lying.

I should have known she would run the first chance she got.

CHAPTER 5

Yelena

THE SOUND of loud music and harsh laughter was jarring as I snuck back into the party through the French door off the patio. It was strange how normal and unchanged everything was considering my whole world had just tilted on its axis.

I stood there for a minute, feeling unsure and self-conscious.

A moment later, there was a blast of chilly night air as the door behind me opened a second time.

My body went on alert, feeling as if I were standing on my tippy toes on the razor edge of a knife.

I could feel him behind me.

I could smell the earthy scent of his cologne and just a hint of tobacco smoke.

I inhaled sharply as the tip of one finger caressed my lower back as he passed behind me.

That was it.

Just the barest of touches.

Not even a caress really.

And yet it practically sent me to my knees.

Forcing myself to breathe, I scanned the room looking for Nadia or Samara. I knew Samara had snuck down the hallway leading to the bedrooms with her boyfriend Peter but that was before I had even gotten on the dance floor. A lifetime ago it seemed. She should be back to the party by now. She wouldn't want to stay away too long or her asshole father would come looking for her.

Finally, I spotted Nadia.

Her face was slightly downturned. Her lips tight and pinched as if she was trying not to cry. My brow furrowing, I shifted my gaze to Mikhail. He was standing close to her. Actually, it would be more accurate to say he was towering over her, with his arms crossed over his chest, looking seriously pissed off.

Poor Nadia.

She was impossibly shy and reserved and had an equally impossible crush on Mikhail Volkov, her family's head of security. There was no way in hell her brothers would ever condone the two of them dating. Mikhail was close to five years older than her for one. He was also an orphan with no family name or connections. The Ivanov brothers would never let their little sister date a man of lower standing, no matter how much they might like or respect him. I knew from my father's drunken ravings that Mikhail was the brothers' right-hand man and the one they relied on for the more dangerous, violent work that needed to be done.

Just then Nadia made a beeline for the other side of the room. Samara had finally returned, looking very disheveled and thoroughly kissed. My upper lip lifted in disgust. I really hated her boyfriend, Peter. He was the kind of boy who was just smart enough to realize he was stupid and to be very defensive about it. Samara could do way better.

The lights dimmed and everyone around me burst into a chorus of the Russian version of Happy Birthday.

It's so sad that a birthday can only happen once a year.

It was an odd little song which mentioned wizards and accordions and ice cream cones, taken from some popular old cartoon.

Her mother appeared in the doorway carrying a large round birthday cake ablaze with candles.

Nadia dutifully approached, as Samara made her way through the guests to stand next to me.

She bumped me on the shoulder to get my attention, then mouthed, "Two a.m."

I nodded, knowing what she meant. We'd all meet at our usual spot. Our childhood treehouse in Nadia's backyard.

Neither of us were in the mood to talk, so we watched silently as a small crowd surrounded Nadia and pulled on her ears, gleefully shouting out the corresponding number. Another archaic Russian birthday custom. My heart went out to her. Although she smiled, anyone who truly knew her could tell she was absolutely miserable.

Unlike me, Nadia wasn't comfortable being the center of attention.

Samara stiffened beside me. Looking at her, I followed her gaze.

Gregor, Nadia's older brother, was staring straight at her.

I wondered what he could possibly want.

Without a word, Samara pivoted and left the room.

What the hell is with Nadia's brothers tonight? Have they both gone mad?

It was like Samara and I were both suddenly very much on their radar after years of being mostly ignored and treated simply as their little sister's nameless friends.

I shook my head. Nothing made sense tonight. All three of us were finally eighteen - adults. Already, I felt ripped off. If this was what it was like being an adult, they could shove it.

Realizing I was wasting precious time while everyone was distracted, I slipped between a few small groups of people and made my way through the kitchen to the side door. Flipping the latch, I turned the knob.

"Going somewhere?" came a deep baritone voice behind me.

Rolling my eyes at getting caught, I pasted a fake smile on my face and turned.

"I was just looking for you," I lied.

Damien's lips twisted into a smirk. "I bet you were."

He stepped close. So close I could make out the five o-clock shadow over the sharp angle of his jawline. I inhaled. Surely, he wouldn't be bold enough to try and kiss me right here in the middle of his family's kitchen?

He raised his arms and stepped even closer.

My eyes widened.

I couldn't move. Frozen to the spot, I wasn't sure if I wanted to run or to let him take me into his arms.

Before I could decide, he swung my black and pink fake chinchilla fur bolero jacket over my shoulders. I wasn't even going to bother asking how he knew that was my coat. He must have been watching me from the moment I'd entered the party, not just on the dance floor like I had assumed.

"Let's go."

I protested as I pushed my arms through the jacket sleeves. "I need to say goodbye to Nadia!"

"No. You don't. March."

He placed the flat of his hand against my lower back and ushered me out the door.

Bypassing the waiting valet hired for the party, Damien walked me across the driveway to where his car was parked off to the side, partially hidden by the trees. My mouth opened on a gasp which I quickly swallowed by pulling my lips between my teeth.

Holy shit!

His car was magnificent.

It was a silver Mercedes-AMG GT.

I wasn't exactly a car person—in fact I knew nothing about them—but I did know my luxury sports cars, especially when they appeared in Jason Statham movies.

Trying to keep the excitement from my voice, I asked, "Is this the same car that appeared in *The Fast and the Furious Eight*?"

Damien chuckled. "As a matter of fact, yes, it is."

Guiding me to the passenger side, he opened the door for me. As I settled onto the soft leather seat, Damien reached down and picked up the trailing hem of my dress and tucked it inside before closing the door.

My heart skipped a beat.

So this was what it was like to be with an actual gentleman?

Flashes of the last time I had been bored enough to go on a date ran through my mind. When Johnny Newston insisted on going Dutch at the movies and picked me up in his run-down Camry. Both the driver's and front passenger side doors were broken, so he'd made me get in the back seat and climb over the seats to the front to let him in. I'd torn the mesh trim on my McQ sequined tank dress doing it. I had saved up all summer to buy that dress from Alexander McQueen's ready-to-wear line. I'd sworn off males, asshole high school boys in particular, that night. I realized with a start that that was over a year ago. No wonder I was about to graduate high school an eighteen-year-old virgin.

Damien slipped into the seat next to me and filled the car with masculine energy. Since it was only a two-seater sports car, his wide muscular shoulders took over the space. Self-consciously, I scooted as far as possible over to my side.

Damien started the engine and adjusted the volume on the stereo as loud pounding piano music resonated around us.

I couldn't keep the shock from my voice. "Is that Rachmaninoff?"

Putting the car into reverse, he placed his hand on the

back of my seat as he looked over his shoulder through the back window. If I moved my head slightly, my cheek would brush his knuckles.

"Yes. Piano Concerto Number Two. My favorite."

"Mine too," I blurted before thinking. I really didn't tell people about my love of classical music. It wasn't considered particularly cool at my age. When I was a little girl, I'd desperately wanted to take piano lessons, but my stepfather had refused to pay for them.

"This is from a live concert of Anna Fedorova's I attended a few years ago."

I didn't know who Anna Fedorova was but nodded sagely and pretended I did.

Meanwhile, I was secretly jealous he had heard Rachmaninoff performed live, probably with an entire symphony accompaniment. He would have been dressed in a tuxedo for the occasion. Looking sexy as hell. With all those tattoos, he'd look like a hotter David Beckham in a suit. I could just imagine him with some tall, professional model on his arm. She probably only spoke French and had a silly name like Mimi or Fifi. I bet she wore a vintage couture Dior gown to match the diamond necklace and earrings he had probably given her earlier.

I looked down at my lap. The pink velvet of my Miu Miu gown was slightly crushed near the right thigh. Miu Miu was Prada's cheaper ready-to-wear line. So far it and my McQ gown were the closest I had gotten to owning something by a true designer, and now they were both ruined.

The overture of the piano concerto filled the car with dramatically intense music as the violins began. It gave our winding drive through the dark woods on Rock Creek Parkway a gothic feel, which felt right since I was basically sitting next to the perfect villain duke from a romance novel.

Demon Damien.

That was what they called him.

I wasn't supposed to know that.

Apparently, it was because he had the charm of the devil and a temper to match. While Gregor had a reputation for exhibiting a deadly calm when angered, Damien did not. He was known to lash out violently and without warning.

Something I was also not supposed to know.

For all his gentlemanly manners, it would be wise for me to not forget that behind his designer clothes, fancy car, and elegant musical tastes, Damien was a dangerous criminal and second in command of an even more dangerous Russian mafia family.

No one messed with the Ivanovs.

No one.

It reminded me of what Damien had said earlier about me being in real trouble. My racetrack scheme had pissed off a lot of powerful people, apparently the Ivanovs included.

I swallowed.

What if he isn't taking me to a hotel?

What if this is all a ruse?

What if he's really just driving me out into the middle of nowhere to kill me?

How could I have been so stupid as to blindly follow him just because he was Nadia's brother?

How could I have thought being his little sister's friend would somehow protect me?

The Ivanovs were about family honor and making money. Lots of money.

Me and my racetrack scheme had disrespected both of those things.

Oh my God.

Oh my God!

He is going to kill me.

He is going to fucking kill me!

I shivered.

Damien noticed and turned my heated seat on.

I rambled as my hand slid along the door panel searching for the handle in the dark. "Did you know the song *All By Myself* from the *Clueless* soundtrack sampled a large portion of this concerto?"

We were getting closer to the city, but just because he wasn't taking me deep into the woods didn't mean he wasn't still planning on killing me. He probably had some super creepy warehouse somewhere on the Southside. Someplace in a basement with a drain in the center and the walls stained with rust-colored blood splatter. A torture room.

Fuck! This was bad.

My mind raced out of control with all the ways he could kill me. I turned to stare at his profile. He had the strong nose and jaw that people usually called Roman, like those marble busts of cruel despotic dictators from history. They also were said to have strong noses and profiles.

Yep. This was really bad.

Damien smiled as he adjusted his grip on the leather steering wheel. Glancing in my direction before returning his gaze to the road, he replied, "Can't say that I did."

Pretending to adjust my skirt, I slipped the leather ankle strap over my heel and placed it to the side. "Did I remember to grab my purse?" I reached down to my other side pretending to fumble for it. I pulled the other strap free, kicking that shoe to the side as well. "Oh, here it is!" I held my purse up then placed it on my lap.

Tense, I waited for my moment.

Soon, I knew there would be a loud crescendo of music with a dramatic ending that included cymbals and then hopefully thunderous applause. That would cover the sound of my opening the door. It would give just a half second advantage but that coupled with the element of surprise would hopefully be all I'd need.

He pulled off the parkway as the music began to rise in pitch.

I leaned forward. Ready.

On Virginia Avenue he slowed the car as we neared a traffic light. I could see the bright glow of the Kennedy Center to my right. It was Saturday night. At this time, there was surely a concert or some event letting out.

The car came to a complete stop.

It was now or never.

I wrapped my fingers around the car door handle.

The violins screamed and strained as the deep notes of the piano reached a fevered pitch.

My heartbeat pounded in frenetic time with the music.

Taking a deep breath, I threw the car door open… and ran.

CHAPTER 6

Damien

"Dammit! Yelena!"

Her slim form bolted straight into the path of an oncoming car. Her body bowed to the left as she placed her right hand on the hood, only narrowly avoiding a fatal accident. The car's horn blared in protest. She ran on, her pink velvet gown occasionally shimmering as she passed under a streetlamp.

Throwing the car into gear, I veered right. The force of my turn swung her passenger door shut as I crossed two lanes of traffic and raced down the nearest side street after her. I could tell she was heading straight for the Kennedy Center. I passed her running on my right. Before I could stop, she sprinted across the street. Jumping the curb, I abandoned the car on the outskirts of a small park nearby and took off after her on foot.

I caught up to her just as she approached an elderly couple.

The woman, who was dressed head to toe in a musty old fur with some yellowing pearls, greeted her kindly. "Hello, dear! Were you at the performance too? Wasn't that dance troop marvelous, the way they jumped in the air and banged on those trash can lids?"

Placing her hand to her side as she struggled to catch her breath, Yelena blurted out, "Please, I need your hel—"

"There you are, sweetheart," I intoned directly behind her.

Yelena swung around.

Her body tensed to bolt again. I wrapped an arm around her waist and snatched her close to my side. "Darling, I told you I would find us a cab. No need to bother these nice people."

Her bright blue eyes were wild with fear. The sudden run had sent a dark pink flush over her high cheekbones, giving her face a primal, animated look like a rabbit caught in a trap.

The elderly gentleman gestured toward the nearest traffic intersection. "Don't go back to the Center. The taxi line is too long. If you want a cab, you need to do like us and walk a few blocks."

The elderly woman chimed in. "It's such a nice night for a walk. The slight chill feels wonderful. Those concert halls can be so stuffy."

Yelena shook her head. "No! You don't understand, I —"

Placing a firm grip under her jaw, my head swooped down and claimed her lips. Her mouth opened on a shocked gasp. I took advantage, sweeping my tongue inside. Her fingers clawed at my chest as her body tried to twist out of my grasp. Shifting my hand lower, I palmed her ass and pulled her in closer.

The older man sighed. "Young love! Come on, Doris. Let's leave them alone."

The elderly couple shuffled away none the wiser.

Still, Yelena fought back, clipping my lower lip with her sharp teeth. The copper tang of blood mixed with the sweet taste of her. Driving a hand through her now-tangled curls, I forced her head back as I took complete possession. I didn't stop till her body went slack as she submitted to the inevitable force of my assault.

Breaking free of our kiss, I growled, "How dare you endanger yourself by running like that! You could have been killed."

"What do you care? You're going to kill me anyway!" she shouted.

"Dammit woman! I'm not trying to kill you. I'm trying to save you!"

How many times would I have to explain to her that I was on her side in this mess?

I should've just laid it out for her. Tell her what the men who were after her were capable of in order to get what they wanted. That they would snatch her off the street with no warning. Lock her in some godforsaken hole where no one would hear her scream. They'd pump her veins full of drugs and deprive her of food and water. They would beat her and probably even rape her for days, weeks, till she became no more than a feral animal willing to do anything to make the pain stop.

And that's when the real torture would begin.

It wasn't her name or just her stash of cash that they were after. They needed her math skills. They needed to know how she was able to beat the odds and win big without risking detection by messing with the horses. They needed to get inside of her head. They would keep her prisoner until they had drained everything that made her human, and then they would kill her and discard her like trash.

I knew all this, because I was one of them. I knew how they thought and operated.

I might draw the line at women, but I wasn't above violence to get what I wanted.

I knew what it felt like to crush a man's bones and spirit.

To watch the will to live drain from his eyes.

In my world, there was no such thing as a line I wouldn't cross.

The Ivanovs were all about the Machiavellian end game.

Fear and power.

It was the only way.

I should have told her all of this, but something held me back.

At least for one more night, I wanted to still be the man she thought I was.

Nadia's protective older brother. The man who bought her a funny McDonald's toy.

For just one more night, I wanted to not see fear and disgust in her beautiful blue eyes when she looked at me. I wanted to be that knight in shining armor, even if my armor was a little tarnished.

Still, I had to get through to her.

Perhaps violence really was the only way to make her see reason.

It was, after all, the only way I knew.

Cursing low in Russian, I swung my head to the right and observed another group of people making their way down the wide sidewalk. They too must have given up on the taxi line. Not willing to risk any more public encounters, I kept my grip on her hair and marched her back to the car. Without her heels, she once more barely reached the top of my shoulders, making her seem slight and vulnerable in my grasp. I would have to keep reminding myself of that as I ruthlessly tried to keep my anger in check.

She could have been killed.

Her sprinting out of the car into traffic was foolish and extreme and just another example of how undisciplined and wild she had become without any proper supervision over these last few years.

Well, that was all about to change.

My abandoned car was slightly hidden from view on the street by a small copse of high bushes and young trees. Dragging her over to the car, I prevented her from reaching for the passenger door as I pushed her past the front.

"What are you doing?"

Using my grip on her hair, I forced her to bend over the hood of the car.

"Damien! Let go!"

Ignoring her shout, I reached for her dress. Fisting the

thin velvet, I dragged it up over her hip, exposing her ivory skin to the moonlight.

"Stop! No!"

She had the most amazing ass. Just curvy and luscious enough to fill a man's hand. I raised an eyebrow. I wasn't sure how I felt about her wearing thongs, as much as I was thoroughly enjoying the view of that tiny scrap of white lace. The scalloped edge highlighted the cleft between her cheeks before slipping between.

"Let me go!" she cried as she tried to reach and pull her dress back down.

I pulled sharply on her hair which immediately quieted her protests.

"It's very simple, Yelena. You misbehave. You get punished."

"What?"

I smoothed a palm over her left ass cheek. "I warned you earlier what would happen if you defied me."

Her body stiffened. "You wouldn't dare," she spurted out as she tried to push herself off the hood. My grip held her in place.

Leaning down, I whispered into her ear, "Try me."

Raising to my full height, I lifted my arm and brought the flat of my hand down on the soft curve of her ass. Her shocked scream was cut off by my other hand, which I quickly wrapped around her mouth. She was such a little thing, it was easy to restrain her. Keeping my hand over her mouth, I spanked her ass over and over again. I watched her flesh blossom into bursts of pink and red with each strike. Her cute bare toes dug into the grass as she raised up on them and occasionally tried to kick out.

My cock swelled to painful proportions as I pictured all the illicit things I wanted to do to her lush body. It was wrong. Completely wrong. She was far too young for me. Naive and innocent despite her bravado.

They may call me Demon Damien in certain circles, but that didn't mean I had to live up to the reputation as far as Yelena was concerned. To take advantage of her now would make me the worst kind of a monster. I knew deep in my soul such an act would push me past any redemption.

Still, I was no angel. Far from it.

Her tears wet my fingers as her open lips pressed against my palm. I spanked her several more times, wanting to make sure the next time she even thought about doing something so foolish, she would remember this punishment and reconsider.

Her ivory skin was a harsh, mottled pink. There were several areas where I could practically make out a full handprint. My mark.

Placing myself behind her, I kicked her legs wider.

"If I remove my hand, do you promise not to scream?"

She nodded.

I rubbed my right hand over her ass then squeezed her flesh, knowing it would send sharp pins and needles of pain up her spine.

She rose up on her toes as she squealed.

"If you do, I punish this ass all over again."

She nodded her head vigorously, signaling she understood.

I removed my hand.

Remaining prone on the hood of the car, her cheek

resting against the warm metal, she hiccupped as the tears continued to roll down her cheeks. I pushed her soft curls aside. Hushing her, my low soothing tone belied my words. "Next time, I'll use my belt. Do you understand?"

She didn't answer.

"Otvet' mne."

"Yes," she sniffled.

I was pleased she remembered that phrase meant *answer me* in Russian. Something told me I would be using it a lot around my malen'kiy angel. She had a quick ear for language. Perhaps I should start teaching her more Russian phrases. Far more dirtier ones.

I stopped myself. There was no point in thinking along those lines. In less than a month, I would have her shipped off to Europe. Safely locked away in the remotest, all-girls, convent-like university I could find.

Looking down at her prone form, I traced the outline of her lace thong. I caressed the crease between her ass cheeks, placing a finger under the small strip of fabric. I pressed deeper till I could feel the soft ridges of her dark hole beneath my fingertip. Yelena inhaled sharply and stiffened.

My cock swelled even harder.

Until then....

What harm could there be in giving the devil just a tiny taste of heaven?

Going down on my haunches, I caressed the backs of her thighs with both hands. "Push your hips out for me."

I was shocked when she obeyed.

Pressing into her inner thighs with my thumbs, I guided her legs open a bit wider as I tilted her hips back.

Pulling on her thong, I moved the scrap of fabric out of the way.

She was slick with arousal.

My babygirl was turned on from the spanking she had just received.

I stifled a groan.

Christ. She was going to be the death of me.

Her pussy had a thin dusting of baby soft blonde curls. Slipping my hands deeper between her legs, I used my thumbs to open her up to me. Leaning in close, I swiped my tongue over her pussy from behind. I groaned. "You taste so sweet, baby."

A sudden sharp and swift stab of jealousy hit my gut. Rising, I took her by the shoulders and spun her to face me. Grabbing her chin, I tilted her face up to meet mine. "Tell me the truth, has any other man touched you there? Tasted you?"

Yelena bit her full bottom lip.

"Otvet' mne, angel."

She shook her head.

That was good. If she had said yes, I might have demanded a name and who knows what I would have been capable of.

I reached over and pulled open the passenger side door. Lifting her against me, keeping her dress pulled up high over her hips, I swung her around and placed her inside with her legs dangling over the seat edge. A breath hissed through her teeth as her punished bare ass hit the soft leather seat.

Kneeling down into the thick sweet grass, I wrapped

my hands around her calves and lifted her legs over my shoulders.

"What are you — Oh God!"

Using the edge of my thumbs to once more open her to me, I leaned down and flicked my tongue over her clit, using the tip to play with the tiny nub. Swirling and tasting. Yelena groaned as her fingers delved into my hair, holding me closer.

The sweet musky scent of her almost drove me over the edge. Shifting, I had to push the heel of my palm along my hard shaft just to ease the throbbing ache.

I slipped a finger into her wet heat. Christ she was so impossibly tight. There was no way my cock wasn't going to tear her. I clenched my teeth and reined in those sublime thoughts.

One taste of her was all I was going to allow myself.

If I sunk my cock into her wet heat, I knew deep in my bones I would never let her go.

She'd be mine forever.

I would drag her deeper into my dark and violent life, using her as my only light source.

It wouldn't be fair to her.

No matter the cost to my sanity, I was determined to walk away from her.

This had already gone way further than I'd ever intended.

I would relish this one taste of her.

Burn the memory of her orgasm into my memory as the one and only time I glimpsed heaven.

Stroking her with one finger, then two, I flicked my tongue over her swollen nub till she cried out in ecstasy.

Her hips rose as her thighs clenched close to my jaw, surrounding me with the soft feel of her skin and her warm scent.

Without a word, I lowered her dress over her exposed thighs and stood. Gently swinging her legs to the left, I placed them inside the car and closed the door. I noticed her discarded purse on the ground and picked it up. Before entering the car, I flicked it open and took out her cell phone, slipping it into my trouser pocket.

Silently, I got back behind the wheel and started up the engine. Throwing the car into reverse, I pulled back onto the street and turned toward the hotel.

She dutifully didn't say a word as I checked her into a suite at the front desk under my name. She didn't even protest when I ordered her to sit as I went into the gift shop. Since I had her purse, I was at least confident if she ran this time she wouldn't get as far. The hotel was mostly deserted so I wasn't worried about her approaching anyone. If she tried to flag down a staff member, she wouldn't get far with them. The Ivanov family kept a house account here. Our money was worth far more to them than the ravings of a young woman in a ruined gown in the middle of the night.

Selecting a few items, my mouth quirked as I imagined the look on her face when she saw the cheesy tourist t-shirt I purchased for her to sleep in. Knowing her, she wouldn't be caught dead wearing it outside the room. I thought about forcing her to strip out of her dress when we got to the suite as an extra precaution but then thought better of it. I had put her through enough for one night.

Grabbing a fashion magazine on impulse, I added it to my pile of purchases, shaking my head and internally admonishing myself over my foolishness.

If any of my comrades could see me now, I would never live it down.

I couldn't even really explain it.

There was just something about her that had instantly drawn me in.

It wasn't just her beauty and obvious intelligence.

It was something else.

A vulnerability.

She hid it well. Most would never notice it. They would see her pretty looks, brash mouth and bold manner and move on, but it was there. Hidden deep in the depths of her eyes. I'd seen it that day when I'd caught her stealing and it was still there.

Even earlier tonight. When she was taunting me on the dance floor from across the room. At first, I thought she was being a typical young woman, testing her flirting mettle on an older man. Granted, I was only older by less than ten years, but still. As I got closer and held her in my arms, I realized I was wrong. There was something deeper at play.

A desperation.

She didn't want me to see past the pretty face and flirtatious looks.

To see her.

That was what all the makeup and cheap designer dresses were about.

On that dance floor, I hadn't just seen the black eye no

one else bothered to notice. I had truly seen her, like no one else had.

Shaking off the destructive thoughts, I exited the gift shop and wrapped my hand around her slim upper arm, leading her to the elevators. Once inside, she sagged slightly against me. Shifting the bag to my wrist, I bent down and lifted her slight body into my arms, ignoring her half protest. I set her down when we were just outside the room.

She still hadn't said a single word.

Swinging the door open, I picked her up into my arms. Carrying her past the expansive lounge area, I marched through the double doors that led into the bedroom. I gently placed her down on the covers.

Placing a palm on either side of her head, I leaned down. Her usually bright blue eyes looked a darker sea blue with a hint of green in this light. Every ounce of my being wanted to crawl into bed beside her and hold her warm body close to mine. Thoughts of waking up next to her in bed each morning floated across my mind but were quickly chased away.

Those were thoughts for normal people with normal lives. Not for me.

"I want you to promise you will be a good girl and stay here."

She nodded.

"I mean it, Yelena. You can't fully appreciate how much trouble you are in right now or the caliber of the people who are looking for you. Hopefully, you won't have to. I'm going to handle everything, but I need you to stay put.

Do you understand me? Not one foot outside that door, or I swear to God you'll be sorry."

She nodded again before turning on her side and curling up like a little chipmunk. She looked so adorable. Reaching for the blanket folded neatly at the end of the bed, I shook it out and placed it over her half-asleep form. Tucking her in.

Allowing myself one last caress, I touched her blonde curls. She really did look like a beautiful angel.

For all her faults, Yelena was a lost angel with a slightly tarnished halo who didn't deserve to be defiled by a demon like me.

Clenching my jaw, I curled my hands into fists and strode away.

An angel.

Little did I know how wrong I was.

She was no angel but a she-demon sent to torment me.

She fooled me that night.

Tricked me into believing in her innocence.

I wouldn't make the same mistake twice.

CHAPTER 7

Yelena

I WAS LATE.

The moment the door closed, I threw off the blanket he had placed over me as I'd pretended to fall asleep. I raced over to the door and pressed my ear against the heavy wood, straining to hear any sounds of movement in the hallway. Hiking up my dress, I went down on my knees and leaned on my palms against the thick carpeting. I tilted my head and peered through the tiny slit under the door. After verifying there wasn't a pair of designer men's shoes on the other side, I watched closely for any shift in the light or shadow that would indicate someone standing nearby.

Nothing.

Leaning back on my haunches, I brushed off my palms

with a grimace. Thank God this was at least the Four Seasons and not some scummy motel room. Still, that didn't make kneeling on essentially a public floor that much less distasteful.

On edge, I paced the confines of the room from one side to the other. Instinctively, I reached into my purse for my cell phone, forgetting Damien had taken it from me.

Grabbing the grey plastic bag on the bed, I dumped out its contents. Damien had disappeared inside the gift shop before bringing me to the room. Lifting up the folded piece of white cotton, I shook it out and laughed at the *I heart Washington, D.C.* decal on the extra-large t-shirt. He'd also gotten me a toothbrush, toothpaste, a few snacks, and a copy of *Vogue*.

It was extraordinarily thoughtful.

He was still an overbearing, exceedingly arrogant Neanderthal for dragging me away like this, but I had to begrudgingly admit it was a nice gesture. True, my experience with men was basically non-existent, but I couldn't imagine many would have thought of such necessities, especially the magazine.

After waiting an eternity, I grabbed my purse and bolero jacket and marched to the door. My heart was in my throat as I reached for the doorknob. My hands were shaking so bad, I had to grip it harder than usual. Taking a deep breath, I turned the knob, cringing at the loud metallic click when the lock slid back. I held the breath I'd just inhaled.

Waiting.

Listening.

There was nothing.

I pulled on the door, shifting it open a crack, then hopping back just in case. I had this image of Damien slamming the door against the wall as he stormed in, catching me mid-escape — and in the nose with the door.

One black eye was enough, thank you very much.

I waited again.

Still nothing.

Pulling the door open, I stuck my head out to peer down the left side of the hallway before snatching it back. I repeated the gesture and checked the right side.

The hallway was empty.

Everything was still and quiet, which wasn't surprising given the late hour.

If I delayed much longer, I would be crazy late meeting Nadia and Samara. I took the first shaky step into the hallway. Quickening my pace, I took several more steps, nearly jumping a foot when the hotel door behind me finally closed shut with a loud thunk. The sound spurred me to run the remaining distance to the elevator. Constantly swinging my head left and right, I pressed the elevator down button several times, ignoring its steady red light. I probably should have taken the stairs, but I was an impossible number of floors up and still in heels.

Just in case, I got out one floor above the lobby level and walked down the final flight of stairs. Emerging through a small side door, I surveyed the lobby as best I could before venturing forth.

The lobby was mostly deserted. Nevertheless, every man I saw, regardless of his attire or appearance, looked like Damien to my overwrought eyes.

The cold night air stole my breath as I emerged from

the warm confines of the hotel. Ignoring the doorman's offer of a cab, I raced down the street to hail one at the corner.

Once inside, after giving directions to the intersection closest to Nadia's house, I kept turning and looking through the back window, certain I would see Damien's big black Mercedes barreling toward me.

It was only once we left the lights of the city behind and moved onto the much darker Rock Creek Parkway that I finally relaxed.

Looking down, I smoothed my wrinkled dress over my lap. I would have changed out of it, but all I had to wear was that oversized I Love Washington, D.C t-shirt, which I wouldn't be caught dead wearing out in public.

Once more, I checked over my shoulder. The road behind us was dark and deserted.

What would Damien do if he caught me?

Would he spank me again? Maybe this time over his lap?

The thought brought a heated blush to my cheeks.

Closing my eyes, I could practically feel the press of the warm metal of his car as it pushed against my stomach. I could feel the cool slide of velvet as he pushed my dress up over my hips. Would he push down my white lace thong or leave it on like last time?

I could practically feel the first impact of his palm again as the heated sting radiated over my lower body to settle between my legs.

It was sick and twisted, but the threatening way he kept his hand over my mouth, cutting off my breath and preventing my screams turned me on as much as the pain.

I wanted him to hurt me. To make me feel. To pull my hair and call me his good little girl in that deep, dark growly voice of his.

The image of his intense blue gaze boring into me as he pulled open my thighs and lowered his head between my legs to take that first taboo lick had me pressing the heel of my palm against the juncture of my thighs.

Glancing up, I made sure the taxi driver's eyes were on the road and not peeping at me in the rear-view mirror.

Closing my eyes, I thought of Damien towering over my prone form.

Reaching those large, tattooed hands down to the fastening of his trousers.

Unbuttoning the top button, then slowly lowering the zipper.

His fingers would disappear inside the flap, to wrap around his heavy, thick…

"Miss, we are here."

"What?"

"We are here, at your destination."

"Oh, uh. Yes. Yes, sorry. How much?"

"Sixteen fifty."

Flustered, I pulled out a twenty and tossed it to the driver. "Keep the change."

I made a wide circle around Nadia's house, hoping the night air would cool my cheeks and give me time to collect myself as I avoided the now-dark windows of her house. The party had ended over an hour ago. Just in case, I also peeked down the drive to make sure I didn't see Damien's car. I crept along the side hedge to the backyard and kept along the tree line until I could scurry across the lawn to our old childhood treehouse.

I called out in a harsh whisper. "Nadia? Samara?"

Samara poked her head out and waved me up.

Slipping off my heels, I put the ankle straps over my wrist and hiked my dress hem between my legs before gripping the first rough wood plank that was nailed into the wide tree trunk as a makeshift ladder. Gingerly, I made my way up into the close confines of the small one room cabin.

Pushing my unruly hair out of my face, I made myself comfortable on one of the many, slightly worn pillows we had strewn about the place.

Glancing to the left, I made sure the small backpack I had stashed in the dark corner under some old dolls was undisturbed. Everything looked in place.

I huffed, "No offense, Nadia, but that party sucked," then turning to Samara I raised an eyebrow, "and what were you and Peter up to for so long?"

Samara shrugged. "We broke up."

Nadia patted her shoulder as she made a sympathetic sound.

I shook my head. "Never liked him. Never trust a Gemini."

My best memory of my mother was how she would sit every morning sipping her tea and reading our horoscopes from the newspaper. She would tell me over and over how I was a Sagittarius, which meant I was destined to take risks and dream big. My sign always chased the impossible. *It's written in the stars, Yelena, so it must be true*, she used to say.

I missed her. Even years later, it felt like a constant empty ache in my chest.

I didn't think it would be so hard if I'd known that she was at least happy and content when she died. She wasn't. Unbidden the memory creeped back.

The smell of disinfectant.

The constant squeak of the nurse's shoes on the linoleum floor.

The harsh glare of fluorescent lighting.

Me sitting on a cold metal chair in the hallway, staring at my sneakers as my legs swung wildly but didn't touch the floor. The sneakers had been my favorite. Pink with silvery glitter on the toes and in the shape of a heart on the sides.

Now they were splattered with blood.

My mother's blood.

In hushed tones, the two policemen stood nearby and whispered to one another. Talking about how my mother couldn't have missed seeing the on-coming car and how there was no evidence of swerve or brake marks on the asphalt.

On the other side of a partially closed hospital room door, I could hear her begging my stepfather. Saying she was sorry over and over again and pleading with him to take care of me and not treat me as badly as her. At the time, I hadn't known what she meant; I was too young. All I understood was the fear and desperation in her voice which, as a child, scared the hell out of me. It was only later, when he started to lash out and hit me too that I understood.

Finally understood it all.

How my mother would get nervous when he came into a room. The heavy eye make-up and long sleeves she would wear even in summer. I shook off the bad memory. It was in the past, best forgotten.

He didn't honor her wish, but I could honor her memory by escaping.

Take a risk.

Dream big.

Chase the impossible.

Samara broke into my morose thoughts. "Listen, I don't even know how to say this, so I'm just going to blurt it out."

Her tone immediately alerted me that something was wrong. Very wrong. Grabbing the edges of my pillow, I shimmied closer to her along the floor. Then I leaned close and rubbed her upper arm reassuringly.

Nadia started. "Oh my God, Samara, what's wrong? Is it Peter?"

I chimed in. "We've been besties since we could walk. You can tell us anything."

Samara turned pleading eyes on Nadia. "I don't want you to get mad at me."

"Samara, I could never be mad at you. Tell me, what's wrong," reassured Nadia.

Samara blurted everything out. I couldn't believe what I was hearing. It was positively medieval! Her parents were cold unfeeling people, but never in a million years would I have thought they were capable of selling their only child to maintain their selfish lifestyle.

Samara brushed away more tears. "I'm sorry, Nadia, but I don't want to marry your brother."

Nadia hugged her. "I don't want you to marry my brother either!"

Samara's mouth fell open. "What?"

"I know you had this big crush on him when we were younger, and I know girls think he's cute and stuff…."

Cute and stuff?

It was jarring to hear Nadia refer to her brothers as cute and stuff.

I thought of the feel of Damien's forceful embrace. The intense scrutiny of his dark sapphire eyes. The way he towered over me and demanded I submit to his fiery kisses. My arms crossed over my chest, to hide my now-hard nipples. Damn, that man was really in my head!

With Samara's insane revelations, now was not the time to tell Nadia about my encounter with her *other* brother.

Especially since I hadn't had a chance to process any of the crazy thoughts and emotions I was feeling.

I mean Damien had kissed me — *there*.

Damien.

Nadia's scary older brother, Damien.

Demon Damien.

No matter how many times I said his name in my head, it still didn't seem real.

Actually, he hadn't *just* kissed me. If he hadn't been the one to stop, I'm fairly certain I would have happily lost my virginity in the front seat of his car.

Not exactly the romantic scene I had always pictured for the pivotal moment but still…

Damien.

Damien Ivanov.

The passionate way he had embraced me, even his anger over my black eye, had taken me completely by surprise. I didn't think the man knew I was alive. I mean, of course, he knew my name and that I was one of his little sister's best friends. He knew my stepfather as one of his minions but that really should have been it.

We'd really never spoken except for that time when he caught me stealing and bought me McDonald's. I was so upset and nervous, I don't think I'd spoken two words to him. I just remember wondering how someone so nice could be so terrifying at the same time.

Years later, that still summed up my feelings about Damien.

On one hand, it was hard not to be drawn to the whole protective vibe he was giving off. Even if it was in a rather arrogant and overbearing way.

On the other hand, there was the terrifying way he took control. The way he didn't ask for but demanded my obedience as if he had a right to it.

Fuck. My mind was all over the place and now was not the time.

Samara needed me.

And fortunately for the both of us, I had plan.

CHAPTER 8

Yelena

GIVING MYSELF A MENTAL SHAKE, I forced my brain to focus.

We could only handle one troublesome Ivanov brother at a time and clearly Samara's situation was far more pressing than my current predicament with Damien.

Still, I couldn't resist saying, "Uh… Nadia. Your brothers aren't cute. They're hot as fuck. Even though they're both a pain in the ass, especially Damien."

They both gave me a startled look. I waved them off. "We had words earlier." *That's the understatement of a lifetime!* "I… might be in a little trouble."

Samara swiped at her eyes. "Wait. What? Why?"

I waved her off again. "It's nothing. We're talking about your problem right now."

Samara cocked her head to the side and gave me a probing look. "Yelena…."

"I'll tell you both later."

Nadia nervously played with the fringe on her pillow. "I love Gregor, but he can be really old-fashioned. I know what he wants in a wife, and Samara is not it. No offense!"

"None taken!" Samara assured her.

"It's just. Look. It's not like I wouldn't love it if you were truly my sister and all that, but… you're not the only one he scares. He terrifies me sometimes, too, and he's my brother! The guy's intense! I still don't know why they sent him back to Russia. It's a big family secret, but I know it was something bad… really bad."

Samara whispered dejectedly, "I'm in real trouble, aren't I?"

In that moment, I blurted out my plan. "You have to run."

I really wasn't sure if I was talking to Samara or myself. Either way, the answer was the same. We had to run. Both of us. Together. There was no other option. It wasn't a great plan, but it was a plan.

They both trained startled looks on me.

Samara's brow furrowed as she shook her head. "What?"

"You have to leave. It's your only option. If you stay, your parents will force you to marry him."

"I don't know anyone. I don't have any money. Where would I go?"

"I have money, and I'm coming with you."

Never in a million years would I have wished anything

bad to happen to Samara, but this really was the perfect solution.

Damien had made it clear my escapade at the track had been found out, although for the life of me I had no idea how. I'd used a fake driver's license and social security card when picking up the winnings. I probably should have worn some kind of disguise, too. I'd known there were cameras all around the track, especially near the betting windows. Still, even good disguises are so conspicuous, and I didn't want to give the teller the slightest doubt about cashing in my ticket. I was already conspicuous enough cashing in a Pick Six for the second then third time in a week as it was.

Maybe someone had watched the security video and recognized me?

Could it have been Damien?

I gave myself a mental shake. No.

He said I had pissed off factions with both the Italians and the Columbians with my betting scheme. There was no way, if he had somehow gotten his hands on the security tapes, that he would have told them who I was — and that's assuming he recognized me. Despite being Nadia's brother, I had barely seen him over the last eight years. Once or twice when he was still in college but after he graduated and joined his brother in running the family business, I'd never seen him again. Until tonight.

We never talked about it, and I was sure both Nadia and Samara only had the barest idea of the dark dealings both of their families were involved in. Nadia especially had no idea her brothers ran one of the scariest Russian mafia families on both sides of the Atlantic. The Ivanovs were infamous, known for being ruthless and unbending of purpose.

If they wanted something, they took it. No apology.

And Samara's family was little better.

Nadia and Samara may be blissfully ignorant, but I didn't have that luxury.

My stepfather was a low-life, hanger-on to the Ivanovs. He had never made any attempt at hiding from me the various criminal dealings he was involved in.

He used to get drunk and complain about how they only trusted him to fix the horses for the races and keep an eye on the activities of the Italians and Columbians at the track. Apparently, all three mafia had their fingers in the racetrack pie. It was an easy way to launder money fast. They each had an interest in keeping things balanced to make sure that none took too big of a piece. That would have attracted the attention of the Feds, something none of the three factions wanted.

He would always grumble about how one day he would be in on the *big deals*. He was so low in the hierarchy, I didn't think even he'd known what the big deals really were, but from snatches of overheard cell phone conversations and his own drunken ramblings, I was pretty sure it involved some kind of gun smuggling.

Which could only reaffirm what I had overheard in my stepfather's drunken rants over the years. Gregor and Damien were two seriously dangerous criminals.

Samara and I had to run.

We had no choice.

As their little sister, Nadia was safe.

We had no such protection.

Nadia leaned in. "What do you mean you have money? How much money?"

My mouth quirked up. "Over a hundred grand."

Samara covered her mouth then asked from behind her palm, as if she was afraid to ask the question. "Yelena! How?"

At the same time, Nadia exclaimed, "Seriously?"

"That racetrack scheme my piece of shit stepfather was working on. I reworked the algorithm and hit big. Really big." I turned to Nadia. "By the way, it's why your brother Damien is *pissed* at me. Something about bringing the attention of the feds to some mob scheme."

"So, we're really doing this? We're running?"

"All kidding aside. If Damien is right, I could be in some real trouble with some pretty nasty people because of what I did. I need to get out of town. Now."

I didn't really have a plan other than to hop on a plane and never return. Now with Samara in tow and knowing I was being pursued, we would need to be more careful. We'd need fake IDs; all the ones I used to place my bets were obviously burned, but those were easy enough to come by. I'd just need two weeks to set it up.

We both turned to Nadia.

Tears streamed down her cheeks. She shook her head. "I can't go," she whispered.

While I was sad we would be separating, deep down I was relieved. If Nadia wanted to go, we never would have told her no, but it would have made an already complicated situation impossible. Gregor and Damien would have torn the world apart searching for their baby sister.

Samara made a weak attempt to reassure her. "We

won't be separated forever. All this will blow over. Gregor will marry someone else, and whatever Yelena did will be forgotten. And then we'll come back, okay, Nadia?"

Samara might come back, but I never would.

We hugged one last time.

I warned them both that I would be reaching out from a different cell phone number in the upcoming days and that I wouldn't be in school. I couldn't go back there. If what Damien said was true then, Monday morning, that would be the first place everyone would be looking for me. We were only two weeks from graduation. For all intents and purposes, I already had my diploma.

Not that it would do me much good with the life I was about to lead.

I watched them both descend down the worn plank ladder. After they were gone, I crawled over to the corner and tossed our old dolls to the side and dragged out the heavy black canvas bag hidden there. To reassure myself, I unzipped it and stared at the stacks of one-hundred-dollar bills. No wonder the bag weighed close to twenty-five pounds. It was a lot of cash.

I had a lot of research to do in the next few days. I had to figure out where the best place was for us to hide out for a few months. Probably Mexico. I also had to figure out how I was going to hide all this cash. If the suitcase got searched at the airport there would be questions. I could risk shipping it ahead of me to some PO box. Worst case scenario was if it got stolen, I would just pull off the same scheme at some other racetrack.

It would be risky. For starters, the men after me were probably watching for Pick Six wins around the primary tracks. They were uncommon enough to monitor. Plus, with my current scheme, I knew in advance what the fixed races were because my stepfather was one of the ones who fixed them. This time, I would just have to rely on the favorite to win, but it could still work.

All of this could wait. For now, I needed to find a place to hide out until Samara was ready to leave. I obviously couldn't go back to the hotel or my house.

My mind raced with everything that needed to be done.

Then all my thoughts came to a screeching halt.

Damien.

What was I going to do about Damien?

Nothing.

That was the only answer.

I was nothing to him.

He'd probably only said all that super sexy protective shit about making my stepfather pay for hitting me to get me in bed. The racetrack thing was obviously an annoyance to him and whatever operation he had going on at the track, but since I was skipping town, I wouldn't be pulling off any more Pick Sixes at Colonial Downs.

There, problem solved.

Damien could go back to taking long-legged, beautiful models named Fifi to live symphony concerts and not spare me another thought.

Never in my life had I underestimated a man before.

Never in a million years would I have thought I would become his one driving obsession.

Demon Damien Ivanov went on the hunt that night — and I was his unwitting prey.

CHAPTER 9

Damien

I STRETCHED out the fingers of my right hand and hissed as fresh blood oozed from the cuts on my knuckles. Usually, I preferred to punch my victims in the kidneys or break their ribs, making it difficult for them to breathe and keep fighting, but this time I had to go for the face. It's not that I had any problems with hitting anyone in the face, I just found it annoying how their teeth tore up my knuckles.

The purpose of this beating was to put on a show of force, in order to truly terrify Yelena's stepfather into talking when he arrived, and for that I needed visible signs of damage, which meant the face.

Mikhail, my head of security, sauntered in.

He kicked at the bloody mess of a man lying prone on

the cement floor. The pile of skin, broken bones, and blood groaned but did little else.

Reaching into his suit jacket, Mikhail pulled free the slim, black and gold packaging of Sobranie Black Russian cigarettes. They were barred from import in the United States but prized among us elite Russians for whom smoking was a pleasurable esthetic not a nasty habit like some Americans considered it.

"Strelyat' sigaret," I said, using the Russian slang for him to shoot me one.

Mikhail nodded and opened the flap, offering me one of the black paper and gold-foil tipped cigarettes. He lit his own before tossing me his Zippo. I did the same and took a long drag.

The body on the floor moaned, capturing our attention.

"I see you started the fun without me," quipped Mikhail as he took a drag then lowered his arm.

Turning, I reached into my wool overcoat pocket and pulled out my silver flask. It was dented and scratched but still a prized possession. It had been my father's. He would be rolling in his grave if he knew I was filling his favorite flask with scotch not vodka, which was precisely the point.

The entire man's life was the motherland and family honor. The happiness and wishes of his sons and only daughter were nothing to him. Even dead, he still ruled over our lives. Gregor consented to an arranged marriage with Samara Federova because our father wished it. We were both in this violent bullshit business because of our father.

I lifted the flask in mock salute.

Fuck you, Father.

I took a sip then offered it to Mikhail with a nod.

He raised an eyebrow. "Vodka or that shit you like to drink?"

"That *shit* is Macallan Rare single-malt scotch. It's aged close to twenty years."

He shook his head again. "I've got my own."

The flask he retrieved from his pocket shone like polished sterling.

"Pretty. Does it come with matching earrings?" I taunted.

He laughed. "Fuck you."

I took another swig. "I noticed you talking with Nadia earlier."

Mikhail stiffened but didn't meet my gaze. He took a swig from his flask.

When he still remained silent, I continued. "You know, my friend, it's not possible."

Gregor and I both thought of Mikhail like a brother. We trusted him with our lives. Unfortunately, that didn't change the fact he had no family name. While it was honorable how he managed to get out of that Siberian orphanage alive and make something of himself, in our culture, a family name still meant everything. No matter how important or how much money one may have, and after working with Gregor and me for several years now, he had plenty. We had made him a very rich man, but that didn't mean we would allow him to court our little sister.

Mikhail tossed his cigarette aside then checked his watch. Neither of us had cell phones on us for a reason.

Cell phones were small tracking devices. We didn't want to leave a trace of our activities here tonight. "They'll be here soon with Levin. We need to hide him."

Tossing my cigarette aside, I nodded in the direction of the beaten man. "You get his feet. I'll get his head."

The key to psychological warfare was to not show all your cards at once.

And the key to the effective use of violence was to never forget the psychological warfare element.

Otherwise, it was just violence for violence's sake, and that was wasteful and unnecessary.

Everything should have a purpose, even violence.

Whether it was a show of strength, to send a message, or to extract information.

It had to have a purpose. At least for me.

Although tonight's purpose was something I usually didn't do.

Tonight was also about revenge.

Revenge was tricky.

Used in a calculated way, it could strengthen your power.

Let your emotions get in the way, which they often did, and revenge could quickly become messy and counterproductive.

Tonight, I didn't care.

This man had hurt Yelena. More than once.

He was going to pay.

I was having Levin Nikitina brought to our warehouse in D.C., down by the docks at the Naval Yard. A place where no one asked too many questions and everyone minded their own business. There had been attempts at gentrification over the last few years with some swanky condos along the river, but the criminal heartbeat of the neighborhood had remained unchanged, which suited my purposes just fine.

Nestled inside a u-shaped stack of wooden crates was a small card table and two metal folding chairs. I took my seat at the one facing the door and pulled out my Smith and Wesson Model 66 .38 revolver. I dumped the six bullets in the chamber out onto the table. With its stainless-steel barrel and black synthetic grip, it was by far my favorite handgun. I preferred the classic revolver to a Glock which had a habit of jamming at the worst times. Plus, it was a useful tool for my method of psychological warfare.

Levin was brought in flanked by two of my men.

They tossed him into the chair opposite me.

He straightened his wrinkled and filthy shirt. "The armed escort wasn't necessary, I'm always happy to meet with a friend."

"I'm not your friend."

"Sorry, Damien. I meant a business associate."

"I don't recall ever giving you permission to call me Damien."

Levin squirmed in his seat. "Sorry, Mr. Ivanov." His upper lip twitched, belying the respectful tone he was trying to achieve.

Levin Nikitina was a shell of a man. The first word that came to mind was *twitchy*. He had oily, pock-marked skin and a bulbous nose too big for his face, with chapped lips he kept nervously licking. The stench of sweat, stale smoke, and horse manure clung to his unwashed clothes.

It was difficult to stomach that this was the man Yelena had lived with alone for the last eight years. Beautiful and intelligent Yelena, who liked designer clothes and classical music, with this poor excuse for a father. Thank God the only thing she shared in common with him was his last name. Even that was too much. It upset me to know she even carried his name. I would make her change it when I got her new identification.

Yelena Ivanova had a nice ring to it.

The thought crept unbidden into my mind.

Yelena Ivanova, my wife.

It would solve many of my problems.

As my wife, the Italians and Columbians wouldn't dare try to kidnap her. I wouldn't have to go through the trouble of getting her a new identity and finding a suitable college in Europe. All of this was nothing compared to the real reason why the idea appealed to me.

She would be mine.

Mine.

All that fiery spirit... mine.

That beautiful body with those big, bright blue eyes... mine.

It wasn't in my nature to deny myself something I wanted.

Why was I doing it now?

Because she was my little sister's friend? Nadia would be made to understand.

Because of some false idea of playing the knight in shining armor for once?

I looked down at the tarnished and dented flask in my hand. A symbol of my own honor.

Who was I kidding?

Yelena would probably fight the idea, but I could be very persuasive when I wanted to be. Besides, in the end, I wouldn't give her a choice.

I was a rich man. I could buy her jewels and all the designer gowns and shoes her little heart desired. Under my protection and as my wife, she would have whatever she desired.

And I would have her.

Levin took out a crushed foil pack of Marlboro Reds. "Mind if I smoke?" he asked as he pulled out a cheap gas station plastic lighter.

"Yes."

Levin leaned to one side to stuff the cigarettes into his back pocket. That was when he noticed the wide bloody drag mark on the cement floor. A mark like that was unmistakable. It was made by one thing — a body.

He wiped the sweat off his brow with the sleeve of his shirt and licked his chapped lips. "I heard you had a party tonight. Please tell… uh… um… Natalie… happy birthday for me."

I picked up one of the bullets on the table and tossed it from finger to finger in my right hand as if it were a coin. "Levin. We have a problem."

He sat up straight, and his beady eyes became animated as he jammed a finger onto the surface of the table, punctuating each word. "I know you found out about what that sneaky bitch did, and I'm here to tell you

Dami — I mean, Mr. Ivanov — that you can do whatever you think is necessary to her."

He made a slashing motion across his neck and then winked at me.

I clenched my jaw, fighting for calm. "That sneaky bitch?"

He waved his hand. "Yeah. Yelena."

"Your daughter."

Making the supreme mistake of getting comfortable in my presence, Levin leaned back in his chair, tossing an arm over the back. "Stepdaughter," he corrected. "She's no blood of mine. I got stuck with her after that bitch of a wife offed herself a few years back. Ruined a perfectly good car doing it too. Good riddance. She was a terrible fuck but a good cook with the proper motivation."

I nodded. Tapping the bullet against the table, I raised an eyebrow. "The proper motivation?"

"Yeah. Yeah. You know," he raised his arm and made a swiping motion with the back of his hand. "A little motivation. Men like us need to keep our women in line." He gave me another exaggerated wink.

My stomach roiled with disgust, which was saying a lot. I had done business with some of the worst sociopaths in the world but the man before me made me want to retch. The guilt tore me up inside. I saw Yelena as she was, that little girl gobbling down a crappy hamburger. The idea that I'd then sent her home to this piece of shit made me want to howl with rage.

Yes. I would make Yelena my wife.

I would drag her kicking and screaming down the aisle, if necessary.

She might defy me at first but in the end, it would be for the best because I was going to spoil her rotten. I would give her the world. Diamonds, gold, furs. Whatever she wanted. And maybe, if there was a God, each time her sea blue eyes would light with joy, it would chip away at the memory of her as a little girl being sent back to this monster — by me.

I sat back in my chair, a casual gesture that belied my mood. "So, you're aware she pulled off three Pick Sixes in one week, winning over one hundred thousand dollars?"

Levin shook his head. He reached into his back pocket and pulled out his cigarettes out of habit before casting a look at me and tossing them aside. "Yeah. Yeah. Who knew, right? I thought she was a dumb bitch like her mother. Turns out she has a brain in her head. Yeah. Yeah."

He once more leaned forward and pounded the table with his forefinger. "But I promise you. I'm as loyal to the Ivanovs as the day is long. Hand to Jesus. I didn't know what the little bitch was up to, and I've pulled the house apart looking for the money. You know... to hand it over to you. But the bitch has it hidden somewhere good, and as soon as I get my hands on her, I'll find out where."

If I had my way, and I always got my way, he'd never lay eyes — let alone his hands — on Yelena again.

This time, I leaned forward. "You're aware in addition to the missing money that this also caused several red flags and some regrettable chatter at the local FBI office?"

Levin waved his hand in front of his face. "I heard something about that yeah, yeah, but that will all die down. The feds got nothing on us."

Us.

There was no us.

There were the Ivanovs.

And him.

I smiled. "I'm not concerned about the FBI, Levin. They were handled immediately. I also took the liberty of confiscating all security footage of Yelena at the track collecting her winnings before anyone, including the feds, ever had a chance to review it."

Levin wagged his finger at me. "That's good. That's real good. I wouldn't have thought of that." He pounded the table again with his bony finger. "That's why you're the boss, Damien. You're always thinking." He tapped his temple.

"I *am* always thinking. For instance, right now, I'm wondering how both the Italians and the Columbians managed to learn Yelena's name and that she was responsible for the Pick Six wins."

Levin leaned back and wiped his sweating upper lip with his sleeve.

I stroked the cool metal barrel of my gun. "You see, I have the only copy of the surveillance tapes. The feds have been bribed not to talk. And she used several fake IDs to collect the money."

With a shaking hand, Levin reached for his cigarettes but then stopped.

"So what I'm *thinking*… is some disloyal piece of trash approached them with an offer to do business in exchange for Yelena's name, so they could get their hands on her betting method."

Levin rubbed his sweating hands along the top of his thighs on his grease-stained pants. "Mr. Ivanov, I can explain."

I picked up my revolver and flicked open the empty chamber. "You ever play Russian roulette, Levin?"

CHAPTER 10

*D*amien

LEVIN STOOD UP.

Both of my men sprang into action. Each placing a hand on his shoulder and forcing him to sit down.

"Mr. Ivanov this is all just a big misunderstanding."

"You didn't answer my question, Levin."

"I'll get you your money back. Hand to Jesus. If I have to beat the girl bloody. She'll tell me where she put it, and then it's yours, all yours."

Thank God Yelena was safely tucked into bed at the hotel. I didn't want to think about what would have happened had I not learned about this mess in time, and she had been allowed to return home after my sister's party.

After I took care of Levin, maybe I would head back to the hotel. Just to check on her. Now that I had decided to marry her, there was no impediment to finishing what we had started. The idea of holding her warm body in my arms had my cock once more stirring back to life, but now was not the time.

The corner of my mouth raised in a mockery of a smile. "You think this is about a paltry hundred grand?"

Levin's eyes shifted around the warehouse as if looking for an escape before landing back on me. "Look I have no idea how the Italians and Columbians found out, but hand to Jesus, it wasn't from me!"

I turned and met Mikhail's eyes. He nodded and slipped out of the room. A minute later, he returned with two more of my men dragging the man I had beaten earlier back into the room. He was suspended between the two men by his arms. His legs limp and dragging. He was bruised and bloody, but he would live. Not with all his teeth, and with a severely broken nose, but he would live.

Mikhail grabbed the beaten man by his hair and lifted his head.

I nodded in the broken man's direction. "Fredo and I had a little chat before you arrived. He says you approached him. Offered Yelena's services to the Italians if they banked the bets and gave you a percentage of the cut."

"He's lying! I'd never do that!"

Fredo Rossi was on par with Levin Nikitina. A low-level thug paid by the Bianchi family to muck around in the horse shit at the race stables and fix races. The Bianchi family would be justifiably annoyed I had beaten up one of their men instead of going through the usual diplomatic hierarchy, but a sizable tribute payment would smooth over any ruffled feathers. After all, Fredo meant about as much to the Bianchis as Levin meant to the Ivanovs. He was an easily replaceable piece of trash who wasn't blood, wasn't true family.

Levin gestured wildly in Fredo's direction. "You're not going to believe that dirty wop over me, are you?"

I motioned for them to take Fredo away. Mikhail nodded. I knew without having to say so that he would return Fredo to the Bianchis and arrange for a payoff as a sign of respect from the Ivanovs.

I slipped a bullet in the chamber and spun it. "This one is for lying to me."

I placed the gun with the barrel facing me and slid it across the table toward Levin.

"Pick it up," I ordered.

He looked at the gun and then me and then back at the gun. "I'm not doing this."

"You are, or I will see that you die a slow and painful death. I will string you up by your wrists and cut you just enough to make you bleed. Over and over and over again. And when you think your prayers have been answered and death is finally approaching, I will bring you back from the brink just to start over again. You will bleed slowly to death over days from a thousand wounds, all the while begging me for mercy. Your pleas will fall on deaf ears."

Levin swallowed. His eyes wide, he looked back at the gun. Finally, he snatched it up, but instead of holding it to his temple, he trained it on me.

My men took a step forward, their hands going to the guns strapped to their sides. I waved them off.

My eyes narrowed, meeting Levin's frenetic gaze with a glare. "Go ahead. Pull the trigger."

His hand started to shake.

"According to the law of probability, you have a sixteen-point six percent chance of killing me. Of course, if you pull the trigger and don't kill me, there is a one hundred percent chance I'll kill you. Slowly," I warned. "You're a gambling man, Levin. How do you like those odds?"

Levin licked his lips then swallowed. "Shouldn't a man have some vodka for this?"

I nodded to one of my men. One of them left and quickly returned with a bottle of Smirnoff and two shot glasses from the warehouse office. He put the bottle and one shot glass in front of Levin and placed the other in front of me. After I motioned with my hand, the man poured a shot of vodka for Levin, but I waved him away from my own glass. Pulling out my flask, I filled it with scotch. Not the way such a fine liquor should be drunk, but I wasn't exactly a gentleman sitting by a fire in his study reading Shakespeare right now, was I? Far from it.

Levin took the shot, splashing half of it down his front.

He held the gun to his temple.

Opening his mouth on a guttural scream — he pulled the trigger.

A hollow click.

Then nothing.

Misfire.

Slamming the gun on the table, Levin picked up the vodka bottle and sloshed some more into his shot glass, spilling it all over the table in the process. He tipped back his head and drained the contents. He then tossed the shot glass on the table and looked at me triumphantly.

I pulled the gun toward me and flicked open the chamber. Without lowering my gaze from his, I reached for a second bullet and slipped it into the chamber. I spun it. "This is for your betrayal in trying to make a side deal with the Bianchis. Defying the family."

I slid the gun back toward him.

Levin poured himself a third shot. Then he raised the gun to his temple. He took several breaths through his nose, his chest puffing out with each one.

Finally, he pulled the trigger.

Another hollow click.

Another misfire.

Levin shouted out in joy. Turning around in his chair in search of validation from my men. He was met with stony silence. "Yeah! Yeah! You see! I have proven my loyalty! I have fired twice and lived!"

I sipped from my shot glass before pulling the gun back toward me.

His whole body twitched. "Hand to Jesus. I've always been loyal to the Ivanovs." He waved his hands in the air. "Yes! Yes! Yeah! Yeah! You caught me. I may have made a deal with Fredo, but it was nothing! I was going to tell you about Yelena and give you the money. I swear!"

"And what about the Columbians?"

Levin's eyes twitched to the right, searching the other side of the room from where we had taken Fredo. No doubt nervous we were about to drag in his second accomplice. "The Columbians?"

The truth was we hadn't found that man yet. As of right now, I only suspected he talked with the Columbians because of Levin's own movements. I'd been tracking him since I was tipped off about this whole mess by my contact at the FBI, who told me about the tapes in exchange for a sizable payout.

While the Italians were easily handled, the Columbians would be a different matter entirely. The Ivanovs had a long-standing mutual respect for the Bianchis. We even partnered together on the occasional arms deal. I would trust their word when they said they considered the matter finished.

That was not the case with the Columbians. There was no central family to approach. No one I would trust to keep their word. They were who I really feared with regards to Yelena. The only way to truly protect her from the Columbians was to make it a matter of war if they touched her.

If she were my wife and they harmed her, it would mean war.

And if there was one thing no one wanted, it was war with the Russians.

No one fucked with us for a reason.

"Yes. The Columbians. I hear you made the same deal with them. I must say Fredo was not happy when he learned that not only was he taking a beating because of you, but that you had planned to double cross him all along."

"I'm telling you, they're all lying! This is a big setup

against me. That bitch Yelena is probably behind it all!"

Once more holding his gaze, I flicked open the chamber. I selected a bullet and held it up. "Do you know what this bullet is for, Levin?"

He screeched. His voice rose several octaves with panic. "Please, Mr. Ivanov. I didn't talk to the Columbians!"

Ignoring him, I continued. "This bullet is special. *Very special.* You see, this bullet is for Yelena."

Levin's eyes widened. "Yelena?"

"Yes, your stepdaughter. Yelena. The girl who was entrusted into your care."

Levin sputtered as he reached for the vodka bottle. "You can't make me pay for what that bitch did! It's her fault! It's all her fault! Kill her! She deserves it. Set an example with her. Kill her, not me!"

This time, he didn't even bother with the shot glass but drank straight from the bottle. He guzzled down the clear liquid as it sloshed over his cheeks and jaw, drenching the soiled collar of his shirt.

"Yelena is very important to my sister, which makes her important to me. I've seen her black eye, Levin."

Levin shrugged. "She gets mouthy. Always complaining about something. What do you expect me to do? A man shouldn't have to listen to that in his own house! And then when I'm going through her room for some money, you know for her upkeep, I find all those cashed-in Pick Six racing tickets. The selfish bitch knew how to make thousands, and she was keeping it from me."

I slipped the third bullet into the chamber. Flicked it

closed and spun it. I pushed the gun toward him. "Only a spineless coward would punch a woman."

Levin hesitated. The false courage given to him by the vodka was starting to wear off. He knew the gun now held three bullets in its six chambers. The odds were severely against him.

He reached for the gun. Wrapped his fingers around the black handle. Leaving his fist on the table, he lifted the gun up.

It was now pointed directly at me.

His cloudy brown eyes narrowed.

If the odds of death increased for him if he pulled the trigger, they also just increased for me.

With a tremble, he lifted the gun higher.

It was still pointed at me.

My men, who were positioned directly behind him, stirred.

Without shifting my gaze, I raised a single finger from my hand which was lying flat on the table, warning them without words to stand down.

Staring down the barrel of the gun, I reached for my shot glass and calmly drank the rest of the scotch. I flipped the glass over and returned it to the table.

Sensing his own defeat, Levin wrapped his dirty hand around the neck of the vodka bottle and took another long swig.

He then held the gun to his temple… and pulled the trigger.

It was fitting that it was Yelena's bullet.

Rising, I reached for my overcoat and put it on. I then pried my gun from the dead man's grasp. Walking away without a backward glance, I said to my men, "Throw out the trash."

Just being in that man's presence made me want to shower. I was going to go home, shower, burn these clothes, and then head to the hotel.

I needed to see Yelena, my future wife.

CHAPTER 11

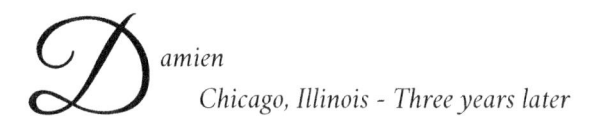

Damien
Chicago, Illinois - Three years later

I HADN'T SLEPT through the night in three long years.

Every time I closed my eyes, I pictured Yelena.

She's chained to a basement floor. Naked on some filthy mattress, crying as a shadowy figure stands over her.

Every night.

Every time I closed my eyes.

I would see her crying and would be powerless to stop it.

I stared at my reflection in the knife blade I was holding. Hard eyes stared back. Three years. I'd caused a lot of pain and suffering in those years. Each time, it chipped another piece of my heart away. I doubted there was anything left.

Three years ago, I'd still had a semblance of a conscience. I had still at least felt guilty for some of my actions. Still weighed the consequences against my immortal soul.

And now? Now I no longer cared.

With Yelena by my side, I had had a chance to hold on to a glimmer of my humanity. I would have drawn from her warmth and kept that small spark alive. In her eyes, I might have salvaged a piece of the man I wanted to be. The man I would have become had family honor and loyalty not demanded the extreme sacrifice of my soul.

But she'd run, and it had all turned to ice.

Three years had turned me into the same cold, unfeeling man my father was with his same narrow-minded ideals of family and duty.

"You're sure it's them this time?" asked Gregor, breaking into my dangerous thoughts.

I answered without turning around. "I'm sure."

Our private plane had a large lounge setup and a bar in the main cabin. I was seated toward the front in one of the large, swiveling leather seats. Gregor was behind me, a file filled with photos of Samara on his lap. I had a similar file with photos of Yelena.

Yelena in Mexico, in Boston, in Los Angeles, in Montreal, and now in Chicago.

Always, I was too late.

Always one step behind.

She continued to cash in on her racetrack algorithm. She thought she was getting away with it. Thought she was safe by only hitting a Pick Six once every few months and each time at a different racetrack in a different state. She was wrong. You didn't take millions of dollars out of the pocket of several mafia rackets without anyone noticing and tracking your movements.

The Italians had been convinced to let her be. Usually with large, continuing payoffs from me.

The Columbians refused.

I knew they wanted to get their hands on Yelena. Badly.

I also knew that, just like me, they had been tipped off she was in Chicago.

There was a large race coming up in a few days. The first thoroughbred race of the season, The Sham Stakes. The race was held at the Santa Anita Park in Arcadia, California but betting would take place worldwide. She would want to be in a major city where she'd be able to cash in her winning ticket quickly with the ready cash on hand from all the heavy betting, but not a place so visible, like Las Vegas. Chicago was perfect.

This time I had her.

This time there would be no escape.

I was not sure when my pursuit of her had become such an obsession. Probably the moment I'd returned to her hotel room to find her gone. I had underestimated her. It wouldn't happen again. I should have told her what she was facing. Should have laid it out to her in stark terms she'd understand.

If I had, would she still have run?

If I had asked her to marry me, would she have said yes?

I'd never know.

I'd returned to find a cold bed.

Two weeks later, Samara was gone as well.

It was galling to realize Yelena must have been hiding out nearby waiting to leave the entire time. My only consolation was she certainly would have learned the fate of her stepfather before she went on the run. I had hoped, perhaps, she would see that as at least a sign I could be trusted to protect her but no.

She'd still run.

Gregor and I had been chasing the girls ever since. In a strange way, it brought us closer together as brothers. A common goal. To retrieve our runaway brides.

I took a sip from my drink as I spun the chair around to face Gregor. He was holding up a photo of Samara taken on the street outside the art gallery where she now worked.

"Rockabilly," I said absentmindedly.

"What?"

"The dress. It's a rockabilly style. Trim waist. Nice flare. High collar."

"What the hell?"

"What? You fuck enough models you learn about fashion. It's obvious Samara is all about the vintage 50s look. Red lips, cuffed jeans, the whole nine."

"Worry about your own girl, Versace."

I raised my glass in a mock salute and turned my chair back. We'd be landing at Midway soon.

Soon, I would have Yelena in my grasp. My cock stirred at the thought. I couldn't remember the last time I'd fucked a woman. At first, I had tried to erase her memory. Any beautiful woman with blonde hair and blue eyes was fair game. But they all paled in comparison to Yelena. They all were false. Their beauty brittle. Their intellect a thin veneer. Their eyes didn't have the same sparkle of defiance that Yelena's had. Their skin wasn't as silky soft. Their lips lacked her sweetness.

Before, I had hesitated because of her age. She had been barely eighteen. Still a child.

Now there was no such barrier.

I wouldn't make the same mistake twice.

This time, when I found her, the first thing I was going to do was claim her for my own.

Once and for all.

Before, I was drawn to Yelena because of her beauty and intellect and her fiery spirit.

Now, I was obsessed with the idea of possessing her simply to own her.

To control her.

To show her the Ivanovs have all the power.

To show her *I* have all the power.

To make her pay for taunting me with the notion that salvation was possible for a man like me.

And she would pay.

I still had every intention of marrying her. She would be mine in every respect of the word.

Except now, I wouldn't bother asking first.

CHAPTER 12

Yelena

Picking up my phone, I listened to Samara's voicemails.

They all had essentially the same message.

Run!

I knew what that meant. We would scramble for our safe house in Montreal. Until then, we would have no choice but to go off the radar. Radio silence. No phones unless absolutely necessary. Taking a deep breath, I reminded myself to focus.

I needed to get the hell out of town. We would figure out our next move when we were safely in Montreal. It was a shame; like Samara, I was starting to like Chicago and the idea that maybe we could stop running.

Heading to my desk, I withdrew every scrap of paper. I kept all important documents in a lockbox in a bank in

Los Angeles, but you never knew what someone could glean from a few receipts or scraps of paper.

Carrying the bundle to the sink, I opened my junk drawer and searched for matches. Lighting one, I held it to the corner of several papers till they started to brown and curl. Eventually, they caught the flame. I lit another match and repeated the gesture. As they started to smoke, the fire alarm went off. Grabbing a broom, I smashed it with the handle till it went silent.

Grabbing a bucket from under the sink, I went into the bathroom. I wrenched the top drawer out and dumped its contents into the bucket. I did the same for the second and third, watching all my expensive Mac and Chanel makeup pile up. It broke my heart, but it was bulky and I needed to travel light. I then took my hairbrushes and toothbrush and curlers into the kitchen. I opened the dishwasher door and pulled out the dish racks. I dumped my makeup and the rest of my beauty products into the bottom. Opening a bottle of bleach, I poured it over the pile. Closing the door, I started the dishwasher. I then stripped the bed of its sheets and put them in the washer. That should take care of any DNA. You could never be too careful.

It would be better to just burn the whole condo, but that wasn't really an option.

Wrenching open the door to my closet, I headed to the secret panel behind a shoe shelf and pulled free a small black backpack—my go bag.

Checking its contents, I opened up a few shoe boxes which contained some hidden cash and jewels and shoved them into the bag. I also made sure the gun Samara and I picked up in Mexico and my pink pearl-handled stiletto knife were there, as well. On second thought, I snatched up the knife and put it in the back pocket of my jeans so I could access it quickly.

Next, I went into the living room and ran my arm along the mantle, tossing my favorite lucky charm Happy Meal toys into my bag. Although admittedly the little plastic toys had yet to bring me much luck. Taking one last look around, I picked up my car keys and pulled open the door.

And screamed in terror.

CHAPTER 13

Yelena

Every instinct in my body went on high alert.

"No!" I screamed as I tried to slam the door.

Damien shoved his foot over the threshold to prevent me.

Despite that, I tried to slam the door again anyway. It just bounced back open. I took a few steps backward.

Nervously, I licked my lips. My voice cracked as I asked, "How did you finally find me?"

He gave me a wink. "You're not the only one with skills, malyshka."

Tilting my chin up, I inhaled a shaky breath. "I want you to leave."

"Listen carefully, Yelena. You are in way over your

head, so be a good girl and come with me and don't give me any more trouble."

I shook my head.

Damien sighed. "Apparently, you don't remember what happens when you tell me no."

Oh, I remembered.

I remembered very clearly what happened.

Dropping my bag, I ran deeper into the condo.

He followed.

Racing down the hall, I bolted into the bedroom and slammed the door shut. After locking it, I turned to push the heavy bureau in front of it.

There was a loud thud as the door rattled on its hinges.

He was trying to break it down.

I pushed harder on the bureau. It began to slowly slide across the carpet.

Another loud thud. The frame splintered as the flimsy lightweight door buckled from the pressure.

The bureau was only a few feet away. Crying out in frustration, I bent my knees and pushed harder.

Too late.

The door crashed open.

"Tsk. Tsk. You are being a very bad girl, malen'kaya shalun'ya," Damien said sardonically as he pushed the door — which was now only hanging by one hinge — out of the way and stepped into the room. The black combat boots, cargo pants, and form-fitting long sleeved shirt made him look even more menacing than before.

It had been three years since I had seen him.

Everything about him was bigger and scarier.

The man was huge. Really huge. He was so tall and his shoulders so wide, I couldn't even imagine how he found clothes to fit him. And they really, *really* fit him. I bit my lip as I tried not to glance down.

And the tattoos! Jesus, Mary, and Joseph! There seemed to be more of them now. They covered both arms. I could even see a few new black swirls peeking out above the neckline of his t-shirt which meant a pretty sizable chest tattoo. With his dark hair and dark eyes, Damien could have been Jason Momoa's brother.

His face was more angular, giving it a hard, uncompromising look. The only problem was he'd become even sexier. There was something about the harsh glint to his gaze and the confident arrogance he exuded. As if he had settled into the reality of his violent life and embraced it where before, three years earlier, he was still at a crossroads.

Well, he would find me changed, too.

Three years ago, my fight had been all bravado, a flimsy house of cards easily tumbled by a harsh word or glare from him. I had put on a tough exterior while hiding my fear and pain. No more.

I wasn't that same girl who took a punch from her stepfather as her due for being a *useless brat* who burdened him after her mother's death. I had done a great deal of growing up these last few years, and I now knew my self-worth. I was independent and strong and didn't need anyone to survive.

I shrieked as I reached for my stiletto knife. "Stay away from me." With a press of a button, the sharp, four-inch blade sprang out.

Damien put his hands up. "Yelena, baby. Listen to me. I'm here to protect you."

"I don't believe you!"

No. Damien was here for revenge. He had to be. He was mad I'd run with all the money and left him to face the Italians and Columbians. Not to mention the fact that my partner in crime was his brother's intended bride. If it hadn't been for me and my money and resources Samara would never have run, let alone stayed just one step ahead of the Ivanov family's grasp for three years. Now we had finally been trapped. For all I knew, Samara was in a worse situation than me as she faced off with Gregor.

This is bad.

Very bad.

I had to get away from him.

Holding up my knife, I threatened Damien. "Come one step closer, and I swear I'll fucking kill you."

He laughed.

The bastard laughed!

"You really are adorable, but you are as threatening as a chipmunk."

Apparently, Damien and Gregor hadn't gotten too deep into how Samara and I had spent the last three years. He obviously didn't know about the time I spent in Mexico training or he wouldn't be scoffing at my threat.

While Samara tried to forget and lose herself in painting, I had taken a different route, taking as many self-defense classes as I could find. I wasn't the same beaten-down teenager who couldn't protect herself against the blows. Not anymore. And no one was going to get the upper hand on me ever again.

A stiletto did not make for an accurate throwing knife. The blade was too thin and the handle too weighted, but it was my only option.

Keeping my eyes trained on Damien, I took a step back with my left foot as I flipped the knife in my palm so I was holding it by the blade. Raising my arm, I aimed for his chest and pitched it forward, releasing my grip on the knife. The weight of the handle arched the knife downward.

I watched as it sunk into Damien's side. His face registered shock before looking down at his wound.

Seizing the moment, I raced through the bathroom door, slamming and locking it. The bathroom connected with the other bedroom I used for a closet. I could hear Damien's roar of outrage and what could only be the sound of the bureau being toppled as he raced after me. Running through the converted bedroom, I deliberately tossed my many designer clothes racks onto the floor to slow down his progress. I spared a moment of regret for all the Prada, Dior, and Chanel dresses and shoes that were now scattered on the floor about to be trampled by Damien's big combat boots.

Hazarding a glance over my shoulder, I could tell he followed me through the bathroom as opposed to retracing his steps back into the hallway. I actually smiled when he cursed as he fell over the fallen racks.

In the living room, I glanced left and right.

Right was the front door.

He would expect that.

I turned left.

Opening the balcony door, I placed one foot over the threshold.

A strong arm wrapped around my middle and dragged me back into the condo.

My scream for help was cut off by his palm.

Damien rasped into my ear, "You're going to pay for that little stunt, malen'kaya shalun'ya."

I remembered my defense training. With my feet planted wide, I lifted my bent arms up, breaking his hold. Bending down, I twisted my body right then left, using my elbows to jab him in the sides. With this distraction, I reached between my legs and grabbed his leg and pulled.

Off-balance, Damien crashed to the floor, and I took off running again. Stepping onto the cushions, I vaulted over the back of the sofa and headed for the front door. I was reaching for the knob when I, too, fell to the floor.

I glanced back to see Damien was stretched out with his hand around my ankle. Trying to kick him free, I reached for my go bag which was still lying in the front entrance. As Damien deflected my kicks and started to move his body over mine, my hand scrambled for the side pocket.

Finally, my fingers closed over the handle of my revolver.

Damien growled as he leaned over me. "Give up, baby-girl. You're mine now."

My response was to raise the gun and cock the hammer.

Damien moved back slightly, his eyes going to the gun in my hand. Shimmying out from under him, I moved along the floor till my back was against the wall.

Holding the gun before me, I sneered, "I don't think so."

His dark eyes narrowed. In our struggles, the neck of his t-shirt had torn. I could see the intricate pattern of a tattoo that crossed his shoulder and crept up his neck. My eyes lowered to his midsection. His black shirt was wet with blood from the knife wound I had given him.

Gesturing with my gun, I said, "You're going to bleed to death."

He smirked. "You're not that lucky. It's only a scratch."

I could only imagine how insane we both looked. My beautiful condo was completely trashed. The two of us were sitting on the floor in my hallway with torn, bloodied clothes. And me with a gun trained on him.

"Is that a Smith & Wesson .38?" he asked as casually as if he were requesting the time.

My brow furrowed, sensing a trap but not knowing what it could be. "Yes. Why?"

He winked. "Good girl. It's a smart choice in weapon. Very reliable. That's my favorite gun, too. Another thing we have in common."

Another thing.

It brought to mind that night a lifetime ago in his car, listening to Rachmaninov's Piano Concerto Number Two. I didn't have to be reminded of what had happened next. Those moments had haunted my dreams every night for three years. The feel of his hand as he ruthlessly hiked up my dress skirt and spanked me. The shock of how arousing I'd found it. The feel of his tongue between my legs bringing me to my first real orgasm. If I closed my eyes, I could still feel the scrape of his five o'clock shadow against my inner thighs. Still feel the warmth of his breath against my pussy.

I shook those thoughts free.

I had to remember; Damien wasn't Nadia's sexy older brother anymore.

He was the man who had been hunting me down for years.

A man bent on revenge because of the trouble I caused and continued to cause with my racetrack schemes. But more importantly, for my role in embarrassing his family by whisking Samara away before his brother could force her into marriage.

We weren't completely without friends. We had heard plenty of times over the years how obsessed the brothers had become in finding us. How obsessed Gregor was to finalize the marriage contract agreed to by his father and hers.

It was a matter of family honor and respect, and everyone knew a Russian never forgot or forgave a slight to their honor. Revenge and retribution was the only option to set things right. Damien was here for one thing and one thing only.

Revenge.

I had to remember his nickname. Demon Damien. The man with the charm of the devil and his same propensity for violence and evil.

"So, what now?" I asked.

Damien shifted. I inhaled sharply and raised my gun. He put his hands up as he slowly moved to lean his back against the opposite wall. Looking down at his side as the movement caused a small gush of blood, his mouth quirked. "This was a Varvatos."

I absolutely *refused* to be impressed that he knew the designer of his t-shirt or that he even bought expensive designer t-shirts — even though I was. There was just something fucking sexy about a man who gave a damn about his appearance.

My chin tilted up in defiance. "I'm not going anywhere with you."

Damien sighed as he ran a hand through his hair. "Yes, baby, you are."

"Are you forgetting? *I'm* the one with the gun!"

The bastard smiled. "I've never played Russian roulette with a female before. Could be fun."

I threatened as I adjusted my grip on the gun and raised it a few inches higher. "This is not a game, Damien. Don't for a second doubt that I *will* pull the trigger if you don't let me walk out of here right now."

Would I?

Could I really pull the trigger on him?

Could I really put a bullet in his chest?

Could I bear to see the light go out of those amazing sapphire blue eyes of his?

Oh God.

Why can't he just let me leave?

As if reading my inner thoughts, he warned, "You're going to have to shoot me, because I'm not leaving here without you."

Gritting my teeth, I fired back, "I *will* kill you if I have to."

A look of sympathy crossed his features.

No. It was a trap. Don't fall for it. *Demon Damien.* Don't fall for his charm. He's not sympathetic. He was a cold-blooded killer bent on revenge. Remember that, I admonished myself over and over again.

Dammit. Why did he have to be so damn sexy? Why couldn't he have a beer belly or a bald spot? Or at the very least have been shorter than me! Why did he have to be tall and muscular with chiseled features and all those hot tattoos?

"Do you have Samara?"

Ignoring my question, he asked, "Why does this place smell like bleach?"

Ignoring his question, I demanded, "Answer me, do you have Samara?"

Damien moved toward me.

I raised the gun.

Angrily, he stormed, "Will you put that thing away?"

"No!"

"Dammit," he cursed as he lunged for me.

Startled, I pulled the trigger.

CHAPTER 14

Yelena

A HOLLOW CLICK.

Nothing.

Damien grabbed my legs and spread them wide as he pulled me toward him. Flat on my back, I tried pulling the trigger again.

A hollow click.

Nothing.

Then again.

Grasping the muzzle in his large fist, his smile not quite reaching his eyes, Damien said, "It's not loaded."

With a screech, I tried to wrench the gun out of his grasp while I beat his chest with my fist.

Tossing the gun out of reach, Damien grabbed both

my wrists and wrenched my arms high over my head. "Listen to me!"

Still, I struggled.

Placing my small wrists into one hand, Damien shifted. His right hand palmed my breast.

Instantly I stilled, my eyes going wide.

"That's better," he soothed as he lowered his hand to cup the full weight of it. At that moment, his hips ground against my pussy as he took full advantage of his position between my open thighs. I could feel the threat of his hard cock against my stomach.

Rubbing the edge of his thumb over my traitorously erect nipple, he lowered his voice to a harsh grumble. "We can talk, or I can give you the fucking you clearly deserve."

My mouth opened in shock. Recovering, I sputtered, "How dare you?"

Damien smiled. "You'll find, baby, I'll dare just about anything where you are concerned."

This wasn't real.

He doesn't mean it. It's all just a pretense to get my cooperation. Remember how he got the best of you the last time? By making you think he actually desired you. It's all just an act. Think of Samara.

"Samara is with Gregor. She's safe, but we need to get out of here. If I found you, then the Columbians will have, as well. You screwed up, babygirl. You started working in a pattern. Hitting major races in major cities. They've been expecting you to show up here."

Fuck.

The Sham Stakes.

He was right. I had wanted to lessen my exposure, so I started only hitting the really big races. But to do that, I also had to be in a major city that would have the type of cash on hand to cash out the tickets more quickly than a little podunk, off track betting center could. The Sham Stakes was the first major race of the season, and it happened in two days. It was an easy money bet that I'd be in Chicago, New York, or Los Angeles for it.

Tilting my chin up, I tried some of my old bravado. "You're a liar."

Damien cupped my cheek. "I'm a lot of things, baby, but a liar isn't one of them. Lying is a pitiful sign of weakness."

I shook my head. "No. No. This is all some elaborate revenge plan."

"It's not, but we do need to get the hell out of here. You *are* in danger."

"How would you know?"

"I don't have time to go into that right now."

I lowered my eyes. I desperately wanted to ask him how he had found us despite all my schemes, but held my tongue.

"I need to get you someplace safe."

"What about Samara?"

"I told you, she's with Gregor."

I scoffed. "You actually expect me to believe you're here to save me? Why?"

Damien didn't answer at first. He just pierced me with a hard stare. Stroking my cheek, he finally said, "You fascinate me. You're an intoxicating mixture of intelligent badass and vulnerable babydoll. My malen'kiy padshiy angel."

His little fallen angel.

Fitting I'd be pursued by a demon like him.

A badass babydoll. Damn if that wasn't the best compliment I think I had ever been given.

Too bad it was a lie.

I didn't believe him. I couldn't believe him. There was too much at stake.

I needed to get away. Searching his face, I remembered his own seduction tactic. Knowing I would talk myself out of such a risky plan if I hesitated, I just acted.

Leaning up, I kissed him.

At first, it was just our lips innocently meeting.

Then Damien took over.

Moving both his hands to clasp my head, he deepened the kiss. His tongue swept in to claim my own. He tasted like peppermint and scotch. The weight of his body pressed down on mine. It was hard not to feel completely possessed by him. Instinctively, I raised my hips to push against his erection.

His growl of approval reverberated between us.

"Christ, Yelena. I need to get inside of you now," rasped Damien as he reached for the zipper of my jeans. "I've waited an eternity to feel you around my cock."

With his body tilted at an angle, all I had to do was swivel my hips to throw him onto his back. Now I straddled his lean hips. His cock pressed between my thighs.

Looking down at him, I was once more struck by his hard-lined, handsome features. His eyes were so dark sapphire blue that they appeared almost black. His strong jaw and angular profile were elegant in their severity. From his face to his thickly, muscled body - every inch of this man screamed *don't fuck with me*.

Too bad that was precisely what I planned to do.

Leaning down, I raised up on my knees. Whispering huskily, I asked, "You want me?"

Damien bared his teeth as he sucked in a breath before exclaiming, "God yeah, baby."

"Too bad."

I put all my weight on my right knee and raised my left, only to bring it straight down onto his still-bleeding knife wound.

Damien's body pivoted and curled up as he howled in pain.

With his large body blocking the front door, I ran once more for the balcony. Clearing the doorway, I swung over the wrought iron railing and grabbed hold of the drainpipe. I had already shimmied up at least one floor by the time Damien reached the balcony. He grasped the railing and surveyed the drainpipe before realizing it would not hold both of our weights.

He disappeared back into my condo.

I knew without a doubt he was racing through my building looking for the rooftop access. Hopefully, I would be gone by the time he found it.

Reaching the top of the building, I swung my leg over the brick edge onto the roof. I scanned the area, and I could see Damien was still inside. I reached for the iron ladder of the fire escape. The rusted metal wouldn't budge. Leaning dangerously close to the edge, I stretched for the top rung with both hands and pushed down with all my might, but it wouldn't slide to the ground.

The rooftop metal door slammed against the wall.

I was out of time.

Damien was here.

Looking over my shoulder, I saw his tall figure thunder toward me. I leaned over the edge of the building, looking for a drainpipe I could perhaps shimmy down. It was dangerous and reckless, but I was desperate. I had seen them do it in the movies, so why not? I had swung my leg over the balustrade when he reached me.

Wrapping one arm around my waist from behind, his hand went to my throat. He wrenched my head back to rest on his shoulder as he whispered into my ear, "You should be very scared right now, malen'kaya shalun'ya, because I'm going to hate fuck you into next week."

CHAPTER 15

*D*amien

GOD DAMN it was I fucking pissed right now.

Damn if this woman didn't infuriate me.

Three years had changed nothing. She was still stubborn and reckless. Foolishly diving headfirst into dangerous situations that were going to get her killed.

At the same time, three years had transformed her from a pretty girl to a stunningly beautiful woman. Her svelte body had softened just a little bit, giving her curves more of a lushness that begged for a man's hands. She still had the same gorgeous blonde hair, but instead of it being one long shimmering length, it was layered. It was now a riot of curls and waves which better framed her heart-shaped face.

Mostly the change was in her eyes.

Countless times, I thought I was misremembering.

Thinking they couldn't have been that bright of a blue. And I was right. They were brighter. The tiny flecks of gold twinkled through a sea of blue that made them shine. Desperately, I wanted to gaze down into them and watch to see if they would change into a deeper blue as I sunk my cock into her.

From her response when I spanked her, I knew she liked to play rough. A girl like Yelena wouldn't be satisfied with a missionary fuck in bed, I was certain of it. No, my girl would like to be thrown over the back of a sofa and fucked hard from behind as I pulled her hair.

My girl.

Yep, that's right.

Mine.

I had thought of her as such for so long it was almost a shock when she fought me. I had forgotten that she didn't know that she was mine now. Didn't know that I intended to make her my wife. Something I would have to remedy and soon. No man should just let a woman like Yelena get away. No smart man at least.

But right now, my interest in Yelena, beyond wanting to fuck her and make her mine, was the mystery around how she operated those racetrack schemes. With that knowledge, I could maybe neutralize the Columbian threat against her. Her actions impacted Samara and anything that impacted Samara impacted Gregor, which impacted me and our entire enterprise. It was a deadly game of dominoes.

The threat needed to be taken care of for both Yelena and Samara to be safe. That was my job. Gregor was the front man of the company. I was the one who operated in the shadows and made sure no one fucked with us. While Gregor thrived on information as a weapon, I relied on both information and muscle.

I had vowed three years ago that no one was ever going to harm her again. Not on my watch, and I fucking meant it. I protected what was mine.

My fists still clenched when I remembered the dark purple bruise she had tried to cover up with makeup. A little rough play with a woman was one thing. I was even okay with a good hard spanking every now and then but hauling off and punching a woman was a big hell no in my book.

And now I had her in my arms. She was alive and safe, and cursing a blue streak at me as she desperately tried to kick me in the shins.

Shifting, I had to adjust my hardening cock. All I could think about was Yelena's petite frame bent over my lap as I spanked that pert little ass of hers red. She was so small I bet I could get both cheeks with one hand.

Yelena screamed as she struggled. "You rat bastard! Let me go!"

"Damn if you don't need an over-the-knee lesson in manners."

She stilled for a moment. Then began to once more thrash as she tried to break my grip. "Hell will freeze over first before I let you spank me again."

I decided to humor her and released my grip.

Yelena immediately swung around to face me. With her feet planted wide, hands on hips, and her long blonde hair falling in wild tangled curls over her shoulders, she looked like a really angry Tinker Bell and about just as dangerous.

That is until she tried to disable me with a 540 kick.

I damn near got my clock cleaned as I watched her in stunned awe. Not many could pull off the complicated martial arts jump kick. It required launching your body weight, kicking and landing all on the same leg as your body did a 540-degree spin. I watched as she smoothly propelled her lithe body into the air. Her legs spun in a circle as her waist twisted before she landed like a cat back on the rooftop. I barely had time to swivel out of the way.

"Where the hell did you learn a move like that?"

She raised her cute chin defiantly. "Wouldn't you just love to know?"

A sharp stab of jealousy hit me straight in the gut. A man. Another man taught her. Probably someone she'd dated — and fucked.

God damn it. It was stupid to think she had remained untouched all these years, a beautiful woman like her, but the idea of another man putting his hands on her made me want to tear apart the world to find him and kill him. There was this hard, driving need to erase from this earth anyone who had touched her skin or looked into those eyes as she came. That was for me and me alone. No other man breathing should be allowed to walk around with that memory.

Keeping my eyes trained on her, I ripped my already torn t-shirt off. I watched as her eyes slid over my chest and abdomen in an unguarded look of appreciation before she shuttered them the moment she saw the knife wound. The knife had only gone in about an inch, not deep enough to hit anything vital but causing a two-inch gash. A scratch. It had already stopped bleeding.

Slowly, I began to walk toward her as I unfastened my pants.

If I couldn't wrap my hands around the throat of the man, any man, who had touched her, I would appease my anger with the next best thing. Erasing the memory of another man's touch on her body with my own.

Yelena held out her hand as she began to back up. "What do you think you're doing?"

Despite our open position on the building rooftop, it was probably around three a.m. by now, so it was unlikely anyone was observing us.

And anyway, I didn't care.

My girl was getting fucked right now.

Sex between us was long past due and had been a forgone conclusion from the moment I'd seen her sway those hips and play with her hair on the dance floor three years ago.

"What do you think, beautiful?"

Her big blue eyes burned with an arousing mixture of hate and desire.

I knew her next move before she even made it. As Yelena pivoted on her heel and took off for the east side of the roof, I leaped over the AC unit and met her at the raised wall edge.

Her breath misted in the cool early morning air with her rough exhale as the weight of my body pressed her against the low brick wall. Grabbing a fistful of her hair, I pulled her head back. "I know you like it rough, baby," I breathed against her neck as my hand reached in front for the fastening of her jeans.

"Fuck you," she countered through clenched teeth as she forced her hips outward to try and dislodge me.

"Promise?" I growled.

The movement only aroused me more as her ass brushed my painfully hard cock. With a flick of my thumb, the brass button on her jeans popped free, and I lowered the zipper. The tips of my fingers could feel the soft silk of her panties. I couldn't wait to see what color they were. Would they be a pretty feminine pink? Or a sexy red? It was one of the things that drew me to Yelena. She had this intoxicating mixture of innocence and experience. *A baby doll who bit.*

Moving my hand around her trim waist, I fisted the loose waistband of her jeans and wrenched it down over her ass.

Christ. Her silk panties were a pale pink with a tiny white bow right at the top of the lower back.

She kept her legs tightly closed so the jeans only fell to the tops of her thighs. No matter. I could definitely work with this.

I placed my palm over her right cheek. She visibly jumped from my touch.

"Why don't you be a good girl and open your legs?"

Her sharp inhale was all the answer I needed.

Tightening my grip on her hair, I moved her body backward and then down so she was forced to bend at the waist, her hands gripping the wall. Raising my arm, I slapped the lower curve of her right cheek. The sound was harsh and striking in the stillness.

Yelena cried out, but I knew it was more from shock than any real pain.

"How dare you?" she sputtered as she tried to turn around to face me. My grip on her long, blonde hair prevented her.

I spanked her ass again. Then again.

Usually, I would want to feel her skin beneath my palm, but damn if I didn't like the sight of that pretty white bow at the top of her ass. I watched as goosebumps formed on her pale skin from the cool air caressing it. I would warm her up soon enough.

Shifting to the left for more leverage, I spanked her left cheek then right, always hitting the same spot, the delicate curve of her ass right above her thighs.

Yelena went up on her tiptoes as I knew the slow burning pain was starting to build.

"Are you going to open your legs?"

Her only response was to grab my fist and try to dislodge my grip on her hair. This earned her a swift volley of hard swats on her vulnerable ass.

Yelena cried out. "Stop! Stop!"

"You know how to make it stop," I answered as her hips bounced up and down trying to avoid the strike of my hand.

I began to focus on the tops of her thighs, watching as her skin turned a bright, warm pink.

"Ow!" she cried. "Fine! You bastard!"

Yelena shimmied her hips till her jeans fell to her feet.

"Kick them off." My command was sharper than I intended, but the sight of her bent over and at my mercy was almost more than I could take. Never in my life had I wanted to fuck someone so badly.

After a moment's hesitation, which earned her a vicious slap on the top of her ass, Yelena obeyed. Kicking off her shoes, then jeans.

She was now dressed only in a simple long-sleeved purple shirt and her pink panties. As much as I enjoyed the sight of them, the panties had to go. The small white bow was crushed within my grip, as I wrenched them off her body. There was a primal sense of satisfaction when I heard the soft silk tear. Balling them in my fist, I lifted them to my nose. I could smell her arousal. I knew it. My baby liked it when I played rough. I positioned myself behind her. Pulling her head back using her hair, I ordered, "Now spread your legs."

"Please! Why are you doing this?"

"You know why. Now do it." I fired back as I pulled my already raging hard cock free from my pants.

Yelena spread her legs.

Reaching between her slim thighs, I ran two fingers along the seam of her cunt. Back and forth till her soft lips parted. I pushed just the tip of one finger in, feeling for her clit. Applying just the barest of pressure, I rubbed the small nub in circles. Her back arched. I rubbed harder. Yelena tried to stifle a moan, but I heard it. Shifting my hand, I found her tight entrance. I pushed in one finger, then two.

Damn, she was tight.

Almost too tight.

Deep down an alarm bell sounded, but I ignored it.

My thick cock was going to be painful for her to

accept. I thrust my fingers slowly in and out to prepare her, just at her entrance, feeling the clenching muscles of her cunt start to soften and relax. I moved my hand faster.

This time, Yelena didn't even try to stifle her moan. Her hand moved between her thighs. The tips of her fingers brushed my hand before she found her own clit and began to caress the delicate bundle of nerves.

"That's it baby, come for me," I breathed against her left shoulder as I leaned in. Sheltering her body from the chilled air.

She began to make the cutest mewing sound. Like a kitten purring. My cock pressed between her ass cheeks. She rocked her hips back.

I pushed a third finger in. Fuck, it was tight.

Yelena's breath hitched.

I couldn't wait another moment. Moving my hand, I fisted my cock and placed the head at her entrance. Releasing her hair, I then used both hands to grip her narrow hips and slowly pushed in.

She cried out.

I froze.

It couldn't be.

It wasn't possible.

I stopped breathing as I shifted my hips back then thrust forward slightly. Again, I felt the push back. The tension. The barrier of her maidenhead.

Yelena was still a virgin.

Jesus Christ.

An intense mixture of cold shock and red-hot primal possessiveness raged through my blood till I wanted to kick my head back and howl to the moon.

This meant no one had touched her.

Only me.

Mine.

And I was the fucking savage who was about to take her virginity on a rooftop like a god damn animal.

I tried to pull out but could only focus on the feel of her wet heat gripping the tip of my cock. With an extreme effort, I pulled my hips back and out of her tight body.

Yelena pitched forward. Her upper body rested against the top of the roof wall. My fingers pressed into her skin so hard I could see white halos around the tips as I tried to calm my heavy breathing.

Yelena moaned as her hand returned to her clit. It drove me mad with lust. This was no longer about sex. I reined in my vicious need to pound violently into her. Claiming her.

Her head pitched back as her body arched. Her lips opened on a soft mew.

Reaching between her legs, I took over. With my right hand, I played with her clit then thrust two fingers inside as I wrapped my left around my cock and ruthlessly stroked it. My hips pushed into hers with each rocking motion. I knew the brick edge of the wall must be scraping the soft skin of her stomach, and I didn't care. I could feel the knife wound reopen. The small drops of crimson blood which dripped onto her pale skin only spurred me on. Shifting my hand, I smeared the blood with my thumb. Thinking of how ancient cultures would smear blood on the skin as a hunting rite… a symbol of successfully conquering your prey. It might not be virginal blood, but it soon would be.

She needed to know.

She needed to understand that I was in control now.

I may not have claimed her virginity yet but that didn't mean she wasn't now mine.

Releasing my cock, I gave her ass a few more spanks to heighten her own climax. Then I fisted it again. My balls tightened while the pressure built as I reacted to the sounds of her own climax. With a roar, I came onto her lower back. Pulling her panties out of my pocket, I used them to wipe off her skin and my cock as I tried to get my breathing to slow.

I had just come and already I could feel my cock hardening, eager for more. My hand was a weak substitute for the tight, wet heat of her body. Unfortunately, that would have to wait till I got her to safety and into a proper bed.

I couldn't wait to spread those thighs again and taste….

I never finished the thought.

Everything went black.

CHAPTER 16

*Y*elena

I HIT HIM WITH A BRICK.

Oh God! I just hit him with a brick!

Damien staggered back. He put a hand to his head and then looked at the blood dripping down his fingers.

"You hit me!"

My hands fluttered in front of me as I tried to explain but couldn't. "I know! I'm sorry! It's just... I... I...."

This whole situation was so fucked up. For all I knew, he was a murderer! Samara could be tied up in his car trunk at this very moment. So how could I have possibly enjoyed almost having sex with him?

No. I hadn't enjoyed it.

I'd freaking loved it.

Holy shit!

The way he'd grabbed me and forced me to bend over while he ripped my jeans off.

Who does that??? No one!

That only happens in the movies or romance novels. No man nowadays would be ballsy enough to do the whole caveman routine and yet… wow. Damien didn't seem to give a damn about social niceties. He was all about the throw a woman against the wall and fuck her senseless.

I would have gladly surrendered my virginity to him then and there.

It's not like I had been saving it for the right guy. It was just that in the last three years, no one seemed to measure up. Any man who approached me always seemed to lack… something. I now had to finally admit to myself what it was… no man compared to Damien. He was the only man I ever wanted to touch me, to make me feel, *to see me*.

That's why, if he hadn't stopped, I would have surrendered completely to him. Willingly.

Up against a damn wall in the middle of the night on a freaking rooftop.

What was it about us and outdoor sex?

First the gazebo, then his car, now the rooftop.

All close encounters but never….

But oh my God! I couldn't imagine what a climax would be like from his cock if that was what the man could do with his fingers! I kept telling myself that that time with his mouth was only amazing because it was my first time but I was wrong. It had been amazing because of him. Damn him.

I had to bite my lip to keep from screaming out. My ass still stung from the spanking he had given me. Just the thought of his large, scarred hands handling my pink panties had me blushing all over again. There was something so arousing about being taken by a man. To being held down and having an incredible, mind-shattering orgasm forced upon you by his expert hands.

And then I had to go and hit him with a brick.

I watched as Damien took a step toward me, his arm out.

I backed away.

He collapsed.

Putting a fist to my mouth to stifle a scream, I quickly looked around. Everything still seemed to be quiet. No lights were on in any of the surrounding buildings' windows. There was a good chance despite the encroaching dawn that we were still unnoticed up here. Creeping over to his prone body, I looked for signs of life. It wouldn't do to leave a dead body on the roof of my building after I had trashed my own apartment. The cops would be on me before I got within a few miles of O'Hare.

Hesitantly, I reached out to lift his wrist to check for a pulse.

I waited.

Nothing.

Of course, I didn't really know how to check for a pulse, this was just what they did on television.

Walking around to his side, I nudged him with my foot.

Nothing.

Placing the pad of my bare foot against his side, I pushed harder. His body shifted and rolled onto his back.

Damien groaned.

Still alive.

Reaching for my jeans, I quickly put them on, then slipped into my sneakers. Keeping a side-eye on Damien, I moved to the fire escape and pulled again. This time, after a rusted groan, the iron ladder careened toward the pavement below, stopping with a loud, rattling clang. This way would be faster than trying to go back through the condo and risk getting trapped in an elevator.

Looking down, I could see the white pavement of the alley below. Shifting my head forward, I concentrated on moving down one metal rung at a time. I repeated the move till my feet finally hit the pavement. I needed to move quickly. The sun was already starting to peek up over the horizon. People would start stirring soon.

As I started in the direction of the Brown line, there was a shout from above.

Looking up, I saw the shadowed outline of Damien. "Don't you dare move, Yelena. I mean it," he called down.

I took a few steps.

"Baby, I *will* punish that ass," he shouted.

I thrilled at his words. There was just something about pushing this man's buttons that did it for me. I had never found a man who could take me on. It was a rush. Unfortunately, I couldn't stick around to explore it further. I needed to get the hell out of town and figure out my next move. Damien had said Samara was fine, and for some stupid reason, I believed him.

I couldn't resist taunting, "You'll have to catch me first!"

I took off running. Sticking to the alleys, I zig-zagged through the residential part of Lincoln Square as I made my way to the Western Station for the Brown Line Metra train. I would take that to the Blue Line to O'Hare Airport. I could steal a car, but it would be better if I just blended into the morning rush crowd.

Besides, I needed a target to lift a wallet and phone since I had to leave my go bag with my extra IDs and cash behind. Since I needed to get on a plane, I would need to make sure the woman at least was my same build and age.

When I got to the Metra station, I climbed the stairs and slowed my breathing, concentrating as I scanned the crowd. Searching the sea of faces for the right one — the perfect mark. Someone who was distracted. Were they on their phone? Late for work? Still thinking about an argument they'd just had with their boyfriend? Worried about a big project? It would be written on their faces, and in the way they walked. After a moment, I spotted her. A petite blonde in a Diane von Furstenberg crepe jumpsuit, ugh dreadful coral pink, and a Balenciago leather tote. She had money. I never stole from people who couldn't afford to miss a couple bucks.

I moved closer.

She was on the phone arguing with someone as she dug through her tote. "I don't care if your mother's in town. I'm not going to blow this promotion because of your fucking mother."

Jackpot.

Keeping my eyes straight ahead, I moved to intersect with her. The moment I was lined up, I shifted my right foot out and shouldered her.

"Hey! Watch it, bitch!" she shouted.

"Oh my God, I'm so sorry! I wasn't paying attention, are you all right?" I asked, feigning concern as I patted her arm. Then I slipped my other hand into her tote.

"I'm fine. Just watch where you're going," she grumbled as she stormed off.

I smiled as I pocketed her wallet. "I will."

Using cash from the woman's wallet, I bought a Metra card. I could hop the turnstile but that would bring attention. As I walked towards the trains, I swiped a jean jacket resting across a man's gym bag on the floor. It would be big, which was what I wanted. It would help conceal my size. I resisted the urge to look around me, as I nervously waited for the next train to pull up.

As the doors opened, and several groggy morning commuters mixed with drunken bar patrons, I pressed in to grab a spot and swiped two more wallets and a cell phone. In the scuffle, I knocked off a guy's baseball cap and hustled to the other end of the train, putting it on as he searched the train's floor hoping to find his missing hat untrampled among the countless pairs of random shoes.

Keeping my head low, I counted the seconds till the doors closed, scanning the platform for any signs of a large, tattooed man. If I was lucky, he would give up his pursuit. Somehow, I thought that was unlikely. He knew I'd had to leave without my bag, so he was probably lying in wait, assuming that after an hour or two, if all seemed quiet, I would return.

Too bad he was wrong.

Finally, there was the beeping warning as the doors shifted.

The doors closed, and with a jerk, the train pitched forward.

I was on my way to the airport.

If all went well, I would be in Montreal by early evening at the latest.

Once more, I thought of Damien. Of his heavy, muscled body as he pushed his fingers inside me. Owning me in that moment. I bit my lip.

Damn, it really was too bad I would never see him again.

CHAPTER 17

*D*amien

When I got my hands on her, I was going to wring her little neck.

I touched my hand to my forehead to see if I was still bleeding.

I was.

She hit me with a brick... A brick.

Getting behind the wheel of my Mercedes, I tossed the backpack Yelena had been carrying into the back seat.

I was racing to O'Hare. If I knew my girl, she was fleeing the country. If she got on a plane, it could be months before I picked up her trail. Maybe even years. But I would pick it up. A quick brick to the head was not enough to get rid of me, not by a long shot.

Reaching into the backseat as I drove, I dug around in my gym bag for a fresh t-shirt and the small first aid kit I carried. Feeling the small plastic box in my hand, I put it on my lap and lifted the lid, then sifted through the Band-Aids till I found the butterfly bandage. Tearing the package open with my teeth, I used the rearview mirror to place it on my temple right at the hairline. I would worry about the knife wound later.

In less than an hour, she had managed to give me a knife wound and a head wound.

I smiled.

I did love a challenge.

Just then my cell rang. It was Gregor. I pushed the Bluetooth button to connect it with my car stereo, as I easily navigated around the sparse Chicago early morning traffic on the highway.

"Damien, you there?"

"Yeah. Everything go as planned?

"It was Samara. I took her to the art museum event. Word should spread quickly that she's back under my control. Saw Dimitri. He and Vaska want to meet in a few hours. It's important. Can you make it?"

I cleared my throat. "I can't."

"You grab Yelena, yet?"

I touched the still bleeding wound on my head and grimaced. "On it. She wasn't at the first two locations. I finally found her at the third."

"Is she there with you?"

I paused. "She's… not with me."

"Why the hell not?"

"She got away."

"Got away? Seriously?"

I shot back, irritated. "Yeah. She got away."

"We're talking about the same girl, right? Small little blonde?"

I sighed. "She hit me with a brick."

Gregor said nothing.

"Stop laughing."

"I'm not laughing," he said with a laugh. "I'm just trying to picture it."

"Apparently, some asshole must have taught her some ninja shit over the last few years," I grumbled, still feeling that same stab of jealousy.

"Yeah, I'm sure that's what it is. Well, if it makes you feel any better, Samara would have pulled a gun on me if I hadn't taken it from her."

"That would make me feel better if Yelena hadn't actually pulled a gun on me."

"Damn."

"And a knife."

Gregor started to laugh again. "Perhaps you should have Yelena give you some fighting pointers."

Ignoring his brotherly taunt, I said, "I think she'll head to the airport. That's where I'm going now. I'm also going to send a cleaner crew to her condo. It's a train wreck. Don't need a nosy neighbor calling the police."

"Sounds good. I'll keep you posted about the meeting with Dimitri and Vaska." Gregor paused. "And ah… Damien… do you need me to send you a couple of men? You know. For protection?"

"Fuck you," I said over his laughter as I disconnected the phone.

As I got off the exit for O'Hare, I began to strategize how I was going to extract Yelena in the middle of a crowd full of tourists and police and—just for fun—homeland security agents, as well.

I turned up my radio. Playing on the classical music station was Aram Khachaturian's *Sabre Dance*, fitting for a chase.

For the first time in three years, I felt warm. As if something deep and cold inside of me was thawing, like I was coming back to life again.

The thrill of the hunt always warmed a man's blood, especially when he's after fiery little demon angels with bright blue eyes the color of the ocean.

CHAPTER 18

Yelena

THE DOORS OPENED. I stood back and waited for a few people to get off the train, so I could blend in. Plus, I wanted a moment to survey the crowd. All I saw were tourists with suitcases and annoyed business travelers with laptop bags.

Which reminded me, I needed to procure a suitcase. TSA found it suspicious when you booked international flights without any baggage. Or maybe I'd just swipe some sunglasses and play the sobbing, jilted bride going on her honeymoon alone. That should work for a first-class upgrade, too. And usually stopped people from asking too many questions, like why you don't look exactly like your photo and where is your luggage?

I knew there was a flight in two hours. I just needed to

get a ticket, get past security, and then lay low till I was on the plane.

I stepped off the train and headed toward the double escalators to my left.

As soon as I was through security, I headed straight to McDonald's. I was starving. Maybe I would get lucky and see Samara there. I knew Samara especially would want a mocha fix this early in the morning. That is, if she'd broken free of Gregor and decided to fly.

Once again, my mind turned to Damien. He was just so… big! In *every* way possible.

I needed to stop thinking about that scary overbearing man and start focusing.

Once I got to the gate I would…

I never finished the thought.

Everything went black.

CHAPTER 19

Yelena

I COULDN'T MOVE my arms.

My skin felt hot, and my breathing accelerated as I panicked.

Oh God. Damien had warned me about this. About how the Columbians could just snatch me at any time, even in broad daylight.

The last thing I remembered was heading toward the escalator at the airport and then nothing. Everything went black. Not wanting to alert my kidnapper that I was now awake, I kept my head down and barely opened my eyes.

I could see carpeting and what looked to be the legs of a dining room table. Shifting in my seat, I could tell I was in a wooden chair and my wrists were bound by the hard metal of handcuffs. Moving my fingers, I felt along the spindle back of the chair.

Okay... okay... don't panic.

I know I'm handcuffed to a chair.

I can work with this.

I listened carefully.

Someone was moving around in the other room.

I strained to hear anything else.

It sounded like they were singing, but I couldn't make out if it was a male or female voice. It was more like humming.

Risking it, I picked my head up slightly and looked around the room. On top of the dining room table was a Glock 9mm.

So, I had a weapon near me. I just needed to get out of these handcuffs.

Shifting my hips back, I pressed my ass against the spindles of the chair. I wiggled the fingers of my right hand into my pocket, searching for the bobby pin and paperclip I kept there. Every pocket I owned in every outfit had a bobby pin and a paperclip because, well, you just never knew when you'd want to pick a lock. I'd learned that the hard way after the umpteenth time my stepfather had locked me in a closet or tried to handcuff me to the radiator as punishment.

My fingertip touched the thin metal of the bobby pin. Slowly I pulled it along till I had it in my hand. Keeping my head down, I paused to listen. There was still humming and the sound of metal hitting glass. Kitchen noises?

Using both hands, I straightened the bobby pin. I

scraped the edge with my thumbnail till the small protective plastic nub popped off the end. Now came the hard part. Careful not to rattle my cuffs, I felt along the smooth metal for the keyhole. Once I found it, I placed the tip of the bobby pin in and bent it sharply to the left, then to the right to create a ninety-degree angle. I then pushed the bobby pin edge down till I felt the ratchet release. The jaws of the handcuff on my left wrist opened. Releasing my hand, I brought my arms forward. The handcuffs still dangled from my right wrist, but I would take care of that later.

I rubbed my wrist slowly as I stood up and circled the dining room table. Picking up the gun, I surveyed the space. Walking over to the windows, I pushed the curtain aside and looked out. I didn't recognize this part of town, but I was at least seven stories up. Too high to jump. The clank of a metal pan on a stove had me turning sharply again toward the kitchen.

I only had one choice...

Edging around the dining room table, I made my way to what I thought was the kitchen.

Peering around the doorjamb, I saw a large man dressed only in jeans standing in front of the stove.

Both arms were covered in tattoos.

Sonofabitch!

I raised the gun.

"Not loaded," sing-songed Damien over his shoulder. "How do you like your eggs?"

Just out of spite, I pulled the trigger anyway. It made a loud snapping sound but nothing more.

Damien turned and walked over to the refrigerator.

"Not that I'm complaining, but that is the second time you've tried to shoot me... today."

Taking out a carton of eggs, he returned to the stove.

He had a small bandage on his side and a butterfly bandage on his head.

I had no words.

I couldn't believe this was happening.

And I absolutely *refused* to feel guilty about the bandages marring his incredible, sexy, washboard ab stomach.

He winked at me. "No preference? Scrambled, it is. I thought you'd never wake up, then I heard you rattling those handcuffs enough to wake the dead."

My eyes narrowed as I stormed into the kitchen. Tossing the useless gun on the counter, I confronted him. "The hell you did! I didn't make a sound!"

Damien turned. Taking his finger, he tapped me on the nose. "Despite that rather homicidal temper of yours, you really are cute. And yes, I'm sure everyone in the building could hear your ham-fisted attempt to get out of those handcuffs."

"Listen," I said as I raised my right arm to point at him. The handcuffs rattled as they dangled from my wrist. I quickly put my arm down. "I hate scrambled eggs," I grumbled.

"Too bad. Now sit down like a good girl so you can eat," he ordered, motioning to the small, two-seat kitchen table with his head.

Reluctantly, I took a seat as he put a plate of eggs and slightly burnt toast in front of me. Damien took the seat next to me.

Toying with my fork, I asked, "Is there ketchup?"

"Ketchup?"

"Yes, ketchup. You know, the red stuff."

"Why?"

"To put on my eggs."

"Who puts ketchup on their eggs?"

"Me! Americans!"

Grumbling something in Russian, Damien rose from the table to rummage in the refrigerator before returning with a small bottle of ketchup. He didn't even try to hide his grimace as I tipped the plastic bottle and squirted a generous amount all over my eggs. I put on more than I usually like just to annoy him.

Picking up his own fork, he gave me a sideways glance. "Tell me about this Pick Six racket."

I shrugged. "What do you want to know?"

"Everything."

"How much do you know about horse racing?"

"Nothing."

"Nothing?"

"Nothing."

"But the Ivanovs bet huge amounts on the races each week. I used to hear my stepfather talk about it."

He shrugged. "It's a convenient way to launder money but I have… accountants to take care of such things. We never got involved in fixing the races. Too messy and cruel. Your stepfather, shall we say, freelanced his services as far as fixing the races was concerned. That wasn't on my orders. We only bet on races we knew were fixed by others as a sure thing for the accountants to clean the money."

I nodded and gave him an exaggerated wink. "Sure… *accountants*."

"Eat your gross eggs," he quipped.

After taking a few bites, I took a sip of coffee and grimaced. "Oh my God, that's sweet."

"What? I made it the way I like it," objected Damien as he took the cup from me and took a sip to test it.

I stared down at the heavily sugared and creamed concoction. It was so sweet, the liquid was a light tan. "You take your coffee like a sixteen-year-old girl."

"And you eat your eggs like a toddler," he fired back with another wink.

I rose to dump out my cup of coffee. Reaching for the pot to pour another one, I explained. "The Pick Six is what's called an exotic bet. To win you have to pick the winners in six successive races."

"And that's hard?"

I nodded. "It's rare."

Damien pivoted to face me where I remained standing by the sink. He leaned an arm over his chair. The position put his naked chest and strong, heavily tattooed muscles on casual display as if he wasn't sitting there looking like a scary gangster god in blue jeans. "Rare but not impossible. Don't they offer those at every race?"

"Yep."

"So, what raised so many red flags with your bets?"

"I got greedy. I was anxious to leave home and needed money, so I placed three bets in one week. Up until that point, I had only been placing the occasional bet over a span of several months to try out my system."

Not wanting to meet his gaze, I stared down at the

black liquid in my cup. I didn't usually drink it completely black but the strong bitterness grounded me this morning. I needed to keep my wits around Damien. "I heard he's dead." I didn't bother saying his name or why I was so anxious to escape. We both knew why.

Damien cleared his throat and reached for his coffee. "I was rectifying a past mistake."

I wasn't sure what he meant but knew I didn't want to talk about it further. I had wasted enough of my life on my stepfather. "Thank you," I said simply.

He nodded.

I took a deep breath and continued. "It wasn't just that I won three times in a row. It's that a single bettor won on a single ticket."

His brow furrowed. "Explain."

I returned to the table and sat. "Pick Sixes are complicated bets with countless possible combinations. Usually, gamblers pool their money and go for it. It's viewed almost like a lottery ticket. A large pool of gamblers purchase a large number of tickets with tons of combinations in the hopes they'll hit on the right combination and win big."

He began to spin his now empty coffee mug on the table. I watched as his strong fingers played with the porcelain handle. I bit my lip, remembering the feel of those same strong hands on my body just a few hours ago.

He shook his head. "That still doesn't explain why you pissed off the Italians and the Columbians so badly. You went to three different racetracks. I watched the security tapes; you were careful with how you cashed in the ticket. You played it really smart. Your only mistake was rushing it, but I can't see how any of this would have cost those two families any money as they claim."

I felt a twinge of pride that he seemed to appreciate my plan.

I sat and thought about it for a minute. Then said, "The track takes a cut of the pool."

His intense gaze swung to me. "What?"

"At the end of each race, if no one wins, and usually no one does, the track takes fifteen percent off the top and carries the remaining pool over to the next race. If no one wins for months at a time the pool can get really big."

Damien sat back in his chair. "With the track skimming straight off the top each day. That's found money. Those two families control those tracks. We only use the races occasionally to launder money. It is a much larger revenue source for the Italians and Columbians. Interesting. If we were to take control of the tracks, combined with your betting algorithm…."

A chill ran over my body.

The speculative light in his eyes. The thoughtful tone of voice. The curious glances in my direction. I knew all the signs. I had seen it plenty of times with my stepfather. It was the look men gave you when they realized you could be *useful* to them.

Stupid girl.

I had actually started to believe Damien cared and was truly trying to protect me.

He just wanted to use me like all the rest.

Now that he understood *why* I made the bets, he'd want to know *how*. The how was where the real skill came in… where my method came in. He was no better than the

Italians or the Columbians or even my stepfather. They all just wanted something from me. No! Damien was worse. He didn't just want my betting skills; he wanted my body, as well. And if I let him have it, soon he would take my soul.

I would have run straight back into the life I was trying to escape.

My first instinct to run three years ago had been correct.

I needed to get as far away from Damien Ivanov as possible.

This time for good.

Before I made my escape, I needed to learn whatever I could about Samara's whereabouts. With any luck, she'd been able to run before Gregor could catch her, and she was already halfway to Montreal.

"Where's Samara?" I asked with no preamble.

CHAPTER 20

Yelena

Picking up his fork, he asked, "Is she missing?" before scooping the last of his eggs into his mouth.

"If Gregor hurts one hair on her head, you'll both be sorry." My threat was all bluster, and we both knew it. I was powerless against him, let alone him and his brother and the whole Ivanov crime family juggernaut.

Damien leaned over and put a finger beneath my chin, lifting my head. "Babygirl, I'm trying really hard to be nice because I know you are scared, but my patience will only stretch so far." His dark eyes glittered with leashed anger. I had touched a nerve.

"I don't know what you mean," I evaded as I lowered my eyes, breaking eye contact. "I'm not scared."

The kitchen was so quiet I could hear the tiny clicks of

the minute hand from the clock on the wall. The tines of my fork scraped against the porcelain plate as I tried to dispel the awkward silence.

Finally, he spoke. His voice was so low it was more a rumbling growl. "What I mean is if you don't want me to toss you on this table and spank that tight pussy of yours while I shove my thick dick down your throat till you beg for mercy between gasps of air... you had better stop asking questions that will just get you into trouble."

I remembered the rumors about how his anger could flash hot without any warning.

Demon Damien.

My eyes widened at the vivid picture he had just painted. My thigh muscles tightened at the idea that he was capable of doing just what he threatened. Flashes of us on the rooftop flickered across my mind.

I harrumphed. "You're totally a Scorpio."

Damien sat back in his chair. His forehead furrowed in bewilderment. "What?"

"A Scorpio. Were you born in November?"

Damien nodded. I could see the look of tempered curiosity cross his features. He was going to indulge me, but for how long?

"I figured as much. Scorpios are very intense signs. Very focused. Like dogs with boners... I mean bones."

Damien raised an eyebrow as his eyes lowered to his crotch. Mine followed. I instantly regretted it when I saw the outline of his heavy cock pressing against the fabric of his jeans.

I stood up so quickly the chair toppled onto the floor behind me. Bending over to pick it up, I heard Damien's harsh inhalation. Looking over my shoulder I realized he was staring at my ass, probably remembering the last time he saw me in this position. Oh God.

"A… shower! I need a shower!"

"Baby, we don't have time for this. I don't have anything concrete yet, but I have little doubt the Columbians are in town, and they will be looking for you."

"Please," I pleaded.

Damien ran his hand through his hair. For a moment, I thought he was going to say no and follow through with his threat. He surprised me by saying yes. We walked down the narrow, bare hallway to a master bedroom.

It looked like an Ikea catalog had thrown up. Like someone had chosen page twenty-three out of the catalog and had it shipped, right down to the plastic demo room plant.

"Is this your place?" I asked, trying really hard to keep the judgment out of my voice.

Damien turned and gave me a nasty look. "You can't seriously think I live here? What kind of tasteless Neanderthal do you take me for?"

I shrugged my shoulders as I followed him into the bathroom. It had an odd Ikea slash I Love Florida theme with a palm tree pattern shower curtain and pink flamingo wallpaper. I covered my mouth to prevent a laugh at the pink fluffy toilet seat cover.

"It's a safe house we occasionally use when we have *delicate* business in Chicago," explained Damien with a twist of his lips as he pulled the curtain aside and started the water.

Business. That's all I was to him.

Business.

A tool to be used to make money and perhaps fuck once in a while.

I'd be smart to remember that.

Turning back to me, he put his hands on his hips and ordered, "Strip."

It took me a moment to realize what he had said.

The dangling handcuffs rattled as I put my hands protectively over my breasts as if they were already bared to his gaze. "What?"

His voice, though quiet and calm, held an edge of annoyance. "Take off your clothes."

Shaking my head, I tried to back away but he leaned over me and closed the door.

"I changed my mind. I don't want a shower," I blurted out.

"Too late. You're getting one. You're still covered in dust and dirt from the rooftop."

Self-consciously, I brushed a hand over my dirty jeans. Still, I refused to obey.

Apparently in no mood for arguments, Damien tried to grab me.

I screamed and reached for the doorknob.

His body pressed me in. Fuck, he was so much taller than me. His size and bulk overwhelmed me. Grabbing my arms, he pulled them high over my head. I could feel his rough hand on my stomach as he fisted the hem of my shirt and ruthlessly pulled it off. He lowered my arms. There was a tension around my ribcage as he pulled on the clasp of my bra before that too hit the bathroom floor.

"Please!" I cried.

He didn't listen. Turning me to face him, he kept his hard eyes on mine as he unfastened my jeans. The brush of his warm knuckles against my cool skin made me suck in my stomach in a vain attempt to avoid his touch.

Taking a step back, he crossed his heavy arms over his chest. With a nod of his chin, he said, "You should know the drill by now. Kick them off."

I brushed the back of my hand across my tearing eyes. I knew I was caught. There was nothing in the bathroom I could use as a weapon. Hell, if a brick to the head didn't slow him down, I doubted hitting him with a fucking soap dish would do the trick. Hesitantly, I dug the toe of my right foot into the heel of my left sneaker and kicked it free. Then did the same with my left foot. As I looked down to push the jeans off my hips, I saw the blood.

"Blood! I'm bleeding!" I cried out, as I twisted to examine my side and back. The dark crimson smears of dried blood looked gruesome against my pale skin.

"That's my blood," uttered Damien calmly.

My eyes went to the bandaged wound on his side. The white bandage looked stark against his deeply tanned and inked skin. He must have gotten blood on me when we were on the roof when he did that thing with his fingers. I clenched my thighs at the memory.

"Oh," I responded lamely. Biting my lip, I shimmied the jeans off my hips. My cheeks flamed a bright pink as I remembered my silk panties had been left on the rooftop earlier, covered in Damien's come. I was a natural blonde, so the curls between my legs were so light the seam between the folds was visible. I might as well have been completely bare.

"Now spread your legs."

The bathroom had started to mist from the hot water running in the shower. The mirrors and small window fogged up. His skin glistened, making the bright colors of the tattoos on his arms vivid and almost lifelike. They were done in bright golds, oranges, yellows, and blues. Mythic beasts and symbols all intertwined. I knew Russians put great meaning behind their tattoos. It made me curious as to what the meaning was behind his. Looking at his hands, it was more of the same, but none of the usual prison tattoos like you'd see on my stepfather's friends. No religious symbols, or knives, or suit symbols from a deck of cards.

Placing my hands against the wall for support, I slid my feet open.

"Wider," he barked.

I obeyed. I couldn't recall a single moment in my life where I had felt more vulnerable or more aroused. Fuck, what was this man doing to me? This was so freaking messed up.

Damien took a step toward me; I inhaled sharply and held my breath. I closed my eyes as I watched his arm reach out. A single finger traced my collarbone, then the upper swell of my right breast, then over my navel. My stomach quivered from the warmth of his touch. He continued to caress lower till his large hand cupped my pussy. That same finger pushed between my folds to press inside my tight passage.

I bit my lip to keep from crying out as I kept my eyes screwed tight.

He shifted closer. Then a whisper in my ear. "You were a very bad malen'kiy angel today, weren't you?"

Without thought, I nodded.

"You made me very angry when I had to chase you across the city," he growled as his lips skimmed my neck, before skimming my jaw to claim my lips.

A Scorpio through and through, he claimed my lips with ruthless possession as if it were his right. The tip of his tongue traced the sharp edge of my teeth before swirling around my own. His hand slid up into my hair, pulling my head back. The sting of pain just brought the consuming kiss into sharper focus.

I tried not to respond. I felt like I was falling, being pulled down into his gravity. Trying to keep my wits about me, I skimmed my hand over his hip and slipped it into his back pocket.

Slightly breathless, he abruptly broke the kiss. "And now you continue to be a brat, petulantly not responding to my orders… or my kiss." He pushed a second finger in and began to pulse.

My whole body started to tremble, and I desperately wanted him to brush his thumb across my clit and relieve the building pressure.

"So now I have to punish you."

My eyes opened in shock as I could only manage a frightened squeak in response.

"Raise your arms."

"Damien," I cajoled as I tried to think what I could say to talk my way out of the punishment I knew I deserved.

Hell, I had tried to shoot the man twice and managed to inflict a knife wound in the bargain. Oh, and then there was the brick.

"Do it," he barked.

Frightened, I raised my arms. The handcuff clattered against the now steam-slick wall. I wondered if he was going to connect them again, but he didn't.

Instead, he leaned in and met my gaze. "Remember, it's never a good idea to make me mad."

The sharp pain took me by surprise.

He had spanked me between the legs.

On my… oh God!

He spanked me again.

I cried out as I tried to smash my knees together. Damien's strong hands forced my thighs apart. "Take your punishment like a good girl."

He spanked me again. The pulsing heat was unbearable. I clawed at the wall behind my hips. I watched through tear-filled eyes as his arm rose and fell over and over again. With each strike, my whole body jolted from the twisted, pleasurable pain. In that moment, I would have given anything for him to take me into his arms and fuck me senseless.

Damien leaned over and cupped my jaw. "Eventually you will understand that I'm actually trying to protect you. And you fighting me won't change that—no matter how many times you try to shoot me," he said sardonically.

Pushing the tangled hair from my eyes, he gently led me to the shower. He checked the temperature with his hand and adjusted it before allowing me to step in. The water felt soothing on my face, but it stung the moment it trickled over my swollen, punished flesh. I hissed in a breath through clenched teeth.

"Do you need help?"

Dazed, I shook my head. I needed to be alone if only for the spare minutes the shower would provide. Needed to think about how I'd almost given my body to the demon devil himself.

Damien ran his hand over my shoulder and down my arm in what I thought was a calming caress, till he lifted my arm high.

Then, a click from the handcuffs.

He had handcuffed my right hand to the metal shower rod.

I opened my mouth to curse at him but started to cough as water rushed in.

"I will be back to check on you in five minutes," he tossed over his shoulder as he turned to leave.

With a cry of outrage, I threw the wet washcloth at his back. It landed against his bare shoulder before falling to the tiled floor with a splat. He just laughed and kept walking.

Well, I would be the one with the last laugh when he returned to find me gone.

CHAPTER 21

Damien

DAMN, that woman was going to be the death of me — literally.

I pulled on the adhesive strips of the bandage on my side. The bleeding had already stopped. The edges of the cut were sealed with dried blood. I pulled the rest of the bandage free before reaching into my bag for another black t-shirt.

This was my last clean one on hand. I was also wearing my last pair of clean jeans; the other pair was covered in tar and grit from the roof. A few more days with Yelena and I would need a new wardrobe. The very domestic thought of strolling through a mall with Yelena as she dragged me into one designer store after another picking out clothes to dress *her man* crossed my mind.

And you know what? It didn't suck.

Especially when I thought about how that beautiful little face would be smiling up at me the whole time. It was amazing that a woman so small and feminine could also be so strong and stubborn. It definitely was one of the things which fascinated and drew me to her. Despite her diminutive size, I knew she would take a pounding from my cock and scream for more.

I reached down to adjust my shaft inside my jeans. Back in the bathroom, I had wanted nothing more than to have spread her legs wide and sink deep into her tight cunt. Just the thought of how the warm skin of her punished pussy would feel against the sensitive underside of my cock had me turning in that direction, but I reined myself in. She needed some space and time alone, if only for a few minutes.

And above all things, I wanted — I needed — her to trust me. It was the only way I was going to be able to keep her safe. The thought of tying her to the bed and strapping that curved ass of hers with my belt immediately came to mind, but that way didn't build trust.

Walking into the kitchen, I picked up the Glock Yelena had set aside and checked the magazine. It was full. Thank God that woman didn't know guns or my crazy babygirl might have actually succeeded in shooting me if she had properly chambered a bullet. I was about to tuck it into my back waistband when I heard a soft knock at the door. Listening to make sure the shower was still running, I raised the gun as I approached the door from the side just in case whoever was on the other side got the funny idea to shoot straight through the door. "Who is it?"

"It is your friend, Vaska Lukovich Rostov," came the muffled response.

Releasing the chain and deadbolt, I opened the door.

"Vaska." I clapped him on the shoulder, and we kissed each other's cheeks. "I haven't seen you since that close call in Uzbekistan."

Vaska winked. "That redhead almost got me killed… but she was worth it."

I shook my head. "You always liked the troublemakers."

He slapped me on the back. "And you my friend are no different. I bring gifts." He held up a duffel bag. "I had to send Jim on another errand, so I offered to bring these to you."

I took it from him and gestured for him to enter. As soon as he crossed the threshold, I double checked that the hallway was clear before securing the door.

With a nod of his head, Vaska gestured to the duffel bag, "It has her clothes."

Taking the duffel, I walked down the hallway to the master bedroom. Tossing it on the bed, I reached for the bathroom door, pausing to take a deep breath before entering. I needed to stay calm and focused since I knew the sight of her wet skin and naked form would likely drive me fucking crazy with lust, especially knowing she was handcuffed and vulnerable to whatever I wanted to do to her.

I opened the door. There she was obediently standing in the shower stall. With the use of only one hand, she'd missed a spot of foamy suds on her right side. The creamy bubbles caressed her butt cheek and hip. Taking a step closer, I kept my eyes trained on hers as I smoothed my hand over her skin, washing away the soap. The dark tan of my hand looked almost menacing against her pale skin tinted slightly pink from the warmth of the water. Her beautiful blue eyes were a dark cobalt blue in the soft morning light that filtered through the glazed glass window.

I leaned in closer.

My cock jumped at the sight of her full lips opening.

An invitation.

Gritting my teeth, I reminded myself to focus. After digging the key out of my front pocket, I reached up to unlock the handcuff from the shower rod. Holding her hand, I also unlocked the one around her wrist.

"Don't make me regret this," I warned as I palmed the handcuffs.

She remained silent.

I wasn't dumb enough to think it was from submissive obedience.

Not my treacherous little angel.

No, she was remaining quiet and still as she assessed the situation.

I placed a towel around her shoulders and held tight to the ends which crossed over her full breasts. "I had some of your clothes retrieved from your place. They're on the bed. Do not leave the bedroom until I come to get you. Do you understand?"

Yelena nodded.

Using my right hand as I kept a grip on the towel with my left, I lifted her chin and shifted closer, every fiber of my being aware of her near-naked state. "I mean it, baby.

Do not cross that threshold, or I will give you the thrashing of your life."

She remained silent.

Stroking my thumb across her jaw, I pushed. "Otvet' mne."

Her blue eyes lit with fire. She knew what I wanted to hear. I watched as she licked her lips. The dark, dusky pink now glimmered, practically begging to be kissed.

The room was so still I could hear her delicate indrawn breath.

"Fine," she acquiesced.

"Good girl," I asserted as I gave her a chaste kiss on the forehead and resisted the urge to wrap my hands around her head to hold her steady for a kiss which I knew would consume us both.

Leaving her to dress, I returned to the kitchen to talk with Vaska.

He had helped himself to a cup of coffee. I poured myself a fresh cup as well, wishing it was scotch. I needed something bracing to cool the heat in my blood. Tossing the handcuffs and key onto the table, I reached for her backpack which I had brought in earlier from the car.

It was filled with cash, jewels, several passports, and IDs, as well as a small revolver.

Tucked in with all the valuables were several small plastic toys. Sifting through them, I found one I recognized. The small Hello Kitty toy she had gotten in the Happy Meal I'd bought her all those years ago. She had not only kept it but placed it among all these items of greater value and apparently had continued collecting the silly toys. Who knew my angel was so sentimental? I felt my cold core thaw even further; if I wasn't careful, I was going to find myself not only obsessed with her but in love as well.

I shook my head. That could never happen. It would be the ruin of both of us. History was filled with the tragedies that ensued when angels and demons dared to tempt fate and fall in love.

Placing the toy back inside, I zipped up the bag and pushed it toward Vaska with a decided shove. "Can you hold onto this for me?"

I knew better than to keep it with me. It only increased the chance my little escape artist would run again — only this time, she would get further. I wasn't stupid enough to think I would have caught her so easily at O'Hare if she'd had her go bag with money and IDs on her at the time. Even then, I'd barely caught up with her. If she had reached that escalator, she would have been close to the main floor of the airport where there was significantly more security than there was at the Metra station.

Disguising a sleeper hold as a hug from an over-exuberant lover, I only just managed to literally sweep her off her feet and carry her back to my car. The whole thing just drew longing looks from the female passersby wondering why their boyfriends and husbands didn't greet them as passionately. If they only knew!

Vaska pushed away my empty plate and sat down. "Gregor wanted me to tell you he's moved up his plans with Samara. There's trouble with the Novikoffs. He wants to know if you've secured Yelena, and if your plan for her was moving forward."

I looked over my shoulder, searching the hallway for

any sign of Yelena. Straining to see a shifting shadow or hear a creak of a floorboard. There was nothing. For once, she had obeyed me. "Tell him yes. Everything is going to plan. What's the issue with the Novikoffs?"

We rarely if ever did business with that family. They were too unhinged. Too prone to violence for violence's sake. It was bad for business.

Vaska took a sip of coffee before answering. "Boris Federov made a second side deal with Egor. Sold his daughter out from under Gregor."

"Are you fucking kidding me?"

Gregor's future father-in-law was a real piece of work, but I never thought he was stupid enough to double-cross us. No one fucked with our family, especially not someone who took millions of dollars in cash for his daughter's hand and then let her slip away right from under his nose. Boris had balls betraying Gregor after my brother had spent the last three years tracking down Samara.

"There's word he sent a crew to Chicago to try and grab her."

"Am I needed?"

Vaska shook his head. "Gregor's handling it. Besides, he says you have your hands full with Yelena." His mouth twitched.

I pointed at him. "Don't you fucking dare, asshole."

He raised his arms, his palms up in a placating gesture. "What? I wasn't going to say anything."

I leaned back in my chair.

Vaska continued. "On a completely different topic, if

you need them, I can get you an extra first aid kit and maybe a bulletproof vest for the wedding night."

I laughed. I should have known Gregor wouldn't keep his mouth shut about my encounter with Yelena. "Fuck you. Besides, you're one to talk."

"What?"

"I hear Dimitri's new wife has a friend who's been giving you a run for your money. "

It was Vaska's turn to look disgruntled. "That woman will be the death of me. Speaking of Mary, are you still using these?"

He lifted up the discarded handcuffs.

"They're all yours."

He rose and tucked them into his suit jacket front pocket. "By the way, Dimitri put a stop to the police investigation over what happened at O'Hare earlier, and the cleaners have been to her condo. There's no trace she was ever there."

I nodded. "Good. We can't afford to have anyone ask too many questions. We need to keep a lid on this. I can't have anyone wondering about her or Samara's disappearance."

Vaska picked up the backpack full of money and jewels and headed toward the door. "I guess congratulations are in order. Will you wait to return to D.C. to marry her or will you marry here?"

I slapped him on the back and smiled. "Haven't decided yet. Probably whatever's fastest. I want the word out as soon as possible that Yelena is under my protection. I don't want to worry about this mess with the

Columbians if we have trouble with the Novikoffs brewing."

Vaska nodded. "In all seriousness, stay safe, my friend. We Russians may be crazy fucks, but the Columbians..." He shook his head. "Shit with them gets... messy."

Russian crime families like ours were known for meting out swift and brutal retribution, but it was only with men and always about business. The Columbians didn't operate by the same code. Everyone was fair game, women and children included. They also favored kidnapping and torture, something I never had the stomach for. The idea that a crew might be at this very moment trying to track down Yelena made me sick with anger and fear.

After Vaska's departure, I relocked the door and went in to speak to Yelena.

Her time had run out.

It was time to inform her of my plans to marry her and that I had no intentions of taking no for an answer. Frankly, she didn't have a choice. She could give me what I wanted the easy way or the hard way. My hand moved to rest on the thick metal of my belt buckle.

As I neared the bedroom, I could hear a hair dryer running. Pleased that she had obeyed my instructions and had just continued to get dressed while I talked with Vaska, I turned the knob and swung open the door without knocking. Half hoping she liked to dry her hair naked.

The room was empty.

The running hair dryer was on the floor, abandoned.

Lifting my head, I immediately saw the open window.

I ran over to it and stuck my head out to survey the

side of the building. There wasn't any sign of her on the wall or ground. Turning my shoulders, I looked up to the roof for evidence of any rope. There was none.

Slamming my fist against the sill, I let out a roar of frustration.

When I caught her this time — *and I would catch her* — I would make sure she regretted ever disobeying me.

The time for games and a light touch was over.

My angel was about to learn it was dangerous to defy a demon.

CHAPTER 22

Yelena

MARRIED!
Married to Damien!
Oh my God!
Married to that man!

After I turned another block and confirmed I wasn't being followed, I began to breathe easier, but I still needed to hustle.

If he hadn't already, Damien was about to learn I had escaped and I just knew the first place he would come looking for me was the airport. I needed to beat him there and get past security where I'd be safe in the terminals.

The conversation I had overhead just kept spinning over and over again in my head.

Married.

He expected me to marry him!

And not some pretty wedding of a girl's dreams. There would be no flowers or Vera Wang wedding gown or ring from Tiffany's. Nope. If Damien had his way, he'd probably drag me by my hair to the nearest courthouse and have a judge marry us at his desk over his half-eaten bologna sandwich at lunchtime. And why not? It's not like it would be a love match. I was a means to an end. A business deal. A way to get the Ivanov family deeper into the horse racing racket with less risk and higher returns. Oh, and bonus for him, he'd get to fuck me.

My hands curled into fists. Here to protect me, my ass. I should have known better.

I was actually lucky Damien hadn't seen me creep along the hallway. There was a moment when he'd turned and practically stared straight at me.

After hearing all I needed, I'd headed back to the room and set the stage. I opened the window and started the hair dryer. I then hid behind the door. When Damien entered and saw the discarded hair dryer and the open window, he did exactly what I thought he would. As he raced across the room to see if he could catch me escaping along the wall, I snuck around the door and down the hallway. I knew the sound of the hair dryer would mask the sound of my steps. I was out of the apartment and headed toward Lakeview before he'd even left the bedroom.

Seeing a yellow car approach, I raised my arm high. After jumping into the backseat of the cab, I gave the driver an address along Montrose Avenue.

Leaning back in the seat, I pulled the wallet out of my

back pocket and opened it. I took out the driver's license and studied it.

Damien Aleksandre Ivanov

Born November 11, 1993

Eyes Blue

Hair Black

Height 6'3

I knew he was a Scorpio! I smiled as I fanned myself with his license. He was going to be so pissed when he realized I'd lifted his wallet. I thought for sure he'd heard the soft thud when I dropped it to the floor among my pile of clothes.

At least I'd had one helluva goodbye kiss.

A goodbye kiss.

Forever.

Why did that idea hurt?

I needed to get a grip. Sure, he was hot as fuck. Sure, the whole prospect of rough, mind-blowing sex with him turned me on. But he was dangerous, and I needed to get as far away as possible from him. The fact that he intrigued me and challenged me like no other man was of no consequence.

But seriously?

Damn him for that.

Damn him for being charming and fascinating.

Damn him for being the type of man who gave as good as he got.

I crossed my arms in a huff. And damn him for even knowing his t-shirt was designed by Varvatos!

It was a little thing, but it really irritated me that I had finally found the holy grail of men. A man who was masculine and aggressive but also appreciated designer clothes and looking good.

Peeved, I dug through his wallet to see what else I could learn. I pulled free an American Express black card. Impressive. I stared at the titanium card with the laser etched numbers. Only the massively wealthy got an invitation for one of these. I wondered if it was true they would send a helicopter for you anywhere in the United States? Unfortunately, I would not find out. There was no way I could get away with buying so much as a coffee with this card. It was so rare it would definitely cause a stir, and they would very quickly realize I didn't look like an over-six-foot-tall Russian.

Curious, I picked up his driver's license again.

No.

Don't do this.

Don't start believing what he said just because you're falling for him.

Falling for him?

Where the hell had that come from?

I wasn't falling for him! That would be the height of stupidity. So what if he was sexy and funny and it was super fun pushing his buttons. *And it really was fun pushing his buttons!* Despite all the danger, I honestly couldn't remember the last time I'd felt such a rush of energy as I had with that big, angry Russian chasing me half-way around Chicago. If I were brutally honest, I was just a tiny bit disappointed that I'd probably managed to escape him for good this time.

What the hell was wrong with me?

Shaking off disturbing thoughts of falling in love with

a man who only wanted to use me to launder his dirty mafia money, I continued to sift through his wallet. Tucked behind a few other credit cards and a gym membership card was a photo. My heart sank. It was a beautiful woman. She had gorgeous green eyes and black hair which made her pale skin glow. I flipped the photo over.

To Damien XOXO Natasha

Natasha. Even her name was elegant and beautiful. A stab of white-hot jealousy pierced my heart.

Well, this was proof he was only playing with me as part of some sick and twisted game of revenge. Forgetting that the entire scenario was in my imagination, I immediately assumed this was the model he had taken to the Rachmaninov piano concert. At least her name wasn't Fifi.

"We're here," said the cab driver.

I opened the cash flap of Damien's wallet. There was probably about three grand in hundred-dollar bills. I took out three bills and paid the five-dollar fare.

"Keep the change."

"Lady are you sure?" asked the cab driver as his eyes widened at the sight of three crisp one-hundred-dollar bills.

I gave him a wink and left the cab.

Having cash was nice but if I was going to catch a flight out of the country, I needed a passport and some better clothes and a suitcase. Showing up in the airport with no luggage and a wad of cash was a great way to get yourself strip searched in some dingy backroom by a TSA guard named Larry.

* * *

As I walked down Montrose, I snatched a baseball cap off the back of a chair as I passed an outdoor cafe. Twirling my hair into a loose bun, I shoved as much of it as I could under the cap and pulled it low over my eyes. I then leaned down and swiped a jean jacket resting over a gym bag as the guy's back was turned while he punched in his pin at an ATM. I put the jacket on over my black hoodie.

I was grateful that whoever Damien had sent to my condo to pick up some clothes had actually pulled them from my bureau drawers and not the closet. The closet was where I kept all my designer labels. The bureau was where I kept my workout clothes, and truthfully the clothes Samara and I wore whenever we hightailed it out of a city for fear Damien and Gregor were closing in.

Flexible fabric for easy movement, nondescript, all black. Mostly yoga pants and hoodies. Nothing that would stand out or be memorable… in other words none of my preferred designer clothes.

Montrose was on the edge of the Ravenswood neighborhood. It was an affluent neighborhood filled with large houses.

Careful to not draw attention to myself, I made a left onto Winchester as I casually strolled down the street, occasionally checking my wrist as if I were checking a fitness tracker. No one would think anything of a woman walking around the block to get her steps in.

I looked for signs that a homeowner was not at home.

I was lucky. It was probably around noon, so it was the

perfect time to break in. It was funny how most people were led to think that burglars only attacked at night. A very silly Hollywood invention. Why would you break in at night when it was almost guaranteed that the residents were home? No. It was far more effective to do it during the day when most of the neighborhood was out and about at work or running errands.

Samara and I had had to *borrow* things occasionally over the last three years when we got jammed up or had to hightail it out of a city without the proper amount of cash on hand in those early months before we got smarter. It had been a few years, but I think I still remembered how.

As I walked past each house, I looked for the signs.

Was there evidence of a dog?

A car in the driveway?

Signs of a security camera?

Finally, I spotted my perfect target. The home was set slightly back from the road. Empty driveway. A large tall fence in the backyard and a massive oak tree in the front. Great for concealment. There were flower beds and dainty curtains in the windows which meant there was probably a female in residence.

Looking around to make sure I wasn't observed, I opened the mailbox of my target house and removed a few letters.

Boldly, I walked up to my target. I would knock on the door and use the excuse that I had received some of their mail.

Taking a deep breath, I raised my fist and knocked.

I waited.

Nothing.

I listened.

No barking dog.

No television.

Perfect.

Tossing the mail on the front porch bench, I made my way around the side of the house.

Grasping the edge of the fence, I easily hauled myself up and over.

The fence was at least five feet tall and provided the perfect cover from any prying eyes from the street or next door. I made my way to the back door. I tried the doorknob just in case I got lucky. Nope. Locked. I didn't have my lock picking kit with me so I would just have to improvise.

The sound of shattering glass carried much further, as it was much more of an alarming sound than a dull thud. When people heard glass breaking, they knew something was wrong. When they heard a strange loud bang and then silence, they just wondered if something was wrong but in the absence of any other loud noises, they tended to move on with their day without another thought.

Knowing this, I took a step back and kicked the door just to the right of the doorknob and lock. The door sprung open with a loud bang. Just to be certain, I stepped to the side and listened for any cry of alarm from inside of the house.

Silence.

Closing the door behind me, I entered the unoccupied kitchen. Immediately, I sprinted to the front hall and looked for evidence of an alarm system. It would be a matter of a few seconds to disable it but fortunately there wasn't one.

Heading back to the kitchen, I walked over to the refrigerator and grabbed the largest magnet I could find.

Without wasting any more time, I headed straight upstairs for the master bedroom. Ignoring the jewelry box proudly displayed on the vanity, I headed straight for the walk-in closet.

I spared a glance for the dresses hung neatly. Pulling one pink and gold dress out, I wondered if it was in my size; it was last season Gucci. This woman had nice taste.

I set the hanger back; I had to get to business first.

The safe was almost always hidden in the closet on the male's side. Pushing aside several suits, I found it. It was a SentrySafe. Perfect.

Inexpensive home safes were ridiculously easy to break into. They weren't really a deterrent to a real burglar. They just made the homeowner feel more in control.

Crouching down, I placed the magnet next to the handle. I knew a nickel solenoid prevented the handle from turning and pulled the bolts into place. All you had to do was displace the solenoid with a magnetic field. I could hear the lock trip. Opening the door, I pulled out the small jewelry boxes and the pile of papers. On top were two passports. I grabbed the female one. She was a brunette and a little taller than me but it should work, especially if I flirted with the TSA agent while he was checking it. I put back the other valuables. The last thing I wanted was for them to think their safe had been cracked and have the police flag the passport.

Looking around the closet, I grabbed a small pink weekender bag and tossed in the Gucci dress and a pair of heels. The richer I looked the less likely anyone at the airport would suspect or stop to question me. After grabbing an Yves St. Laurent jacket and matching scarf, I made sure everything looked in order before heading back downstairs.

Going back into the kitchen, I replaced the magnet and opened the refrigerator. I grabbed a yogurt and apple.

Looking around, I noticed they actually still had a landline. Sweet.

Picking up the receiver, I dialed 911. "Hello, police? Please hurry. I just saw a shady looking man hop over a neighbor's fence. I think he might be a burglar."

After giving them the address, I hung up. Heading through the backyard, I tossed the luggage over the fence and then followed. I was back on Montrose when I heard the sirens. After seeing no electronics or jewelry missing, the homeowners and police would assume the sound of the sirens had interrupted the burglar before they'd had a chance to steal anything. Even if they did check the safe, they would probably be so focused on the valuables, they wouldn't even notice the missing passport.

I bit into the apple as I walked to catch the next Metra train.

* * *

I DECIDED ON THE WESTIN. It was close to the airport but not too close and had a shuttle. After using Damien's cash to secure a room, I had to give the front desk clerk a little extra on the side so he wouldn't ask for ID, but he made me leave a credit card number, so I had no choice but to use Damien's. I probably could have given him more money or talked my way out of it but something stopped me. Maybe it was my way of taunting Damien, pushing his buttons again. Challenging him to find me by just leaving little breadcrumbs.

It was only for one night. I would be gone by dawn on the first flight available to Montreal. Too bad there were no more flights today.

I opened the hotel room door and collapsed onto the bed.

Desperately, I wished I could get ahold of Samara. I didn't have a phone and knew she had probably already ditched hers. I hated leaving Chicago knowing she was in the clutches of Gregor and Damien, but I had no choice. Obviously, I couldn't go to the police, especially after hearing they were in the Ivanov's back pocket. I had to stick to the plan and head to Montreal.

Feeling a little better with a plan, I decided to run myself a bath and order a big bottle of wine from room service. I knew I should eat, but all I wanted right now was a cool, numbing glass of wine.

I ordered the best, most over-priced bottle they had. What did I care about the cost? Damien was buying. The fact that they would charge his card since I paid cash for the room crossed my mind.

I was playing with fire, and I knew it.

CHAPTER 23

*D*amien

SHE LOOKED ALMOST INNOCENT.

Deceptively so.

Her long blonde hair spread out on the pillow. She slept on her stomach with one knee pulled up and the covers kicked off. She was dressed only in a pair of silk panties. This pair was black with a pattern of tiny red cherries. Her skin looked soft and warm. I had to resist the urge to run my fingertips up her spine. Her beautiful full lips were slightly parted. Every now and then, she made the cutest mewing sound.

After seeing she was gone, I'd raced to the apartment door and immediately noticed it was unlocked. Then I realized what the clever minx had done. I shook my head, still not believing I had fallen for such an old tried and true trick. No doubt about it, this woman had me turned around and upside down.

Life from this point forward was never going to be boring. Not with Yelena by my side. And she would be right by my side if I had to chase her halfway around the globe. There were just some women who were worth it. Besides, I'd be lying if I didn't say I loved the chase. It was no fun hunting easy prey. Any other woman in my life was just that, easy prey; the moment I approached, they rolled onto their backs, exposing their vulnerable undersides and just begging me to pet them.

Not Yelena.

Each time I approached, she bit, clawed, and kicked.

Forcing me to overpower her.

Forcing me to compel her submission through my superior strength.

I shifted in my seat as my cock grew thick and heavy at just the thought of it.

Hell yeah, it was way more fun hunting prey that fought back.

Problem was, we were out of time… and I was out of patience.

Standing up, I leaned over her prone form. Picking up one silky curl, I used the end to tease and tickle her soft cheek. Her little nose scrunched and twitched. Her arm came up to brush her cheek. I tickled her skin again. This time with a sleepy huff, she rolled onto her back. Giving her time to settle in, I took a step back and reached into my duffle bag for the padded wrist restraints I had packed especially for when I caught up to her.

Carefully, I lifted one wrist off the pillow and slipped

her hand through. I then secured the belt strap to the headboard.

She slept on. Helped no doubt by the half empty bottle of wine on the room service tray which I apparently bought with my credit card.

That she had managed to lift my wallet without my noticing still rankled me. The worst part was I didn't even know *when* she had lifted it. Was it on the roof? Or later? I would be damned if I would ask her. It was bad enough she had lifted it without my notice, I wasn't going to let her know I didn't have the first clue as to when it had happened. My babygirl would get way too smug over that tidbit of information.

Crossing the room, I stepped to the other side of the bed. Once more, I gently lifted her wrist and put her hand through the padded restraint. After securing the second strap to the other side of the headboard, she was well and truly trapped.

Returning to my seat across from the bed, I took a moment to admire my view. She had amazing breasts, just enough to fill a man's hand. My cock got harder just at the thought of sucking one of those cute pink nipples into my mouth, scraping the delicate flesh against my teeth. Giving my baby the edge of pain I knew she enjoyed. Her lithe body was now stretched out and open. Her legs gently spread. As if she were waiting for me.

Aware the clock was ticking, I decided it was time to wake her up.

I lifted the lid off the ice bucket and loudly dropped two ice cubes into a highball glass.

Reaching into my jacket pocket, I pulled out my silver

flask and poured myself a generous portion of Macallan Rare as I watched her eyelids flutter.

It took her a moment to realize she wasn't alone in the room. I could tell the precise moment she learned she was tied to the bed. I watched as she tested the tight binds and tried in vain to sit up. Then her vivid, bright blue eyes turned on me.

My pretty angel let loose an ear-piercing scream and a string of curses that would impress a drunken sailor.

I had a fairly impressive vocabulary, but I must admit even I learned a few new ones. I think several of them might have even been in French.

Calmly, I raised my glass and took a sip, relishing in the smooth bite as the slightly chilled scotch coursed down my throat. "Yell all you like. I took the liberty of booking all the surrounding rooms. I didn't want to chance that we would be disturbed."

"Fuck you, Damien!" shouted Yelena as she kicked out.

I smiled. "Is that an invitation?" I stood. She immediately quieted as her wide eyes watched my hands lower to undo my belt buckle. With a snap, I pulled the heavy leather free of the jean loops.

"I wouldn't fuck you if you were the last man on earth," she hissed.

I leaned over the bed, my hands falling on either side of her head, capturing some of her hair and pinning her in place.

Looking deeply into her enraged eyes, I warned, "Well then it's a good thing I have no intention of asking your permission."

Her mouth opened on an outraged gasp, and I

swooped down to claim it. Bruising her lips with a punishing kiss. Taking more than I gave.

Breaking the kiss, I stood over her half naked form.

Gesturing with a nod, I said, "I see you helped yourself to the cash in my wallet."

Yelena stayed stubbornly silent.

"Too bad you also used the credit card. That was a stupid, rookie mistake. You had to have known the American Express concierge would call me. That card is heavily monitored." I narrowed my eyes as I watched the play of emotions cross her features. She had to have *known* using that card was a risk. Hell, slipping a quick hundred to the front desk clerk would have solved the issue.

But she hadn't, she'd given him the credit card.

Did she want me to catch her?

Maybe she wasn't even aware of it, but I think she did.

And I had no intention of disappointing her now that she was back under my control.

"I'm not going to marry you," she ground out.

CHAPTER 24

Damien

I RAN a hand through my hair. I couldn't contain a frustrated sigh. "So, you overheard?"

"Are you going to deny it?" she accused. She strained against the binds to raise up her shoulders and meet my gaze. Her chest flushed a delicate pink as she became more agitated. "I heard you talking about me. Dictating my future as if I had absolutely no say in the matter."

She didn't, but that was definitely not the way I wanted her to learn of my marriage plans. But it changed nothing. We would be married as soon as I could arrange it. "Baby, it's for your own protection."

"Liar. You just want to use me. You're no better than the Italians or those stupid Columbians... or my stepfather," she spit out.

Grabbing her by the jaw, I forced her to lock gazes

with mine. "Babygirl, you don't want to test my patience right now," I threatened, holding on to my self-control by a very thin thread. If she wasn't a virgin, I would have fucked her raw by now. As it was, I knew I would have to come first at least once to ease the tension before I even tried to fuck her, otherwise I might hurt her.

"I don't like your tone," she fired back.

"You're about to like far less than my fucking tone."

Tears sprang to her eyes, and she whispered, "I hate you."

I reached for the hem of my t-shirt and pulled it over my head. "We both know that's far from the truth."

"No. I really do fucking hate your guts."

I shrugged. "Guess I'm just going to have to prove you wrong."

Yelena pulled on her binds. "Not exactly a fair fight. Are you so afraid of me that you have to tie me up to win?"

I chuckled. Damn if this little brat didn't relish in pushing my buttons. She could spew profanities and declare her hatred all she wanted. I could see the light in her eyes, the flush on her cheeks. The way her thighs clenched and quivered whenever I stepped near the bed.

She may have hated me, but she wanted me all the same.

Keeping my eyes trained on her, I lowered the zipper to my jeans and stepped out of them. My erect cock sprang free. Her eyes fell to my waist then lower. Taking my cock in my fist, I gave it a few pumps. It was one thing to feel all ten inches press into her lower back like she had on the roof earlier, but it was another to get a good look at it. I knew the sight intimidated her. Good.

Turning, I reached into my bag for the pink stiletto knife she had thrown at me earlier. Making sure she could see the handle and recognize it as her own, I flicked the blade open. Resting a knee on the mattress, I swiftly sliced through the thin silk fabric of her panties over each hip. Gripping the center, my fingers grazing the soft mound of her cunt, I pulled the fabric free.

"Bastard!" she fumed.

Padding barefoot across the room, I dropped four more ice cubes into my glass before pouring a generous three fingers from my flask. I took a sip, as I returned to the bed. Setting the glass within reach on the nightstand, I placed a knee on the mattress.

As I expected, Yelena kicked out at me with her left leg. I easily captured her ankle in a strong grip. Moving to kneel between her thighs, I pushed her legs open wider. I could see her whole body stiffen.

Christ, she was beautiful. Her ocean blue eyes were bright with unshed tears and wild with suppressed arousal. Her creamy skin had a delicate pink flush, as her breasts rose and fell with each frightened breath.

She should be frightened.

I felt the need to claim her as my own.

To put my scent on her, my mark.

Seize her as my treasured possession.

A demon stealing his piece of heaven.

Yelena hissed through her teeth. The slight sheen of arousal glossed the soft curls between her legs.

"My baby did a bad thing running away from me like that," I chastised darkly.

Yelena stayed silent. The hunted assessing the hunter.

"I thought I made myself clear when I spanked this cute cunt of yours pink that I wouldn't tolerate any more disobedience." Using the back of my forefinger, I caressed her pussy… up and down, up and down.

Her breath caught, as she fought her physical response to me.

"I don't take orders from you," she fired back.

I smiled.

Fuck, I loved the fight in her.

"That's where you're wrong, babygirl. I'm in charge now, and you *will* obey me."

"Fuck you!"

"I think it's time I did something about that dirty mouth of yours," I threatened as I rose up on my knees.

Looking down at my fully engorged cock, Yelena threatened me back. "Put that thing in my mouth, and I'll bite it off."

Grabbing her jaw again, I tilted her head back. "When I'm done with you, you'll be begging me to fuck your mouth."

The headboard thumped and rattled as Yelena tried once more to fight her wrist binds.

Raising my hand, I gave her right tit a hard slap. She immediately stilled. A look of pure shock frozen on her face.

Reaching over to the nightstand, I picked up one ice cube.

I held it aloft over her open mouth, watching as the

scotch whisky-soaked drops of ice water coated her lips. The tip of her small pink tongue flicked out to taste the smoky liquor.

I moved to slide the cube over her right breast, tracing the crimson outline of my fingers which had marked her delicate skin. I then circled her pert nipple.

"Stop. It's cold," she moaned as she bit her lip.

I moved the ice over her belly, watching as the muscles of her abdomen twitched from the icy sensation.

I met her eyes as I moved the ice cube lower.

Yelena began to shake her head. "No, Damien. No. I don't like this," she complained.

"This is a punishment. You're not supposed to like it."

I placed the softened, melted edge of the ice cube between her cunt lips, pressing it against her clit.

Yelena's hips pitched off the bed as she cried out. I placed my left hand on her stomach and forced her back against the mattress.

"It's too cold! It hurts!"

I chuckled. "I think you enjoyed the heat of my spanking a little too much earlier. Time to try a different tactic."

With that, I placed the melting cube at her tight entrance and pushed. The ice cube slid in deep with my finger. I could feel her muscles clench painfully around the icy intrusion.

"Stop! It hurts!" screamed Yelena as she tried to twist her hips to escape the pain.

Reaching over her, I picked up another ice cube. Her eyes widened.

"Don't! Please don't," she whispered plaintively.

Ruthlessly, I pressed the ice into her cunt. Yelena cried out as her whole body stiffened. I knew the ice was causing a special kind of pain. A clenching, tight, raw kind of agony as her warm muscles contracted painfully from the cold touch.

I picked up the third ice cube. Holding it over her squirming body, I let the icy drops of water fall onto her flat stomach. A warning of what was to come.

"Please! I'm sorry! Okay? I'm sorry I ran away!"

"Not good enough," I growled. She needed to understand that each time she ran from me, each time she fought me, she put herself in greater danger.

This time, I used the edge of the cube to part the folds of her cunt. I moved past her entrance to press it against the tight rosebud of her ass.

"Don't! Oh God! Don't!" she pleaded.

I caressed her puckered entrance with the ice cube. Her butt cheeks clenched as her thighs tensed with her efforts to close her legs. The watery slickness of the ice helped me push the cube into her dry, tight entrance. I knew this one would hurt far more than the ice in her pussy.

Yelena howled in pain as she pulled on her wrist binds.

"Why am I punishing you?" I demanded.

Yelena didn't respond.

I forced my finger into her pain-clenched asshole. The tip of my finger pushing the melting ice cube in further.

I repeated. "Why am I punishing you?"

Yelena's breath came in frantic gasps. Finally, she blurted out, "Because I was a bad girl."

"Did you disobey me?"

Yelena nodded as she moaned. Her thighs pressed against my sides as she continued to try to close her legs to protect the delicate flesh I was abusing.

"Yes," she whispered, turning her head to the side to bury her face in the pillow. Tears coursed down the sides of her cheeks.

I picked up the final ice cube. Yelena whimpered.

Reaching over her body, I grabbed her jaw and forced her to face me. Holding up the ice cube, I demanded, "Tell me to punish you again. Tell me you deserve the pain. Tell me how you like it rough, baby. Ask me to make it hurt."

Her eyes pleaded with me, but I would not relent.

My fingers pressed into her cheeks. I could feel the sharp edges of her teeth through the skin. "Say it."

"Punish me, Damien. Punish me with the pain," she moaned.

I pushed the final ice cube into her ass. Yelena sobbed as the ebbing agony once more surged.

Placing a hand near her shoulder, I leaned over her prone body. Reaching between her legs, I tried to push a finger into her chilled entrance. The muscles were clenched so hard from the cold, I could barely fit in the tip.

Whispering in her ear, I asked, "Do you know what my cock is going to feel like when I force it into this incredibly tight, virgin cunt?"

Yelena's eyes widened as she began to shake her head. "Please! Please don't! It'll kill me. You'll tear me in two."

I moved my finger down and teased her puckered asshole. "Then how about here?"

"No! I don't… I've never… no!"

I stared into her eyes.

Waiting.

I could tell the very moment my intention dawned. Those beautiful blue eyes turned a striking shade of aquamarine. I watched the play of emotion from anger, to desire, to pride, and finally to submission.

"I'll suck your cock," she conceded, her voice hoarse from her tears.

I said nothing.

Waiting.

She got the message.

Swallowing a sob, she entreated, "Please fuck my mouth."

Leaning over, I ran my tongue over her upper and lower lips, wetting them before I rose up on my knees. Straddling her ribcage, I leaned up as I fisted my cock.

"Say it again," I commanded.

"Please fuck my mouth," she moaned.

Grabbing the headboard with my left hand, I placed the head of my cock between her lips.

"Open wider," I growled.

She obeyed.

I thrust my hips forward. My cock penetrated her mouth straight to the back of her throat.

Yelena gagged and began to struggle.

I pulled back slightly and thrust forward again, feeling the head press slightly into her throat.

Her muffled scream sent vibrations up my shaft, spurring me on.

Gripping the headboard with both hands now, I

leaned my hips into her, forcing her to swallow my entire length.

"That's it, baby. I want to feel your nose against my stomach," I panted from the exertion of keeping myself in check from full tilt fucking her hot little mouth.

I pulled free and allowed her one ragged gulp of air before I thrust again. I could feel the slide of her tongue on the sensitive underside of my cock. I bit back a groan as my balls tightened. I leaned back and gripped my cock, ruthlessly pumping my fist along the painfully hard length. My own breath came in harsh pants as I anticipated the moment I would come on her face and in her mouth.

"Keep your mouth open," I demanded. I could feel beads of sweat trickle between my shoulder blades as I tightened my grip.

Looking down at her flushed cheeks and bright eyes, her lips dark and swollen from the press of my flesh, was my undoing.

With a roar, I felt the rush of release. A thick stream of warm salty come coated her lips and tongue.

Still breathing hard, I leaned back. I placed my large hand over her pussy. Warming it. Rubbing the edge of my palm against her clit, I pushed one finger into her. She was still tight and slightly chilled.

"Lick my come off your lips."

Sliding my body down, I positioned myself between her open legs. My breath warming her cunt.

Hesitantly, her tongue poked out between her lips.

"That's right, baby. Lick it. Swallow it."

Yelena moaned as I forced a second finger into her cunt as my tongue flicked her clit. The heat of my skin and tongue was warming her, creating a beautiful extreme of sensations. Pleased, I stared up over her creamy expanse of skin as her tongue swept her lower lip, lapping up my seed. I thrust my fingers a little faster, swirling my tongue around her sensitive bud with the same frenetic rhythm.

Her hips raised up. I could feel the brush of her inner thighs against my jaw.

Her tongue flicked out to capture the last drop of my come off her upper lip.

Increasing the pressure and pace of my finger thrusts, I rose up over her body. Using my other hand, I grabbed a fistful of her hair.

"You're mine now," I rasped before capturing her lips in a savage kiss. Tasting myself. The proof of my ownership on her lips as I penetrated her with a third finger.

I swallowed the screams of her release.

CHAPTER 25

*Y*elena

I COULDN'T THINK STRAIGHT. What had just happened?

I barely even noticed when Damien released the straps on the padded wrist restraints. Tellingly, he kept the restraints themselves dangling from the headboard within easy reach.

Sitting up, I watched as he grabbed the fluffy white down comforter which had been kicked to the floor. He returned to the bed. Sitting against the headboard, he wrapped his large hands around my ribcage and lifted me onto his lap.

In my defense, I did let slip a small mew of protest but in all honesty, I didn't put up much of a fight. There was just something about him.

His strength.

The palpable edge of danger.

The way he didn't let me get away with any of my usual crap.

It drew me like a moth to a flame.

A very white-hot angry flame.

I couldn't suppress a sigh when he wrapped the comforter around the two of us. I settled into his lap, even resting my head on his shoulder. I could feel the press of his cock against my hip as he reached for his glass of whiskey. Tilting the glass at my lips, he ordered, "Drink."

I scrunched my nose. "I don't drink scotch."

"You'll learn to. Now drink."

There was no point in fighting him. I drank. The burn had an oddly restorative effect. I leaned in to take another sip, but he pulled the glass away.

"Easy, little one. Crawl before you walk," he chuckled as he emptied the glass in one swallow. I watched the sinews of his neck as if I could see the amber liquor slip down his throat.

Fuck. There wasn't a damn thing about this man I didn't find sexy as hell. Even how he drank.

There was a gentle pull on my scalp as Damien slipped his hand under my hair and pulled it free from the comforter. He smoothed the curls down my back. We sat there in silence. A temporary truce, as I was soothed by the rhythmic caress of his hand.

At one point, he pressed his hand against the side of my head as he leaned in to kiss my temple.

Keeping his lips close, he whispered, "I'm never letting you go, baby."

I sighed.

My time was up. Truth be told, I was out of options. It was clear I was not going to be able to escape Damien. It was also equally clear that if his intent had been to kill me, he could have easily done so back in my condo.

Without looking up, I murmured, "I know."

I was expecting to feel this sickening feeling of impending doom, like a big heavy door swinging shut, locking me in darkness. While he hadn't actually asked, and I hadn't really said yes, it was obvious he was talking about marriage. I should be feeling angry and trapped right now. In truth, I felt… safe. For the first time in my life, I felt safe and warm and protected in his arms.

Was this what it felt like to love and be loved?

Were either of us even capable of that emotion?

It seemed almost too tame and common of a word for whatever this fucked up thing we had between us was. This constant battle of wills. The need to push each other to the edge, to push each other's buttons. It was insane and twisted, but at the same time it was exciting and wonderful.

Pushing back a lock of hair which obscured his view of my profile, he asked, "Are you hungry?"

I thought about saying no just to be petulant, but the truth was I was starving. The only thing I had eaten all day was an apple and a few bites of eggs. No wonder two glasses of wine had put me quickly to sleep, giving him the advantage when he snuck into my hotel room.

Damien picked up the hotel phone and asked for room service. I listened as he ordered ravioli with a brown butter and sage sauce.

Later, when Damien set me aside to throw on a pair of

jeans and answer the door for room service, I felt oddly cold and vulnerable, immediately missing his heat and strength.

After grabbing the plate, a cloth napkin, and a fork, he returned to the bed. I started to position myself on the mattress against the headboard but a low rumbled growl from Damien had me changing course. Apparently, we had already gotten to the point where I understood his growled, wordless commands. Hiding a smile, I climbed back up onto his lap.

Resting the bowl with the three large ravioli on the mattress, Damien halved one, swirled it in butter sauce and held it up to my mouth.

"I can feed myself you know."

"Not while I'm around," he said with a seductive wink.

I opened my mouth and groaned as I chewed the creamy, savory bite. As he pulled the fork away, a dollop of melted butter sauce dripped onto the curve of my breast.

"My turn to feast," said Damien with a chuckle as he leaned over to lick the sauce off my skin. His cock was pressed between my hip and his stomach. I could feel it start to thicken and lengthen. It gave me a taboo thrill.

Food was forgotten. I don't think I could have eaten another bite. My earlier hunger had been replaced by something far more primitive. A gnawing need to be possessed by this man. To be overpowered, held down, and taken. I was still untouched because I had never found a man who made me want to sacrifice my freedom for a moment in his arms. Never trusted someone to get that close to me.

Until now.

I wasn't sure if I could trust Damien with my heart, but I knew I could with my body. I wanted him. Needed him. This. If just for now, just for this moment, I wanted to feel as though I belonged and was loved… even if it was just a devilish illusion.

Damien tossed the still-full pasta bowl onto the nightstand and pivoted, pinning me beneath his weight against the mattress.

"I can't wait any longer," he growled.

CHAPTER 26

Yelena

His hand easily spanned my slim thigh and forced my legs open. Shifting his weight, he placed his hips between my legs, pressing his already engorged cock against my core. It was both a threat and a promise. In that moment, I felt... everything. The rough brush of his chest hair against my hard nipples. The warmth of his thigh pressed against my own. The feel of his slightly calloused fingers as they swept over my hip to grasp my breast.

My back arched.

His mouth descended to claim one pert nipple, pulling it deep into his mouth. The sharp scrape of his teeth had me grasping handfuls of the starched white linen sheets beneath us. He sucked hard till I cried out in pleasurable pain before moving to the next nipple, giving it the same torturous attention.

All the while, I could feel the press of his cock wedged between us.

Damien moved to kiss my shoulder, skimming his lips along my collarbone. With the tip of his tongue, he traced my jaw till he reached my ear. He whispered to me in Russian as he flicked the soft shell with the tip of his tongue. I didn't have to understand the language to know they were dark, erotic words filled with even darker promise.

His hand slipped between us to tease my clit. Swirling the tip of his finger, testing my slick arousal before pushing it deep inside of me. I groaned and reached for him. Spanning my hands over his back, I ran my nails over his skin, rewarded with his deep, guttural growl and a push of his hips. Emboldened, I pressed my nails in harder, wanting to mark his skin as he had marked mine.

Lifting up on his forearms, he threw his head back, exposing the thick cords of muscle on his neck and shoulders. His teeth clenched as he swallowed a groan from the feel of my claws on his back. Unable to resist, I leaned up and licked his skin. Tasting him. Loving the astringent sting of his cologne on my tongue.

He gripped my hair and pulled my head back, breaking the contact. "Christ, babygirl. I'm not sure how much longer I can hold on."

Incapable of speech, I shifted my hips, grinding into his cock.

He cursed again, this time in Russian, before pushing a second finger inside of me as he claimed my mouth. His tongue danced with mine, leading as I followed. He tasted of whiskey and warm butter. My arms reached up to caress his jaw with my hands. The harsh scrape of his stubble scratched against the soft skin of my palms. It felt so masculine, so *him*. My lips felt bruised and swollen as he ravaged my mouth, taking and giving.

He pushed a third finger inside of me.

I cried out.

My body strained to stretch around the intrusion as he pulsed his fingers back and forth, opening me. Preparing me. My toes curled and I pushed my knees up, pressing my inner thighs against his hips.

Damien leaned back. His sapphire eyes became dark and stormy. His left arm shifted higher, placing his forearm near my head. His hand reached out to cup my face as his thumb caressed my cheekbone. The three fingers of his right hand slowly pulled out of me and gripped my thigh, holding my legs open.

I froze.

My heart beat a chaotic cadence inside my chest.

Despite the pleasure, I recoiled inside of myself. It was time. I knew it. We both knew it. This wasn't just about him taking my virginity. This was something deeper, the impact of which would define the rest of my life. This was a point of no return. Darkness crept along the edges of my vision. I feared I might faint.

Unaware of my distress or perhaps because of it, Damien threatened, "There is no escaping me now. You will truly be my padshiĭ angel."

His fallen angel.

Fallen into the arms of a demon.

Him.

Pressing against his shoulders, my voice was high-pitched with panic. "Wait!"

His gaze narrowed as his jaw tightened. I could feel the tension and power radiating off his shoulders. "No."

His knuckles pressed against my sensitive skin as he fisted his cock and brought the tip to my entrance. The tip nudged in just slightly.

Scared, I tried to shift upwards and away. He shifted his left hand to grip my hair. Pulling sharply, he wrenched my head back as my body arched upward.

The large bulbous head slipped inside.

Damien was breathing heavy. Leaning down, he growled against my lips, "This is going to hurt."

My eyes widened. I tried to call out *no*, but the word was trapped in my throat.

He lunged forward.

Spearing his thick flesh into me.

Tearing me in two.

I screamed and began to buck and thrash. Damien subdued me with the power of his weight as he held my body, pinning it down. His hips moved. Piercing me again and again, each thrust opening my body more. I felt every heavy inch of his cock as it moved inside of me.

Damien captured my mouth, his tongue taking possession of me as effectively as his cock. His hips pounded into me with each thrust as he clasped my face between his large hands, stopping my head from thrashing from side to side.

"God damn it, Yelena. Don't you do this. Don't shut me out. Not now!"

Tears slipped from the corners of my eyes as the shock of his words hit me. Taking advantage, Damien claimed my lips once more, but this time his kiss was more gentle, almost persuasive.

"Please, baby, open for me."

My mouth softened under his. He groaned and pressed his advantage, cupping my breast as his tongue swirled around my own.

The sharp pain of him breaking through my maidenhead ebbed, eclipsed by a rising tide of pleasure. A throbbing pressure that increased with every thrust of his hips.

It was as if I was trapped inside the notes of Rachmaninoff's Piano Concerto Number Two. The way the music started with slow, dark determination and then built… and built… and built in intensity. The darkness rising like the coming of a storm. It ebbed and flowed on a whirling wind which spiraled and twisted. I no longer had any sense of self or awareness other than the power of the man on top of me, inside of me, claiming me.

Unlike anything I had ever experienced before, fear mixed with pleasure as I clung to him, using his body to anchor my chaotic swirling emotions. His strong arms wrapped around me tightly, holding me close as he drove into my body several more times. Riding my climax to his own.

With a roar, he filled me with his seed. Binding us together.

Afterwards, he insisted on getting me a warm washcloth. Wiping away the evidence did nothing to stop the tightening inside of my chest. I could still feel his hands on me. Feel his weight holding me down. Feel him inside of me. It was as if he had marked my soul, and the imprint of him would be with me forever.

Trapping me.

Slipping into bed beside me, he wrapped his arms around my middle and pulled me close. My back to his front.

"Stop," he whispered into my ear after smoothing my wildly tangled hair aside.

"What?"

I could hear the smile in his voice as he continued. "Stop whatever is racing through that beautifully intelligent, chaotic mind of yours."

I bristled. My body tensing, I tried to pull out of his embrace but his arm only tightened. After a moment, sure he had made his point, his arm shifted. His hand caressed my arm and hip in long soothing strokes.

"How about you don't think of it as being trapped?" he murmured against the nape of my neck.

I started. It was as if he were reading my thoughts. I stayed silent.

"How about we just worry about the next minute and the minute after that? And not let the entire future crash down on us all at once?" he offered.

I played with the wrinkled tag that poked out from the pillowcase under my head. "Does this mean you won't make me marry you?"

His hand stopped moving. The dark hair on his chest tickled the skin of my back as he took a long, deep breath. "No."

I turned and looked over my shoulder. "No you won't make me marry you, or no it doesn't mean that?"

His dark gaze bore down into mine. I could tell by the tightening of his jaw that I was trying his patience. "Would it be so terrible to rely on someone other than yourself for once? To actually trust that someone might care enough about you to want to protect you?"

I turned away. I thought about how I'd once rambled to him that the song *All By Myself* was sampled from Rachmaninoff. That horribly morose ode to loneliness had become sort of a life anthem for me. I could hardly be blamed for not wanting to trust or rely on anyone. My own mother had taken her life, choosing death over me. The rest of my childhood had been spent dodging my stepfather's fists and being told I was useless and unwanted. I had been fending for myself for as long as I could remember.

"When were you born?" he asked suddenly.

I furrowed my brow, trying to figure out what his angle was in asking. Unable to decide, I answered, "December third."

"What does that make you?"

"Make me?"

"Your zodiac sign."

Realization dawned. "Oh. A Sagittarius."

"And what is a Sagittarius like?"

I traced the symbol of an archer's bow onto the sheet with the tip of my finger. "My mother used to say that I was destined to dream big, chase the impossible, and take risks. That it was written in the stars."

Damien shifted, pushing me onto my back as he loomed powerful and large over me. Leaning down, he kissed my shoulder, then the top of my breast. "And how compatible are a Sagittarius and a Scorpio?"

"Terrible!" I said gleefully, my eyes widening as I warmed up to his change in subject.

He frowned. "You're lying."

"Nope. It's true. Scorpios are too darkly intense and controlling, forcing the more free-spirited Sagittarius to run away and chase their freedom." My lips twisted into a knowing smirk.

Damien looked deep into my eyes. "Or maybe the Sagittarius brings light and a breath of fresh air into the Scorpio's rigid life, and instead of taking away her freedom, he becomes a rock, something solid to fix her dreams to."

And just like that I was completely, irrationally, stupidly in love.

Damn him to hell for making me feel this way.

I should have known better than to fall into the path of a stubborn Scorpio.

CHAPTER 27

*D*amien

I WATCHED as Yelena's small nose scrunched in distaste as she picked her wrinkled pair of yoga pants and simple black hoodie up off the floor where she'd left them the night before. She cast a glance at a small suitcase with a designer dress tossed over the side. By the looks of it, it was about two sizes too big for her. It was probably best if I didn't ask too many questions as to how she had acquired it.

It was clear my baby preferred her designer outfits. I was certain she only wore hoodies and yoga pants when she was running from me. Since their innocuous appearance and maneuverability would be prized well above tailored but constricting designer clothes.

With a resigned sigh, she stepped into the yoga pants. Leaving on my t-shirt, which I'd given her to wear last night, she pulled her hoodie over her head and reached for her sneakers.

I liked the sight of her in one of my shirts. It felt strangely normal. Like something a boyfriend and girlfriend would do. It was a funny thought. I had never really thought of myself in relationship terms. Probably because I had never been in one. I didn't count fucking the occasional model and having them on my arm for the random social function as a relationship. More of a quid pro quo.

Yelena was different.

She had always been different. From the moment I'd laid eyes on her on that dance floor, something inside of me changed. I thought it would pass over the years but it had only grown stronger. Then when I saw her yesterday, it solidified, like a fist made of hot iron wrapping around my heart. It was solid and steadfast. My feelings for her were now not just a part of me but the only breathing warmth in my body.

"When this is all over, I'll take you to Paris for the Spring shows. I'll escort you to Dior and Chanel and Yves Saint Laurent, and you can buy whatever you want," I offered as I tossed on my jeans. "Although, please no Gucci. I won't be able to pretend to like boring brown patterns with green and red or all that trashy gold."

It really was adorable to see her eyes light up with excitement like a little girl just offered a treat. Then just as quickly, her look shuttered. Sticking her chin up in defiance, she huffed, "I'm perfectly capable of buying my own clothes."

She had just put her long blonde hair up into a high

ponytail which made it convenient for me. Grabbing her ponytail, I looked down into her petulant upturned face.

"I'm more than aware you can buy your own clothes. That isn't the point. From this moment forward, *I* want to be the one buying you things." I gave her ponytail a tug for emphasis.

"Listen. Just because you fucked me doesn't mean you own me," she snapped as she tried to break my grip.

Placing my hand around her throat, I walked her backwards till her body flattened against the wall. Her small hands tried to wrap around my wrist and dislodge my grip. I pressed my hips against her stomach so she could feel the threat of my quickly hardening cock.

Leaning in close, I stared suggestively first at her open mouth, then into her startled baby blue eyes. My voice was so low it was practically a growl. "Let's get something very straight. I do own you. I own this mouth, that tight pussy, and sometime in the very near future, that sweet ass of yours. *You're mine.* Run as often as you like. I'll find you each and every time and bring you back where you belong. You're never getting rid of me, beautiful. I suggest you get used to the idea."

After giving her a hard kiss, I released her throat.

She wisely stayed silent. I think we both knew if she dared contradict me, I would not hesitate to drag her over my knee and give her ass the spanking it so richly deserved.

These weren't just words to me. I fucking meant every one of them. She was the woman for me. She aggravated the piss out of me, and I would probably wind up with more scars from her than from my enemies, but she would be worth every damn one of them. I wasn't some jackass Neanderthal who didn't know a good thing when it slapped him in the face. I knew I had found a beautiful little gem when Yelena crossed my path, and I had absolutely no intention of ever letting her go.

From across the room, she watched as I tossed the wrist restraints into my bag. I walked over to the hotel bureau and also retrieved my wallet. There was a chortle that sounded very suspiciously like a laugh, which quickly turned into a cough from Yelena. I cast her a look which hopefully signaled I would not tolerate any mention of her easily lifting my wallet without my knowledge.

Noticing my cell phone had died sometime last night, I grabbed the plug from my gym bag and started to charge it. It wasn't like me to let it die. I must have been too distracted by the painfully beautiful woman in my arms. I couldn't recall ever spending the night with a woman. Things got complicated when you spent the night. It sent a message I'd had no intention of ever sending, but with Yelena, it was heaven just holding her warm body in my arms, falling asleep to the soft sounds of her breathing.

Yelena played with the strings of her hoodie. Without looking at me, she asked softly, "What about Natasha?"

My eyes narrowed. What the fuck? "How do you know about Natasha?"

Yelena nodded to the wallet in my hand. Of course, the photo. Shoving the wallet into my back pocket, I grabbed my gym bag and motioned for her to start heading toward the door. "Natasha is none of your business."

Yelena dug in her heels. "That's not fair, and you know it. You expect me to suddenly just trust you… to suddenly just throw my lot in with yours, and you probably have a wife or girlfriend in Russia!"

I tossed the bag onto the bed and paced away, running a hand through my hair.

I turned to see Yelena staring at me, arms crossed defensively across her chest. At least I could take small comfort in the fact that my babygirl was clearly jealous; it meant she wasn't as immune to my charms as she claimed. She obviously felt the same intense connection I did.

Still, I did not want to talk about Natasha right now.

But it looked like I didn't have a choice. Not if I wanted to get Yelena out of this hotel without half the lobby calling the police to report a kidnapping in progress.

"Natasha was a friend of Gregor's and mine from college."

Yelena's mouth quirked up. She all but rolled her eyes. "Oh… a *friend*."

"Yes. A friend. More like a second sister. We lost her several years ago."

Yelena closed the distance between us and placed her hand on my arm. It was the first time she had touched me of her own accord, if you didn't count the knee to my knife wound, which I didn't.

"I'm sorry, Damien. I didn't know."

I shrugged my shoulders, uncomfortable with showing this weak side of my past. "She fell in love with an asshole who got her addicted to cocaine. Every time Gregor and I dragged her away to get her clean, he would appear back in her life and get her hooked again. Realizing we would never get her clean if he was still in the picture, we... took care of the problem. That's why Gregor was shipped off to Russia. The investigation into Natasha's boyfriend's death was hitting a little close to home."

I gave Yelena a hard look, certain I didn't have to spell out what I meant by taking care of the problem. She knew I meant we'd killed the bastard. "Unfortunately, it was too little too late. Natasha overdosed shortly afterwards."

Yelena rested her head against my chest as she wrapped her arms around my waist. "I'm sorry," she repeated, her voice slightly muffled.

I wrapped my arms around her shoulders. She was so small; it was like trying to hold a wild bird. Still, I took the comfort she offered.

"Despite the outcome, I don't regret for a minute that asshole breathed his last in my presence. *I protect those I care about.* No matter the cost." Stroking her back, I kissed the top of her head, hoping she realized I was talking about her too, before giving her ponytail a playful tug.

Before I could press her again about marrying me for her own safety, my cell phone began to ping. As I crossed the room, there were several more pings as it came back online. A knot formed in my stomach. We kept our cell communication as minimal as possible, usually just quick conversations and never any texts. Even after you deleted them, texts left a record that could be accessed by law enforcement.

There was a notification for several voicemails as well as texts.

. . .

From Gregor...
Call me.
We have a situation.
Warehouse.
Now.

From Dimitri...
At Gregor's.
Clean up necessary.
Warehouse.

And Vaska...
Where is your location?
Situation.
Warehouse in five.

"Blyad'," I cursed as I pressed the button to listen to the voicemails.

Yelena crossed the room to stand next to me. "Fuck is a word I do know in Russian. Is everything okay? What happened?"

I wrapped a protective arm around her waist and pulled her close as I listened to Gregor's voicemail telling me about the attack on Samara. He was speaking in rapid-fire Russian, so I wasn't worried about her overhearing the substance, but she did pick up on the tone.

Placing a hand on my chest, the light in her blue eyes dimmed as she asked, "Is Samara okay? What happened?"

Setting the phone aside, I placed my hands on her shoulders. "Samara is fine."

She closed her eyes briefly and visibly relaxed.

I hated to tell her more, but there was no point in keeping it from her. She would learn the details soon enough. "She was attacked last night. Three men broke into Gregor's home."

Her eyes flooded with tears. Her small hands gripped the fabric of my shirt over my upper arms. "What? Is she hurt?"

I shook my head. "Gregor reached her in time."

Her hand covered her mouth. "Oh my God! Oh my God!" Her knees buckled. Leaning down, I swept her into my arms and carried her over to the bed. Sitting down, I settled her on my lap. Rubbing soothing circles over her back, I kissed her temple. "Shhh, baby. It's fine. She's okay. She's not hurt."

Yelena began to rock back and forth in my arms. "This is all my fault. It's all my fault!"

My hand stilled. For just a moment, I considered letting her believe that. If she thought the attack was by the Columbians, then maybe she'd finally listen to me and realize she was in danger. Maybe she'd stop fighting me at every turn and accept my protection. As soon as the idea formed, I discarded it. I had never lied to her, and I wasn't about to start now. Lying was for weak cowards who didn't have the strength to back up their own words.

Gripping her chin with my thumb and forefinger, I forced her gaze to mine. "No. It's not."

She tried to wrench her face away. "You're just saying that to make me feel better."

"Baby, I don't lie. It's not your fault. The attack was by another Russian family. The Novikoffs."

"The Novikoffs? I know them. My stepfather used to drink with one of their bodyguards. Pavel Rasskovich, a real asshole who couldn't keep his hands to himself."

As if it were yesterday, I remembered Pavel touching her on the dance floor at Nadia's party. I'd wanted the man dead then, and apparently last night, I got my wish. "Well, he's dead now."

"Did the Novikoffs attack her because of Gregor?"

The simple question was like a punch to the gut. Although the answer was no, it could so easily have been yes. It was a stark reminder that while I was offering Yelena the safety and protection of my name, it was a double-edged sword. It might protect her from the monsters seeking her but wouldn't protect her from *my* monsters. I lived a dangerous life full of dangerous immoral people. Was what I was offering her really any safer?

My whole body rebelled at the thought. I had to believe she was at least safer in my arms, sheltered by my name, money, and strength, than out in the world alone and vulnerable. Sure, she had made it this far but for how long? It was only a matter of time before someone got to her. If it wasn't the Columbians it would be the Italians or worse.

My motives may not have been pure, but neither was the world we lived in.

At least I was the devil my angel knew.

"Can I talk to her?"

"Not just yet. Soon."

"But she's okay?"

"Yes, baby. She's safe and unharmed. I'll explain it all in the car. For now, we need to get out of here."

I would wait till later to explain to her how the voicemail also mentioned how my brother forced them to marry the moment they'd landed in D.C. No point in putting ideas in her head. I needed to get her on a plane in a few hours and that would never happen if she thought I was planning to do the same… which was in fact precisely what I was planning. I even had the same damn judge lined up.

Yelena nodded and rose to finish dressing.

I gave Vaska a quick call. In Russian, we made plans to meet at Dimitri's. His house had a helipad on the roof and a helicopter they would let me use. Although we were close to O'Hare, private planes left out of Midway. With morning rush hour traffic, it would take far too long to get across the city and to the Southside by car. A helicopter would be faster. By the time we arrived, the Ivanov private plane would have finished making the round trip from Washington, D.C. back to Chicago.

"Where are we going?" she asked as I ushered her out of the room.

"First to Dimitri's. Gregor and Samara caught a private plane out of town a few hours ago. We're going to do the same. I'm taking you home to D.C."

She nodded. "Okay," she answered softly. Her head bowed. Her face hidden behind a curtain of golden blonde hair.

I sighed. The news of Samara's attack must have really

rattled her if she was agreeing with me without a fight. It felt cruel to think it, but I was pleased.

Although I was forgetting that it had also been an extremely long and stressful twenty-four hours for my baby. Starting with my return into her life and ending with a bout of intense sex. I also remembered that she hadn't eaten much of the ravioli before I selfishly decided I wanted a taste of sweeter fare. "I don't think you ate enough. We'll grab some food on the way."

Her voice trembled slightly, probably from exhaustion. "Can I get a Happy Meal? I don't have the Little Bo Peep from Toy Story yet."

I caressed her cheek with the back of my hand. "Whatever my baby wants."

Except for her freedom.

She was truly mine now, and I was keeping her… no matter the cost.

CHAPTER 28

Yelena

DAMIEN'S FRIEND Dimitri lived in a massive sandstone house in Lincoln Park just off of Burling Street. Before Damien could raise the ring in a massive bronze lion's teeth to knock, the glossy black door swung open.

A large man, equal in size to Damien, answered the door. I recognized him as the man I saw in the safe house yesterday. He was just as intimidating with a dark, intently brooding look to his face, and tattoos which covered his hands and crept up his neck. The fact that he smiled in greeting as he called out Damien's name did nothing to change my opinion. He still looked scary as fuck.

I edged closer to Damien, feeling better when he placed a protective arm around my waist and pulled me into his side. I raised my head to look up at him. He caught my gaze and gave me a reassuring wink before greeting his friend.

"Yelena, this is my friend, Vasili Lukovich Rostov."

"Please, call me Vaska."

It wasn't until we were inside the magnificent ivory marble entranceway that I noticed there was a woman standing slightly behind him. She was beautiful. Her impossibly shiny ink black hair was done up in that super cool Rockabilly victory roll style with big glossy curls. It was then held back by a classic bright red bandanna. She had on a cute boat neck, dark blue and white striped sailor shirt and dark jeans with wide cuffs. Her whole look was pulled together with matte red lipstick over a serious Angelina Jolie pout.

Feeling self-conscious, I smoothed the wrinkles down on the front of my hoodie, wishing I at least had my Chanel lipstick to put on.

"And this is Mary."

"Hello." When she raised her arm to wave, I was astonished to see Vaska's arm rise as well.

They were handcuffed together!

I turned wide eyes up to Damien, but he seemed to not even notice.

To not notice his friend was handcuffed to a woman!

"You heard Gregor is already back in D.C.?" asked Damien as if nothing was amiss.

Vaska nodded. "Dimitri has taken Emma to a secure location just to be on the safe side till things calm down. I've already called for the helicopter to take you to Midway. It should be arriving any minute now."

Damien clapped him on the back. "Thank you, my friend. I'm sorry we have caused so much trouble in your city this visit."

Vaska laughed. "Things were getting boring with only the Petrov brothers to kick around. Besides, we owed you for your help with that Morocco mess."

Seriously? Was no one going to even mention the handcuffs?

"I'm sorry but..." I started but Damien squeezed my side and gave me a warning look.

I narrowed my eyes and shot him a warning look right back. He couldn't honestly think I wasn't going to say something.

Vaska pulled on his arm which jerked Mary forward slightly. She pulled right back. "Mary has decided to stubbornly refuse my protection."

"Because *Mary* can take care of herself and doesn't need an overbearing Russian barging into her life barking orders," responded Mary in a sarcastic, almost sing-song tone before her gorgeous red lips twisted into an angry pout.

A quick burst of laughter escaped Damien's lips, and he patted his own chest as if he had just coughed. My cheeks burned. The parallels to our own situation were unmistakable.

Damien raised an eyebrow and looked down at me. "Perhaps I should have kept those handcuffs."

"Mary if you need any tips on how to easily pick a handcuff lock, let me know," I said through clenched teeth.

"Just make sure you don't need to do it quietly or quickly, or you're fucked," fired back Damien.

My mouth dropped open at the insult to my lock picking skills.

"You don't — by any chance — have a gun on you, do you?" Mary asked me before turning to innocently bat her long black eyelashes at Vaska.

Before I could respond, the vibrating hum of an engine and the *thwap, thwap, thwap* of what I could only assume were helicopter blades sounded overhead.

"Looks like your ride's here," said Vaska cheerfully, as if the woman he was handcuffed to hadn't just requested a firearm. "Damien, you know the way?"

"I do. Take care of your own *affairs*."

With an arm around my waist, he led me to the curved staircase.

I tugged against his grasp. "Wait. Shouldn't we help her?"

Damien cast a look over his shoulder. "Why? She's safe with Vaska."

"She's here against her will."

His large shoulders shrugged. "Technically, so are you."

I stopped. He had a point.

Placing a finger under my chin, his sapphire gaze darkened. "And despite being lifelong friends, if he tried to interfere and take you from me, I would kill him in a heartbeat. I would expect no less from him, as well."

The intensity and sincerity of his response took my breath away. I actually believed he would kill his friend if he tried to rescue me.

"Trust me, angel. Vaska is only trying to protect her."

Where had I heard that before?

Casting a quick look over my shoulder, I saw Vaska fiercely kissing Mary.

Damien guided me up the stairs. I caught only a glimpse of a sumptuous bedroom decorated in cream and gold before we climbed a second staircase. Large French doors opened onto a furnished rooftop terrace with large lounge chairs and an open fire pit.

At the far end, a sleek black and red helicopter had just landed gracefully onto the raised helipad.

Despite the chaotic and scary circumstances, I was actually pretty excited. I'd never ridden in a helicopter before. I imagined it would be terrifying and exhilarating at the same time, like a roller coaster ride.

A man dressed in all black with a matching black helmet and sunglasses covering his eyes hopped out of the pilot's side and swung open the back door, motioning for us to enter.

"Let's go!" Damien called out over the din of the helicopter engine and still spinning propellers.

Grasping my long ponytail so my hair wouldn't fly around more than necessary, I ran toward the helicopter, ducking low as I neared the spinning blades even though they were several feet over my head.

Someone called out Damien's name. I turned to see Vaska and Mary both running across the rooftop. Damien motioned with his arm for me to continue onto the helicopter as he turned to see what Vaska wanted.

The pilot grasped my hand and helped me inside. It took my eyes a moment to adjust to the dim enclosed interior. When they did, I was startled to see a second person inside just across the narrow leather seat from me.

The seat was only long enough for two people. I assumed Damien would take the seat next to the pilot up front and was a little disappointed he wouldn't be directly by my side for the experience.

I immediately chastised myself for the silly thought.

What? I have sex with the guy once, and he says something insanely romantic about our compatible zodiac signs, and now all of a sudden I couldn't bear to be parted from him even for a minute like some doe-eyed teenager? Apparently, I was forgetting that yesterday I was throwing knives at him and hitting him with a brick! Or that for the last three years, he and his brother had been ruthlessly chasing me and my best friend down from one end of the country to the other.

Giving myself a mental shake, I pushed all these thoughts away. There would be plenty of time to analyze to death my conflicted and confused feelings for Damien once I was back in D.C. with Samara. Once I knew she was okay, then I could decide what my next step and future was... and whether Damien was included in my plans. Because after all, just because he said we were still getting married didn't mean I was going to say yes.

I turned at Damien's shout.

My brow furrowed. He was yelling and racing toward the helicopter. The pilot swung the door shut and hopped back into the pilot's seat.

"Wait! What are you doing?" I exclaimed.

Damien reached the door and pulled on the handle, but it didn't budge. Lunging for the door to open it myself, I was wrenched back by an arm around my throat.

The silent person who had been seated behind me

stretched his arm past my head. He was holding an ominous looking handgun.

My gaze locked with Damien's through the scuffed and dirty helicopter window. The horror reflected in his eyes froze my blood. Terrified, I struggled against my captor's grasp.

I screamed as he fired several shots through the glass. The bullets penetrated and caused cracks to radiate from the hole but didn't shatter the glass. Given that it was Dimitri and Vaska's helicopter, it must have some type of bulletproof glass. At this close range, the bullet would still penetrate but hopefully the glass and layers of plastic in between slowed it down enough not to harm Damien or the others.

Just then the entire helicopter shook as we began to rise into the air.

"Damien!" I screamed as I clawed at the arm around my neck.

The helicopter pitched sharply on its side sending me tumbling to the floor before I slammed my shoulder against the door.

"He's on the landing skids!" shouted the pilot as he struggled to control the helicopter. He had a heavy Spanish accent.

"Shake him loose!" cried the man who'd held me around the throat. Again, with a Spanish accent.

Oh my God!

My entire body went cold.

Realization dawned.

The engine whined and strained at whatever

maneuver the pilot was trying, but suddenly the helicopter righted itself.

I threw myself against the door, peering through the radiated cracks in the glass. I saw Damien getting smaller and smaller as we rose into the air. Even from this distance, I could see the tortured expression on his face.

As Vaska closed in on Damien, he tossed a black object that looked like a gun to him with his free hand. Damien caught it and turned. Swinging his arm to the right, it looked like he intended to fire at the tail of the helicopter, to try and take out the engine, but it was too high in the air by now and the risk to me was too great.

It was too late.

CHAPTER 29

*D*amien

SNATCHING the manager by the front of his coat, I swung him violently around and slammed his body against the glass partition. The back of his head bounced against the window, shattering it. Sharp shards of glass cascaded over both of our shoulders.

"I don't know his name!" Foamy bits of white spittle had formed in the corners of the man's mouth.

"You're fucking lying. I want his fucking name," I ground out.

"I don't know it!"

Pulling my arm back, I landed a punch against the man's left ribcage. Feeling the thin bones crack under the force of my fist, I punched him a second time in the same spot. This time the bone splintered. I could hear the sickening crunch. The man started to gasp for breath and wheeze as the broken rib bone punctured his lung. His knees buckled.

Grabbing him by the shirt front, I yanked him to his feet and pulled him within inches of my face. "Listen to me, you piece of shit. I will beat you to death with my bare hands, methodically breaking every bone in your useless body, unless you tell me what I want to know."

The man drew a ragged wheezing breath. "They'll kill me."

"So will I," I fired back, "but I guarantee it will be more painful than anything they would do to you."

Yelena had been gone now for forty-three minutes.

Forty-three agonizing, soul crushing minutes.

For the rest of my life, the look of sheer terror on her beautiful face would haunt my dreams.

I had failed her. Again.

I hadn't protected her when she was a vulnerable little girl needing my help, and now — after swearing to keep her safe from the Columbians — it was me who had led them straight to her.

If I lived for a thousand years, nothing I ever did would assuage my guilt.

How could I have been so complacent, so stupid as to let her get on that helicopter without verifying who the pilot was?

Blyad'!

As Yelena headed toward the helicopter, Vaska and Mary had run toward me, but I couldn't make out what they were yelling over the din of the engine. It was only when I got closer that I realized they were screaming *stop*. Without even finding out why, I turned and ran with all my might to reach Yelena, but I was too late. They shut the doors, trapping her inside.

In desperation, I latched onto the landing skids. It had been my intention to pull myself up and somehow force my way into the helicopter cab, but I was thrown off. When Vaska tossed me a gun, I knew it was dangerous to try and shoot it down, but it was a risk I had to take.

I knew what the Columbians were capable of. I knew all the torturous dehumanizing things they wouldn't hesitate to do to her.

It was worth the risk.

I knew I clipped the tail, but it wasn't enough to stop the helicopter. I had to stand and watch in horror as it climbed higher and higher into the sky.

Taking my babygirl with it.

Raising both arms, my fists pressed against my temples, I roared my pain and anger into the swirling wind created by the retreating spinning blades.

When Vaska placed his hand on my shoulder, I turned on him like a rabid dog. I was out of my mind with grief and anger. I didn't even see that Mary was still handcuffed to him. My attack on him made her trip and fall painfully to the ground, injuring her shoulder.

Vaska responded like a man possessed.

I twisted my jaw to the side. It still ached where Vaska was forced to haul off and punch me to get me back to my senses.

It was the least that I deserved.

"What the fuck happened?" I finally asked.

Holding Mary close to his side, Vaska reached into his back pocket for the handcuff keys while he told me. "I got a call from John. He's our usual helicopter pilot. He's provided by the service we use to store and maintain it when it's not in use. We have an understanding with the management because of the... *special circumstances of our business dealings...* that John and only John flies our bird. After doing a final check, his boss called him into the office. Next thing he knew, another pilot was taking off. The boss acted real cagey about why. So John called to warn me."

"Address," I growled, more beast than man right now. My only thought was of Yelena. The thin veneer of civilization slid off me like water, replaced by a single, primal need to find my mate.

Vaska nodded. "I need to secure Mary someplace safe. Then we'll go."

I shook my head. "I can't wait that long."

"You don't know what you're walking into there. We haven't even confirmed who's involved. They could still have a team of men on premises."

"It's them. I know it. They have her, Vaska, and it's my fucking fault. Do what you have to do to protect your girl, but I'm not waiting one fucking second to go after mine."

Cradling her arm against her middle, Mary protested. "I'm not *his girl*, and I'm fine. Go with him."

We both ignored her. As far as I was concerned, if Vaska wanted her protected, that was enough for me.

"I'll text you the address. I'm taking Mary to where Dimitri has Emma." He turned and gave her a harsh glare when she started to protest. "After you learn all you can, meet us at the usual place. We'll gear up with some firepower and go after the bastards."

Less than half an hour later, I was at the private hangar. John, warned of my coming, met me in the parking lot and pointed out where his boss could be found. The rat bastard was sitting at a desk stuffing his face with a sloppy Italian Beef as if everything was normal. As if he hadn't just sent a woman to her death because of his greed.

My boots crunched over a piece of shattered glass as I dragged him deeper into the office. Reaching into my back waistband, my fingers wrapped around the grip of my Glock. I pulled it free. Placing the muzzle against his left eye, I asked him, "What are their names?"

"I can't!" he squealed.

Lowering the gun, I shot him in the kneecap. His considerable bulk fell to the ground as he screamed in agony. A random employee appeared in the doorway. I raised my gun. "This is none of your business."

The employee looked like they were going to protest, but then John appeared and dragged them away with a nod in my direction. I knew he would take care of it, and at the very least, hold back anyone calling the police till I left. He would be rewarded for his loyalty.

Turing my attention back to the bleeding pig at my feet, I warned, "The next shot goes in your stomach."

He held one bloody hand palm up in a placating gesture. "He didn't tell me his name, but we've flown for his boss several times before. The boss owns a horse stable in Oak Park."

"The name."

"They'll kill me!" he whined again.

"You're already dead."

"Santiago. Santiago Garcia. He paid me to let them know when Dimitri or Vaska ordered their helicopter to be ready. I didn't ask any questions. I didn't know they were going to steal it!"

I swallowed down the bile which rose in the back of my throat. Unlike with the Italians, I had never been able to arrange a meeting with the Columbians to sort out the misunderstanding over Yelena and pay them off, because I could never find out which gang or faction was involved. Unlike with the Italians — and occasionally with us Russians — they were rarely organized by family, which made them more fragmented with less of a hierarchy. There always seemed to be someone new in charge.

Santiago Garcia was the current head of the Los Infieles. *The Unfaithful.*

I had already had a run-in with him a few months ago when he tried to renegotiate the price of some German G3 rifles, Israeli Galils and Uzis, and U.S. M-16s we had acquired for him. We never renegotiate. His threats of retaliation for my disrespect to him in front of his men meant nothing to me.

So this explained why, after a year and a half of silence, the chatter about the Columbians searching for Yelena had turned into such a frenzy. I thought it was because she had become active again in some of the major races.

It had nothing to do with her.

This was about me.

Santiago was getting his revenge against me.

He must have learned of my connection to Yelena.

They had probably been tracking me this entire trip.

They had taken a chance I might use the helicopter, and I had played right into their fucking hands.

It would only be a matter of time before he realized her part in the Pick Six scheme which had been robbing his tracks blind these past three years.

Fuck.

John appeared in the doorway. "Cops are at the front gate. I have a buddy holding them back but not for much longer."

"You got a way out of here?"

He nodded.

"I'll make it worth your while."

He smiled. "I know what I signed up for. Bird is gassed and ready when you are." He gave a pointed look to the moaning man at my feet before leaving.

His boss sniveled, "I told you what you wanted to know. You don't have to kill me."

"That's where you're wrong." I fired a single shot straight into his temple.

He had to die.

They would all die.

Anyone who harmed my Yelena was about to find out how I earned the nickname Demon.

CHAPTER 30

Yelena

THE FEAR and adrenaline pumping through my veins made my head spin. I wrapped my arms tightly around my middle, clutching my stomach, scared I would throw up as the helicopter raced over the tops of the city's skyscrapers.

Through the window, I could see the cold, grey waters of Lake Michigan. Whitecaps churned as the waves crashed against the rocky shore.

Should I try and jump?

It would be my death but that would be preferable to what probably awaited me when we landed. I had heard the gruesome stories from my stepfather and his cronies. Sitting around my mother's old kitchen table, letting their cigarette butts burn nasty char marks in the varnish as their sweaty cheap beer cans left hazy water marks, they would compare notes on who was more ruthless — the Russians or the Columbians.

As a little girl, the things I overheard gave me nightmares.

No. I had to stop thinking this way.

Damien would rescue me.

He would move heaven and hell to get to me.

I was sure of it.

I'd never trusted a man in my life before now, but I trusted Damien.

I more than trusted him.

I love him.

The man drove me crazy. He was such a typical Scorpio, far too controlling and pushy and — according to my sign — we shouldn't be the least bit compatible but none of that mattered.

I love him.

I loved how he had the same sarcastic sense of humor as me. I loved that he loved classical music. Or how despite being this big thug Russian with tattoos, he could rattle off all the most popular high-end Parisian designers. I loved how he kept a photo of his old school friend in his wallet and how he and his brother did everything they could to try and save her from herself.

Just like he tried to save me from myself the night of Nadia's birthday party.

I should have listened to him then. I should have taken a risk and trusted that maybe, for once, someone was trying to help me instead of hurt me. Maybe then I wouldn't have dragged poor Samara from city to city and country to country these last few years, convincing her to stay by my side because I was too afraid to face life on my own.

Damien was dangerous and lived in a world I desperately wanted to leave behind but I no longer cared about any of that.

He was also sexy and funny, and for the first time in my life, I felt safe and protected in his arms. Right at this moment, I wanted nothing more than to feel those strong arms around me. Wanted to feel his lips against my forehead as he called me his angel. Wanted to hear him gruffly tell me everything was going to be okay.

I had to hold on to the feeling that he was coming for me.

No matter what happened.

I had to stay alive.

I owed him that much.

I owed him my trust that he would save me.

We left the city behind. Soon there was nothing but large suburban housing developments and strip malls below. Then even those were left behind for large sweeping fields of corn and grass. We must be heading west, deeper into the farmlands of Illinois.

The helicopter slowed and hovered over one such property. It had a large white manor house and a classic red barn. There was also a horse paddock and a long rectangular structure which looked to be a horse stable.

The helicopter kicked up a cloud of dirt and sand as it landed in a field nearby. Several horses in the paddock started to stomp their hooves and race about in a frenetic circle.

A group of men with automatic weapons strapped to their shoulders hunched down and ran toward us. The door swung open. A gloved hand wrapped around my upper arm and dragged me out.

I tripped and fell. The small stones dug into my palms, scraping them. Cursing in Spanish, a man pulled me back to my feet by my ponytail.

Balling my right hand into a fist, I swung out, clocking him on the jaw. The man by his side approached. I kicked out, catching him in the stomach.

That was as far as I got before two men snatched my arms from behind.

I coughed on the cloud of dust and dirt as I was dragged across the open field to a pair of large hunter green wooden doors with white trim.

Both swung open as we approached.

I had to squint as my eyes adjusted from blinding sunlight to the shady interior. It smelled musty, like moldy hay and horse manure. I was forced to march forward, and we stopped before a short, well-groomed man. He stood before me in a rather garish off-the-rack, purple pin-striped suit. At first, he didn't say a word, just spun the gold ring on his pinkie finger.

After inhaling a breath through his small, rat-like nose, he finally spoke in a heavy Spanish accent. "Yelena Nikitina. It is a pleasure to finally meet you. I've heard many... *interesting things*... about you and your prowess at the track."

I remained silent.

"Where are my manners?" he said genially, as if we were at a party and he had neglected to introduce me to the host. "My name is Santiago Garcia, and I believe you and I have a mutual acquaintance."

I thrust my chin out and spoke brazenly, with more bravado than I felt. "I don't know what you're talking about."

He smiled; one of his teeth was gold-capped. It made his demeanor seem even more false, more caricature than man. "Let me show you my babies."

With a firm grip on both of my upper arms, I was forced to walk behind him deeper into the stable.

He gestured to the various horses stalled on either side. They were all beautiful. All with glossy black or chestnut coats. Several with shocks of white on their noses. All obviously expensive thoroughbred stock.

He leaned over one stall to pet the nose of a horse that poked its head out to greet him. Reaching into his pocket, he pulled out a few sugar cubes and held them on his flat palm for the horse to eagerly lap them up. "Isn't she gorgeous? This beauty is going to win me a nice purse in the Sham Stakes this year."

I looked at the horse with sympathy. The poor thing. More than likely, he was pumping her full of steroids and then, on race day, he would force a milkshake down her nose. It was an awful practice of forcing a tube into a horse's nose and then down into its stomach where they would pump a mixture of bicarbonate soda, sugar, water, and electrolytes into it. It prevented the buildup of lactic acid in the muscles so the horse would literally run itself to injury or worse, death. I should know. My bastard stepfather was one of the men who used to torture horses with the concoction as part of his side job to fix races.

Santiago continued deeper into the darkness of the stable.

As we approached the last stall, I could hear a man groaning.

My stomach twisted.

Oh my God.

Damien.

Please God tell me they hadn't captured Damien.

My steps faltered but the men holding me kept me marching forward.

Right before we reached the stall, there was another pitiful groan.

A few more steps, and we were standing at the opening to the stall. I closed my eyes, unable to bear looking.

"Ms. Nikitina, may I introduce Geraldo Gomez."

My eyes flew open.

My knees almost buckled. Thank God it wasn't Damien. The man lying on his side among the dirty hay and filth looked like no more than a pile of rags. Dried blood was matted in his hair and one eye was swollen shut. As he rose onto his knees, it was clear the way his left hand hung limply at his side that either it or his arm had been broken.

"Please, Mr. Garcia. I'll pay it all back. I swear! Please!"

Once more twirling the large gold signet ring on his pinkie finger, Santiago turned to me. "Like you, Mr. Gomez here thought I wouldn't mind him stealing money from my pocket. He thought I wouldn't notice a few fixed races off the books."

"I never stole anything. I never fixed any races!" I objected.

Santiago stepped close. I hissed as he rubbed the back of his hand down my cheek. The ring on his finger was cold against my skin. "You will only anger me by denying what we both know is true. I would advise against that," he said softly. "Things will get... ugly... if you anger me further."

Goosebumps rose on my flesh.

Santiago stepped back and motioned to some of his men who were standing nearby. Swinging their rifles to their backs, they stepped inside the stall and grabbed Geraldo by the arms. He cried out in pain when the one touched his broken left arm. They hefted him high and pulled him backwards till he was propped against the far wall. Another henchman stepped forward and handed Santiago a large, ominous-looking power tool.

"So many people think that stealing from a racetrack is a victimless crime," he said, shaking his head. Lifting the power tool, he aimed it at Geraldo and pulled the trigger.

With horror, I realized it was a nail gun. A long steel nail hit Geraldo in the fleshy part of his right underarm. Pinning him to the back of the wood stall wall.

I tried to turn my head away but one of the men holding me snatched my ponytail and forced my head up and straight.

"They do not think about the cost to me and my family."

He fired the gun again and then again. Each time striking Geraldo in the arms or legs. The man's screams almost drowned out Santiago's next words.

"You must understand, Ms. Nikitina, I am only a humble businessman trying to make a... small profit."

Geraldo was sobbing as the nails pierced his limbs. By now, so many had struck him that the two henchmen no longer needed to support him. He was being held up by the nails in his own flesh.

"This is something Damien Ivanov did not understand when he cheated me on a recent transaction of ours. I don't appreciate being cheated, Ms. Nikitina. It sets a bad example to my men... and makes me very angry."

So, this wasn't just about me. It was about Damien as well. *This was bad, really bad.* I realized with a sick feeling that the best thing would be for Damien not to find me. He would only be risking his own death if he tried.

I wet my dry lips. Santiago had said he was a businessman. Maybe I could make a deal with him.

I inhaled a shaky breath. "I'll tell you all you need to know. I'll teach you my betting scheme. It's really just a simple category forecasting algorithm. You won't need to bother with fixing races anymore. I'll tell you everything, just don't hurt Damien."

Santiago grasped the end of my ponytail. For several agonizing minutes, he didn't say anything. Just stroked my hair. I swallowed the bile in my throat, repressing the urge to pull away from his slimy touch.

"You really are a beauty. Damien Ivanov *was* a lucky man."

"Please. We can make a deal."

He smiled. His gold-capped tooth glinted even in the dim light of the stable. "You don't understand the rules of business very well, Ms. Nikitina. There is no reason for me to make a deal. I will already be taking whatever I want from you," he said as he pulled painfully on my hair and stared at my mouth.

Just then, a groomer approached with a horse. "You asked for Satan's Spawn to be brought out, Mr. Garcia?"

"Yes, put him in the stall," ordered Santiago without taking his snake eyes off me.

The man moved the horse into the stall. Shifting it around till he was facing us with his hind quarters crowding against the pitiful limp form of Geraldo who still whimpered and pleaded for his life.

Santiago placed his hand under my chin, painfully digging his fingers into my jaw. "You are about to see what I have planned for your beloved Mr. Ivanov."

One of his men stepped forward. Taking a stiletto knife out of his pocket, he flicked it open then stabbed the poor horse in the flank with the sharp blade. The horse whinnied and shrieked. First, it reared up on its hind legs but then it began to kick its back legs in anger and pain.

My eyes were wide with terror as I screamed and fought Santiago's grip. Both he and his men held firm.

The sickening sound of bones cracking echoed around the stable as the horse's back hooves pounded over and over into Geraldo's already damaged body. Santiago shifted position, dragging me with him so that I was forced to stare upon the bloody mess that used to be a human being.

The force of the beating had torn his body off the nails. It now was nothing more than a trampled heap of blood and bones on the stall floor. Pounded into the dirt and shit.

Just as I thought I might faint from the horrible sight, Santiago viciously slapped me across the face. My ears rang with the echoes of the dying man's screams.

"It's best you prepare yourself now. Soon that will be Damien Ivanov lying in there," he viciously taunted.

Just the thought of my handsome, strong Damien being kicked to death by a horse and left to die among the piles of dung made me want to die, too. My stomach lurched. I gagged. This time I didn't even try to stop it. Surging forward, I choked out bile onto his shiny alligator shoes.

Disgusted, Santiago stepped back. "Take the bitch away. Lock her in one of the stalls."

I was dragged off to a nearby empty stall and tossed onto a pile of moldy hay, where they wrenched my left arm high. Clapping handcuffs around my wrist, they then attached the second cuff to an iron ring secured to a cement column set in the wooden wall.

Both men stood over me. One gave my leg a hard kick. I stifled a groan.

"Think the boss will give us a go at her once he's done with her?"

The other one laughed and slapped his friend on the shoulder. "By the time the boss is done with her, you won't want anything to do with her, trust me."

They both laughed.

Leaving the stall, they closed and locked the high gated door.

I curled my knees into my chest and rested my forehead on my knees. Tears ran down my cheeks. Misery washed over me. Part of me wished I could feel Damien's arms around me right now. And another part of me desperately wished I'd never lay eyes on him again. At least that way, I knew he would be safe.

I thought of Damien's dark sapphire eyes and how they always shone with stubborn resolve.

A spark of hope lighted deep inside of me.

I had forgotten. He was a Scorpio. The bad boy of the zodiac signs.

Intense and extremely powerful, nothing and no one ever got the better of a fiercely determined Scorpio. *Especially not my Russian Badass Scorpio.*

Feeling my feisty Sagittarius nature start to come back to the fore, I took a deep calming breath.

Despite the pain in my cheek from Santiago's slap, I managed a slight smile.

Suddenly, I was a little sorry for Santiago and his men.

They had no idea the hellfire that was about to rain down on them once Demon Damien Ivanov found me. *And he would find me.* I had no doubt. All I had to do was hang on till then.

CHAPTER 31

Damien

Five hours, twenty-six minutes, and forty-two seconds.

That was how long Yelena had been held captive.

It was five hours, twenty-six minutes, and forty-two seconds too long.

"Target confirmed," said Dimitri as he handed me the high-powered binoculars.

We were about seven hundred yards away on a high ridge which looked down into the sheltered valley where Santiago Garcia's Los Infieles controlled a thoroughbred farm. Looking through the binoculars, I couldn't spot Dimitri and Vaska's stolen red and black Enstrom 280FX Shark helicopter but that didn't matter. I had called in a few favors, and Russian military satellite footage confirmed the helicopter had been here less than an hour ago. Only the pilot was seen departing which meant Yelena should still be on property.

Based on the number of armed guards stationed around the stable, it was our best guess she was being held there.

I prayed to God she was still alive.

Either way, anyone responsible for her kidnapping was dying today.

Vaska pulled his Barret M82 sniper rifle out of its case. He opened the base and arranged several sandbags to stabilize it. It was an anti-material rifle whose ammunition could take down any small aircraft. It could also penetrate through a concrete wall. He connected the ten-round detachable magazine and placed several back up within easy reach. He checked the scope then nodded to us both.

Pulling out my two Glock 17s, I clicked a double-stack, thirty-three round high-capacity magazine into each gun and chambered the first round. I then tucked four more magazines into the lower leg pockets of my black cargo pants. Dimitri did the same. Since we would be coming in hot, we needed a gun that was reliable and light with semi-automatic, striker-fire capability. There was none better than the Glock 17.

Vaska nodded to the Escalade parked about twenty-five yards from the stable entrance. "As soon as you reach the crest, I'll start laying down suppression fire. When you're close enough, I'll hit the gas tank. So watch for the big boom."

Dimitri tossed me a red bandana. We each tied one

around our necks. I tucked an extra one into my back pocket.

I instructed, "After we breach the stable, take out anyone who goes in or out."

Vaska winked. "Just make sure those bandanas are visible."

Since both Dimitri and I were wearing black, as was Yelena, it would be difficult during a fire fight to differentiate us from Santiago's men who were also in dark fatigues. The red bandanas would alert him.

Dimitri clapped Vaska on the back. "See you on the other side my friend."

"Try not to die today. Emma would never forgive me. She looks sweet, but she's hell on wheels when she's angry."

Dimitri laughed. "And we both know what Damien's girl is like when she gets pissed."

They, of course, had both learned from Gregor about the knife wound and the brick to the head, which only made them love Yelena before they had even met her.

"You cannot fault the girl for doing what we've all fantasized doing ourselves," Dimitri taunted.

Vaska placed his hand on my shoulder. "She may not be officially Russian, but she is Russian in spirit. Do not worry, my friend. Chances are that piece of shit Santiago is the one who needs rescuing from her!"

His smile was strained. We both knew that wasn't true. The Columbians were ruthless bastards who'd rip a child from a mother's breast and kill it if it suited their purpose. If Yelena was still alive, there was no telling what condition I might find her in. There was no way to prepare myself mentally for that kind of situation other than to know deep in my gut that I loved her, and if she were alive, the rest we could tackle together.

I just needed her to be alive.

Hang on, babygirl. I'm coming for you.

Vaska pulled out his flask. He held it high. "Chtoby stoly lomalis' ot izobiliya, a krovati ot lyubvi." After wishing us a classic Russian toast of tables that break with abundance and beds that break from love, he then drank deeply and handed it to me.

"Za nashu druzhby." *To our friendship.* I took a swig and passed it to Dimitri.

"Za uspekh." *To success,* Dimitri toasted before doing the same. He grimaced and shook his head. "Damn you, Vaska, and your cheap taste in vodka."

"This is man's work. You need a man's vodka!" Vaska protested before he took another swig and returned the flask to a side pocket.

Dimitri and I met gazes. After a nod, we started down the hill, keeping to the tree line. Within minutes, we were crossing the open field area. The stable was still about three hundred yards off. All was quiet. Vaska, who was watching through his scope up on the ridge, would wait until he saw signs we were spotted before he fired. The closer we got to the stable, the better.

Keeping our bodies as low as possible, we hurried across the field.

By the time we heard the first cry of alarm, it was too late for the man. A bright burst of crimson exploded from his chest as Vaska fired.

Since we'd been spotted, there was no point in being coy. Dimitri and I both started running at full speed toward our target.

"Right. Two o'clock!" Dimitri shouted.

Lifting my right arm, I took out the assailant with a head shot over a hundred-fifty yards away.

Suppression fire popped behind us. Vaska mowed down three of Santiago's men before they even had a chance to raise their M16 automatic rifles.

We were within fifty yards of the stable. The Escalade parked nearby suddenly rocked. I knew that meant Vaska had hit it, and within half a second, it would blow.

"Get down!" I shouted.

Dimitri and I both hit the ground and covered our heads.

The luxury SUV exploded in a ball of fire, sending burning shards of metal and glass flying.

Looking up, I saw one man who had taken cover behind a tractor start to rise to his feet. Closing one eye, I aimed and fired, hitting his ankle from between the massive tires. He hit the ground. I fired a second time, taking him out.

A Jeep came roaring up from around the corner. It stopped in front of the stable doors, blocking them. A man jumped into the back while another positioned a machine gun on the roof.

It was an M134 GAU-17 Gatling gun. It was nicknamed the Vulcan cannon; it was a six-barreled machine gun capable of firing as many as six thousand rounds per minute. It was usually only used in military aircraft for suppression fire that needed increased range and projectile lethality.

I motioned to the left, then Dimitri and I both took cover behind the smoldering metal frame of what was left of the Escalade.

Dimitri cursed. "Who the fuck was dumb enough to sell these assholes a goddamn Vulcan?"

Replacing the empty magazine in one of my Glocks, I ground out, "When this is all over, I'm going to find the bastard and beat the crap out of him."

We may have been illegal arms dealers, but there was a certain code among the better ones. You didn't sell big guns to little boys. In the end, it wasn't worth the trouble. They invariably caused problems and kicked up messes that caught the attention of the authorities, which increased the chances of heat on our operation. I had no problem selling guns and bombs to dictators, despots, and drug kingpins. It was all just business to me. But selling a gun that was too much firepower to someone who didn't know how to use it was dangerous. There was no fucking reason why some thug like Santiago and his crew, who mainly ran racetrack, drug, and kidnapping schemes, needed an anti-aircraft Gatling gun in the middle of Farmville USA.

If they fired it in the direction of Vaska up on the ridge, they could be over twenty-five yards off the mark and still kill him.

"You ready?" asked Dimitri.

I nodded. "Yeah, cover me."

Dimitri stayed low, spraying the Jeep with distraction fire as I went high. Taking the extra half second, I took aim and fired. The bullet went straight through the left eye of the man standing behind the gun. A sickening burst of brain matter, bone, and blood burst from behind his head.

We both ducked behind the remnants of the truck.

"One more?"

"Yeah."

Dimitri fired again.

This time, I aimed down the barrel of the gun, the only way to disable the gun from a distance without matching it in firepower. Breathing out slow and steady to calm my heartbeat, I closed my eye, aimed, and fired. Less than a quarter of a second later, the gun exploded.

Dimitri laughed. "You motherfucker. We'll never hear the end of it now."

He was right. When we got out of this mess, I would make sure to remind them as often as possible of the impossible kill shot I'd just gotten off. This beat the time Gregor took out a moving target in Uzbekistan at over eight hundred yards with only a second-generation model Glock.

The stable yard fell silent.

Before Santiago's men had a chance to regroup, Dimitri and I ran for the stable doors and braced ourselves on either side. I raised an arm and fired at the padlock and chain keeping the doors closed. We paused. Then with a shared nod, we each grabbed a handle and pulled the doors open along the track. The ten-foot-tall doors easily slid back along the stable wall. We waited again. Nothing.

We knew this was not the only entrance to the stable.

There was a good chance there were more men inside guarding Yelena.

Hopefully Santiago himself.

My jaw tightened.

Him, I would personally kill.

Slowly.

"On three," Dimitri mouthed.

I nodded.

One. Two... three.

We swung into the doorway. The interior was dark and shaded. It took a moment for our eyes to adjust. We heard movement to the right and both swung. Arms raised. Guns at the ready. With the sun glare, we didn't see him in time. He got off several rounds, one of them striking Dimitri in the thigh.

He stumbled but caught himself against the door frame.

I turned and fired. Killing the man.

Keeping my eyes trained on the interior for any movements in the shadows, I called out, "Dimitri? You okay?"

He groaned. "Yeah. Just a flesh wound."

Hazarding a glance over my shoulder, I looked at his leg. Fresh blood had already soaked his pant leg. Grabbing the red bandana from my back pocket, I tossed it to him. He caught it with one hand. "Tie it off."

That was supposed to be for Yelena. I would just have to make sure she was close to my side and Vaska's aim was true when we made a run for it.

When Dimitri was ready, we took our first few steps down the wide, dirt-packed aisle. Agitated horses stomped and shook their heads in stalls to the right and left of us.

"Yelena!" I called out.

No answer.

"Yelena, answer me!"

Nothing.

My heart seized.

CHAPTER 32

Yelena

THE BARREL of the gun pressed harder against my temple.

I glared up at Santiago. He placed a finger against his lips as he gave me a wink.

My stomach churned.

On the other side of the stable, Damien continued to call out my name. Each time there was a loud crash then the sound of splintering wood. If I had to guess, he was kicking open each of the empty stall doors, looking for me. It was only a matter of time before he reached us.

My heart raced. My fingers were curled into fists so tight my nails dug painfully into my palms. I didn't know what to do. If I called out, Santiago would kill me. If I didn't call out, he was probably going to kill me anyway.

My decision was made.

Either way, Damien would be warned and that was all that mattered.

I took a deep breath, then screamed with all my might: "He's got a gun!"

Santiago raised his gun and struck me with the edge of the handle.

Pain exploded in my head, momentarily blinding me with a white flash. A small trickle of blood oozed over my right eye. I swiped at it with my free left hand.

The wooden gate to my stall crashed open. Damien stood there looking like a vengeful god... or better yet, a vengeful demon. He was dressed all in black. His front was covered in dirt and mud. Even though it had only been a few hours since I had been captured, he looked like he had aged twenty years. There were shadows around his eyes and deep lines of tension around his mouth. I had never seen him look so filthy and tired... and handsome as hell. Never in my life would I think any other man was as beautiful or sexy as Damien Ivanov was in this very moment.

He had come for me.

For me!

Unwanted and unloved Yelena Nikitina. *Me.*

There had never been a doubt in my mind that he would come. My wonderfully stubborn Scorpio.

His dark eyes practically glittered with malice as he looked first at Santiago then me. I was kneeling prone at Santiago's feet, my right hand still handcuffed to the iron ring. I could tell the moment Damien saw the blood matted in my hair and running down my cheek.

"I'm fine," I mouthed. I didn't want him to get so upset

he lost focus. There would be time to worry about my injury later.

"I'm going to get you out of this, babygirl," he said, his voice low and gruff with emotion.

My eyes filled with tears. I could only nod, afraid to speak.

Santiago taunted him. "Don't make promises you can't keep."

Damien took a step forward as he raised his gun.

Behind him, I could see a second large figure who kept his back to us, watching for any more of Santiago's men. He looked like Vaska, but I couldn't tell with him turned away. All I did know was he was roughly Damien's size and equally as muscled and tattooed.

Santiago grabbed my ponytail and wrenched my body up. He placed the gun barrel against my temple again. This time pressing into the fresh wound. I cringed and hissed air through my teeth as my body braced against the pain.

Damien let out a low growl.

Santiago cocked his head to the side. "Careful. You wouldn't want me to blow her pretty head off now, would you?"

Forced to lower his gun, Damien's eyes narrowed. "You're a dead man."

Santiago laughed. "I do not think so. I have more men on their way. It is you who will die today."

"Let her go. This is between you and me."

"It *was* between you and me. Imagine my delight when I learned that the pretty woman who had been causing me such an annoyance over these last few years was the very same woman you yourself were trying to track down. Fate… she smiled on me that day."

My body started to tremble with fear. I clenched my jaw as I tightened my abdominal muscles, trying to still the tremors. I needed to appear calm so Damien could focus on Santiago. The last thing I wanted was him worried or distracted over me.

I also didn't want to draw any attention to myself as I slowly shifted my left arm behind me. Using my fingernails, I continued to scrape and scratch at the small flat head of a slightly loose nail. Finally, I felt the edge lift from the wood plank floorboard. Getting my fingernail under it, I pinched the top with my thumb and forefinger and pried it loose. Rolling the thin cylinder between my fingers, I realized I was in luck. The iron nail should be just thin enough to work. It wasn't as good as a bobby pin, but I had left that behind in Damien's safe house apartment when I'd gotten out of the pair of handcuffs yesterday.

Never in a million years did I think I would be grateful that my loser stepfather used to lock me up on a daily basis. It seemed my lock picking skills were coming in very handy lately.

Pretending to swipe at the blood at my eye, I transferred the nail to my right hand. This would be extremely difficult. My hand was hanging higher than my shoulder and at an awkward angle. If at any point Santiago turned in my direction, he would clearly see what I was doing. Still, I had to try.

Santiago sneered. "You thought you were such a big man, insulting me in front of my men, but I am the big man now."

Damien fired back. "Kidnapping a defenseless female makes you a big man?"

My mouth twisted at the word *defenseless*. Damien cast me a quick apologetic look.

Santiago pressed the gun harder against my temple. "You! You are the idiot now! I'm the one who bested the great Ivanovs. It was so easy to take your woman from you. Like candy from a little baby."

Damien's shoulders tensed as he planted his feet more firmly. He adjusted his grip on his guns. "So what now, Santiago? If you are such a *big* man, what is your *big* plan now?"

The tip of the nail was inside the lock. I rolled it between my fingers, trying to feel for the pin.

Santiago's voice rose a few pitches, showing his fear. "My men will be here any minute, and then I'm going to see you strung up by your thumbs. I'm going to force you to watch while I fuck your woman."

He pulled on my hair as he made the threat. The sudden jerk to my head made me let go of the nail. My heart stopped. Thank God the shaft was far enough in the handcuff lock it didn't drop to the floor. Gripping the small flat head, I continued to shift it around, waiting for the click.

Santiago continued to taunt Damien. "She will finally know what it feels like to have a real man between her legs."

Inwardly, I shook my head, knowing I was staring up

at a dead man. I knew the only reason why Damien hadn't already killed him was because he was holding a gun to my head. If I could just get out of these cuffs, I could lunge free of him.

I caught Damien's gaze and very deliberately shifted my gaze to the handcuffs. His nod was almost imperceptible to anyone but me.

Damien's brow furrowed. "And who will that real man be?"

Santiago took the bait. Shifting the gun away from my head, he pointed at his chest. "Me, asshole! I'm the real man!"

The handcuffs clicked.

The latch opened.

I slipped my wrist through and launched myself backward till I hit the far side of the stall.

Damien raised his arm and fired, hitting Santiago in the shoulder. He fired again, hitting him in the chest. Santiago fell backward. His body slumped down the wall, leaving a crimson streak along the cement column.

Damien fell to his knees before me. Dropping his guns to the side, his hands spanned my jaw as he tilted my head back. Before I could say a word, his mouth claimed mine. I melted into his embrace, drawing on the strength of his arms, needing it like my last breath.

He rested his forehead against mine. "My God, I don't know what I would have done if I'd lost you."

"Damien. I need to tell you…."

He smoothed my hair as his gaze rested on the wound along my hairline. His eyes hardened, and his lips thinned.

"First, I need to get you out of this hellhole and to a doctor."

I clasped his upper arms. "No! It can't wait. I… I… I'm… I'm sorry about the knife… and the brick."

"That is what couldn't wait? You're sorry about the brick?"

I bit my lip. I had wanted to say I love you but suddenly felt foolish. What would he think if I just blurted out those words?

Words I had never said to anyone.

Words I hadn't heard anyone say to me since my mother died.

He'd think I was some silly stupid girl traumatized by the moment. After all, I hadn't laid eyes on the man in three years. We had only been together for less than forty-eight hours, in the span of which I had run from him twice and tried to kill him several times.

How could he possibly believe that I loved him?

How could he possibly even want my love?

How could I make him understand that I had been a little in love with him since I was ten and he'd caught me stealing that silly tube of lipstick. That I had collected little Happy Meal toys ever since because they reminded me of the one moment in my life when someone seemed to care… when someone had stood up and tried to protect me.

How could I possibly put into words how he'd made me feel that night at Nadia's party? When he was so gruff and overbearing and controlling but also protective and sweet. Would he think it silly if he knew that tucked into that backpack filled with money and jewels was the Hello

Kitty toy and the *I Heart Washington, D.C.* t-shirt he'd bought me? Would he laugh if he knew I'd worn that t-shirt to bed practically every night for the last three years?

Before, when I was so certain that he would come to my rescue, there hadn't been a doubt in my mind that he loved me and I loved him, but now that he was kneeling before me looking all big and dangerous and more than a little scary, I lost my nerve.

Doubt crashed in on me.

He was so much older.

His family was wealthy and powerful.

He and his brother were practically legends both here and in Russia.

He could have anyone he wanted. Including tall, leggy models named Fifi and Mimi.

All I was was the unwanted stepdaughter of a two-bit criminal.

My own mother hadn't even wanted me enough to stay alive.

I was a racetrack railbird who made her money on betting schemes and nothing more.

I tried to lower my gaze.

He placed a finger under my chin and lifted my face to his. "I love you, too, my pretty padshiĭ angel."

How the hell did this man always read my mind? Maybe he really did possess demon powers.

Just as I opened my mouth to respond, there was the slightest movement over his left shoulder.

"Damien!" I screamed.

Without thinking, I ducked under his shoulder and

grabbed the Glock he had discarded near him. Raising my arm, I fired my gun just as Santiago was raising his.

My bullet hit him right between the eyes. A faint mist of blood splattered over my face, shoulders, and chest as Santiago's body slumped lifeless to the side.

Damien stared at me with wide, shocked eyes.

A faint chuckle from the opening at the end of the stall made us both turn.

The large man I saw earlier was standing there surveying the bloody scene. "So I guess technically now we have to say that the damsel rescued you instead of the other way around."

Damien rolled his eyes and groaned as he lowered his head into his hand. "Fuck off, Dimitri."

Damien lifted me into his arms and carried me out of the musty stable into the waning sunshine. The sky was a fiery orange and purple as dusk approached. Wrapping my arms around his neck, I rested my head on his shoulder. "You're not really mad that I shot him instead of you, are you?"

Judging by his friend Dimitri's comments, I had a feeling he was going to take quite a bit of taunting from his big scary Russian buddies over my actions. I also knew that Scorpios could be very touchy about this sort of thing. They liked to be the ones in control, doing the rescuing.

The thing was, even though I may have fired the final shot, Damien did rescue me, and had been rescuing me for some time now. It had just taken me a little while to realize it. To others, his criminal activities may make him a bit tarnished but to me, he really was my knight in shining armor.

He kissed me on the forehead. "Baby, I'm just glad this time the gun was loaded… and for once, you weren't pointing it at me."

CHAPTER 33

*D*amien

IF I LIVED to be a thousand, I would never get over the image of Yelena being forced to kneel in the dirt with a gun to her head.

I looked down at her sleeping form and kissed the top of her head. She was tucked in my lap in the backseat of the SUV as we drove into the city. Thank God there wasn't a real mirror nearby because my little fashionista would faint if she saw herself right now. Her yoga pants were covered in mud and torn in at least three places. Her hoodie was so caked in filth I'd probably have to cut it off her. Her beautiful blonde hair was matted with dried blood from the cut above her forehead, and her neck and front were splattered with blood. I had done what I could with a wet bandana to at least get the blood off her face.

She never looked more beautiful.

I truly could not wait to spend the rest of my life staring down into her gorgeous face.

I knew some men would unselfishly let the woman they loved go after a day like today. They would think that their lives were too dangerous to keep them by their side. That the woman would be better off without them. Safer. They would spend the rest of their lives pining after what could never be but confident in their sacrifice, knowing it was for the best.

Not me.

Yelena was mine, and I was keeping her by my side.

Yes, my life was dangerous because of my criminal activities but so was life in general. So call me a selfish bastard. The devil incarnate. An absolute cad. But she was staying with me. Forever. I would keep her safe. And no one… no one… would love her more. Every day of her life, I was going to show her how much she was wanted and adored. She had spent enough time in her short life feeling unwanted and unloved. The last thing I was going to do was send her away "for her own good." Fuck that.

I was what was good for Yelena.

I may have been stubborn and controlling and a pain in the ass, and I was absolutely certain that I hadn't seen the last time she'd try to hit me with a brick or stab me with a knife, but I didn't care. I was good for her, and she was everything for me. She was the fire and light in my life that chased away the unforgiving cold darkness. I wanted that light and craved her warmth.

No, I had made up my mind several years ago, and I had no intention of changing it.

She was mine.

And I was going to make it official — now — this very day.

Vaska looked over his shoulder from the front passenger seat. "You know, we've started a real mess with the Los Infieles."

Dimitri met my gaze in the rearview mirror. "True. They'll definitely seek revenge. We're going to have a real war on our hands."

All three of us burst out laughing.

I cringed and held my finger to my lips as Yelena stirred but then fell back to sleep. My poor baby was exhausted.

There was nothing a Russian liked more than a good fight. Today was just the start. In a week, we would have the Los Infieles wiped off the map. We would send a very clear message. Don't fuck with us, and never under any circumstances do you fuck with our women.

Vaska held up his phone showing me a text. "The judge just confirmed. He'll meet us at Dimitri's."

I nodded.

"Should we get the girls for the ceremony?" asked Dimitri.

They had taken Emma and Mary to a safe house that was more fortified than Fort Knox somewhere outside of Chicago. It was the primary reason why it was only the three of us that went after Santiago. We knew we could handle the bastard and his men alone, and we wanted every available man in our combined crews guarding the girls. After what had happened to Samara last night and now Yelena today, we weren't taking any more chances with our women's safety.

Vaska shook his head and shuddered. "I'm going to need to get my hands on some police riot gear before even considering approaching Mary after what I pulled this afternoon."

Dimitri rolled his eyes. "You're getting off easy. I had to promise Emma I'd take her to D.C. for a Shakespeare lecture series on the conflicts between platonic love and carnal desire in his sonnets."

Vaska raised an eyebrow. "You don't suppose they have any lectures on that weird vampire show Mary likes?"

Dimitri shook his head. "Doubt it."

We pulled into Dimitri's underground parking garage. I carried Yelena up to Dimitri's master bedroom. I would have liked to have brought her to my own home, but that would have to wait till later today when I took her to Washington, D.C. The Ivanov plane was arriving at Midway in the next twenty minutes.

I stood for a moment in indecision. Dimitri's entire bedroom was in pale creams and golds including the bed covering. Both Yelena and I were covered in dirt, mud, and blood. With a shrug, I placed her in the center of the bed. I would just have to pay him back for any damage. She curled up in a small ball just like a little chipmunk.

I headed into the bathroom and started the shower. It was a large chamber with multiple shower heads. Waiting till the water was nice and hot, and there was a pleasant steam rising inside the glassed-in chamber, I went to awaken Yelena.

"Baby? Sweetheart, wake up."

She opened her eyes and groaned, closing them instantly.

I stroked her cheek. She opened her eyes again. I was pleased to see none of the horror or fear inside the crystal blue depths this time. She rose up and stretched out her arms. My jaw tightened when I saw the harsh red mark which encircled her right wrist from where she had been handcuffed in the stall. If I could, I'd kill Santiago all over again. I would just have to be alright with wiping his entire organization and any family members I found off the map, but that was a plan for later. Right now, my focus was Yelena.

All traces of fatigue gone, she jumped up. "Oh my God!"

I clenched my fists.

Here it comes. The anger. The recriminations. The blame. It was my fault. All of it. Sure, she had annoyed the Columbians with her racetrack scheme, but the real reason why they decided to finally come after her was me. I was the liability, not her. I was blaming her actions when really it was me and my business which had actually put her in danger. Now that the shock of what had happened was wearing off, she was probably realizing just that. She would blame me, and she had every right to. She would probably demand to be set free…

Unfortunately, I couldn't do that. I would never do that. She was mine. I would just have to figure out a way to convince her of that fact.

She looked down at her hoodie and cried out in dismay. "I'm covered in mud!"

"Wait… what?"

She picked at the soiled fabric which was stiff with dried mud and blood. "Look at me! This is disgusting!"

With a shout of joy, I snatched her to me and kissed her. I hope my angel never changed.

She pulled away, straining her head to the left. "Stop! I'm gross!"

"No, you're not. You're the most beautiful, sexiest woman I've ever laid eyes on!" I picked her up and carried her into the bathroom.

The moment I set her down, she yanked on the zipper to her hoodie. It was so caked in dried mud it was stuck. Pushing her hands away, I unzipped it for her and pulled it off her shoulders. The t-shirt underneath had sagged around the V-neck showing a glimpse of her white lace bra. My cock surged to life, but I ignored the urge to strip her bare and carry her into the shower. I may have acted like a Neanderthal around her sometimes, but this wouldn't be one of those times.

"Take your time in the shower. When you're done, there is a closet just to the left in the bedroom full of Emma's clothes. She said to help yourself to whatever you need."

"Thank you," she said shyly.

"Meet me downstairs when you're done."

She nodded.

I turned to leave but not without glancing over my shoulder to see her start to undress. Resisting the urge once more to join her, I forced myself to keep walking. I needed to talk to the judge and sign off on the marriage certificate, so he could marry us the moment she was done getting dressed.

I had almost lost her. I wasn't taking any more chances.

She would be my wife in less than an hour.

CHAPTER 34

Yelena

THE SHOWER FELT HEAVENLY. I twisted and turned, letting the shower heads massage my aching body. The water was hotter than I usually liked it, but this time I relished in the heat and steam as it washed away the nightmare I had just endured.

It was probably the shock but it really did feel like just that... a nightmare. A horrible dream. Like it didn't really happen. Probably because Damien had rescued me so quickly that the terror of my situation didn't have time to truly sink in.

He really was magnificent. The way he'd kicked in that stable door. Guns at the ready. He was like an action movie star. I'd known the moment I heard the first exchange of gunfire that it was Damien coming for me.

Strangely, even as Santiago had come in and put a gun to my head, I knew, deep down to my bones, I knew Damien would get to me in time. There was just something about him.

He was dangerous and stubborn and way too controlling, but all those same attributes made me trust him with my life.

After I washed the last of the dirt and mud out of my hair, I stepped out of the shower and wrapped myself in a soft, fluffy oversized towel. Walking over to the mirror, I combed my fingers through my hair to get rid of the tangles. I found a hair dryer under the sink, dried my hair, and was finally feeling close to human again.

Remembering what Damien had said about Emma's closet, I wandered back into the bedroom, cringing at the smears of mud on their nice bed coverlet. Leave it to a man to not care about such things.

When I reached the closet, I laughed at the framed poster of a book cover titled *The Nympho Librarian* that was hanging to the right of the door. Flicking on the light, I ran my fingers over the various clothes which hung in neat rows. It was clear Emma didn't care about designer labels, but she did have really cute taste. Taking down one of the plaid pleated skirts, I held it up to my hips and cringed. We looked to be the same size, but I was an inch or two taller which would make her already short skirts scandalously short on me.

I decided on a pretty floral maxi dress. I had to add a pale pink cardigan because of the way the tops of my breasts spilled out of the low neckline. Thankfully we wore the same size shoes. I selected a simple black ballet flat.

Finding a notepad and pen on top of the inlaid bureau at the other end of the closet, I wrote her a note thanking her and promising to pay her back. I hadn't met her, but from the snippets I had heard from her husband, Dimitri, I was sure I'd like her. Thinking of Emma made me think of Samara and Nadia. I missed them both terribly. I couldn't wait to be reunited with them.

Exiting the bedroom, I walked down the stairs and followed the muted sound of conversation till I found them in a beautiful study. Every wall was covered in bookshelves which were filled with richly bound books in blue, green, and maroon leather with gold imprints. There was a large marble fireplace which had a roaring fire already going to chase away the winter chill that had started to set in now that the sun had gone down.

Standing in front of the fire was Damien, Dimitri, and Vaska. I was struck by how handsome the three were. Although not related, they all shared that same dangerous mystique which came with the territory when you were over six feet tall, heavily muscled, and covered in tattoos. In short, they all looked like crazy badasses.

Unlike me, none of them had showered or changed yet. They stood casually chatting in their mud-caked black fatigues with drinks in their hands as if they were in designer suits at a party.

"This must be the bride."

I turned at the sound of the voice. An elderly gentleman I hadn't noticed dressed in a terribly misfitting brown suit approached me. He snatched up my hand and enclosed it with both of his, pumping mine up and down vigorously.

"I'm sorry. What did you say?"

Damien rushed over.

Pointing to the elderly man, I asked, "What did he just call me?"

The elderly man continued to talk over me. "Damien, your bride is a beauty. No wonder you are in such a rush to marry her." He laughed giving Damien an exaggerated conspirator wink.

My eyes widened in shock. "Marry? Marry!"

Damien placed restraining hands on my shoulders. "Yelena, we've already talked about this."

I shook my head. "No. *You.* You talked about it. I never agreed to it."

Sure, I loved him, but what did that mean? We had barely been together for twenty-four hours, and he expected me to marry him? This was insane. Besides, this was hardly the wedding of my little girl dreams. There was no church draped in sweet smelling flowers, or Vera Wang dress with a long train or even champagne and dancing. Technically, he hadn't even proposed! It's not like I needed a big expensive ring, but didn't I at least deserve a traditional proposal?

His voice had lowered an octave, a sure sign he was getting angry. "This is for your own good."

I didn't care. I broke free of his grasp. "I'm standing here in ill-fitting *borrowed* clothes." I gestured wildly in his direction. "You are covered in mud and the blood of the lunatic who just *kidnapped* me!"

Damien ran a hand through his hair. "Exactly! You

were fucking kidnapped! Jesus Christ, Yelena, I almost lost you. I'm not going to take that chance again. The Ivanov name brings protection. No one would dare harm my wife."

He just didn't get it.

I didn't want him to marry me to protect me.
I wanted him to marry me because he loved me!

I wanted a pretty wedding not for the sake of having a pretty wedding but to finally feel like I belonged and was worth something. My real father didn't want me. My mother left me, and my stepfather never let a day go past without telling me I was an unwanted burden. Was it asking too much to have something real that was just for me? This half-assed, slapped together shotgun wedding wasn't it.

Angrily swiping at the tears which began to fall, I backed away from him. "Sometimes, I really hate you, Damien Ivanov."

I stormed out of the room.

CHAPTER 35

*Y*elena

Rushing past several doors, I opened the set of double doors at the end of the hall.

The floor of the large square room was covered wall to wall with padded mats. Even the walls were padded. In the corner was a canvas cart on wheels filled with sparring gloves, helmets, and pugil sticks. In the far corner was a punching bag and a pommel horse. It looked to be a private fighting gym.

The double doors banged open. Damien crossed the threshold. With a pointed look at me, he slammed the doors shut and locked them.

Turning to face me, he crossed his arms over his chest. "Start talking," he growled.

"Fuck you!" I fired back.

Damien stalked toward me till I was pressed against the wall. Towering over me, he used both hands to cup my jaw, tilting my head back. "Start talking," he repeated with more emphasis. "Or I take off my belt."

My jaw dropped. "You wouldn't dare! I'll scream for Dimitri and Vaska!"

"Go ahead. Cry out for help. I dare you," he challenged. His dark eyes glittered with rage.

Breaking free, I fell several steps back till I was within arm's reach of the canvas equipment cart.

Placing it between him and me, I shouted, "I don't want to marry you!"

Not like this, my heart screamed.

The truth was I did want to marry him. I just wanted to know he was marrying me *for me* and not for some sense of obligation to protect me, or male pride.

"I got some bad news for you, my malen'kiy padshiy angel. You *will* marry me if I have to toss you over my shoulder and drag you in front of that judge."

Reaching into the cart for one of the padded pugil sticks, I grabbed the red one.

Arching an eyebrow, he asked, "You really want to do this?"

I adjusted my grip on the pugil stick and held it defensively in front of me.

Damien whipped his belt off and tossed it aside. He then ripped off his black t-shirt. *Oh God.* He really was magnificent. All toned muscle and brightly colored tattoos. They ran up his arms and shoulders before creeping up his neck. Twisting and writhing images of mythical beasts, strange symbols, and even flowers. His black cargo pants hung low on his hips, emphasizing his flat, muscled abdomen. I could see the press of his already hard cock against his inner thigh.

Swallowing, I ignored the sick twist of my stomach.

Raising my chin, I challenged, "Bring it on."

CHAPTER 36

Damien

I CIRCLED around Yelena to reach into the bin to retrieve the blue pugil.

Testing the weight of the thick pole with heavy padding on both ends, I kicked off my shoes before walking back to the center of the padded mats.

Without warning, I stepped forward and swung my right arm out, using the pugil stick to sweep her feet.

Yelena flew backwards and landed on her ass.

Before she could recover, I grabbed her left ankle and spread her legs, watching as her dress slid up to her hips, exposing her thighs. I could see my naughty girl didn't have any panties on. My cock lengthened.

Before I could step between her legs, Yelena pulled her leg back and lithely arched her back to force her body upright. She swung out with her own pugil stick and barely missed boxing my left ear. She gave me a knowing smirk before backing up and shifting her weight on bent knees.

Evaluating my target, I feigned right then swung left, tapping her hip with the padded end and sending her off balance. Before she could right herself, I swung my foot out and once more swept her legs. Again, she went down on that cute little ass of hers. I grabbed her right leg and flipped her onto her stomach. I fell to my knees, ready to straddle her. Visions of hiking her dress up and entering her from behind as I pulled on her ponytail momentarily distracted me.

Yelena used that moment to shimmy out of my reach and use her pugil stick to regain her feet.

"You see where I'm going with this?" I taunted.

"In your dreams!" she fired back. The brat.

"Oh babygirl. I'm about to make my dreams your *painful* reality."

I charged.

She parried.

We tapped the center of the poles, angling them left and right before disengaging.

Again, I charged.

She blocked my offense, but I could see she was tiring. The pugil sticks were heavy, and she lacked the arm strength to outlast me.

In a surprise move, Yelena twisted to the left and brought the center of the pole down on my exposed knuckles. The sharp pain forced me to drop one end. She took advantage and thrust the padded end into my side. Before she could retreat to a safe distance, I raised my pugil stick and twisted it with her own, forcing it from her hands and across the room.

I immediately lowered my stick to the floor so the moment she dove for her own she tripped, landing on her stomach. As she tried to crawl towards her weapon, I pulled at the hem of her dress. She twisted onto her back and tried to kick out, but it was too late. The flimsy fabric easily tore straight up to her stomach.

With an outraged cry she fumed, "This wasn't mine! It was Emma's."

I smiled. "I'll buy you both another one."

She flipped back onto her stomach and reached for her pugil stick. I noticed her bottom was red from all the falls she had taken. While I wished that glorious blush was caused by the leather of my belt or my own hand, it still was satisfying to think I would be adding to it soon.

Yelena sprung onto her feet. As she bent her knees and adjusted her weight, I could see the play of muscle on her slim thighs and just a peek of the heaven that laid between them.

"Admit I own your ass, and I'll consider letting you off easy," I taunted her, knowing and loving the fact she would say no.

"Go to hell!" she bristled.

That's my girl.

With her flushed cheeks and bright eyes, it was obvious she was enjoying this battle of wills as much as I was, but it was time to put an end to it.

Swinging the pugil stick to the left and right, I stepped forward and shoved it between her open thighs. Since she weighed next to nothing, I easily lifted her high.

Yelena cried out in shock as she dropped her stick and reached out to steady herself on my shoulders when her body pitched forward.

"I win," I breathed against her mouth. Lowering my voice, I ordered, "Beg me to fuck you."

"No," she rasped defiantly. Her chest rose and fell with her labored breathing.

Suddenly, it was vitally important to my very being that she acknowledge my authority over her.

Call it misplaced arrogance.

Call it possessiveness.

Call it obsessive control.

I didn't give a damn.

Dropping the pugil stick, I wrapped my arm around her back, securing her to my front. Walking a few steps, I moved to the far corner of the room to the padded pommel horse.

My hands easily spanned her small waist as I lifted her high and forced her to straddle the rounded raised stump. With its leather surface close to a foot and a half wide, it stretched her legs open nicely. And with its close to four feet high legs, it was the perfect height for what I had planned.

"Damien, what are you—"

Ignoring her question, I grabbed her hips and pulled her back till her ass was just hanging off the edge of the horse. I pushed the hanging shreds of her dress out of the way.

Yelena reached out and grasped the metal handlebar to keep herself upright. "Get me off this thing!"

"To quote one of your favorite words, no."

Reaching my arm back, I spanked her right cheek. My full open palm made contact with her skin with a satisfying smack.

Yelena howled in outrage as she tried to climb off the pommel horse.

I fisted the loose torn fabric of her dress to hold her in place. Shifting to the side, I used my other arm to vigorously continue her punishment. Raising my arm over and over again, I reveled in the red handprints that began to appear on her pale skin. She squirmed and screamed, but I refused to relent. I loved the feel of her soft, heated skin beneath my palm.

"Beg me to fuck you," I shouted over her screams.

She refused to answer. Pressing with the hand that held her down by her dress, I forced her hips open even wider as they slipped over the edge of the leather horse. The position also spread her ass cheeks and left the delicate folds of her cunt vulnerable.

Directing my aim, I landed the next blow over her pussy.

"Stop! It hurts! Stop!" she cried.

"You know how to make it stop."

I spanked her pussy harder, wanting the lips to swell and pulse so when I finally entered her, she would feel every thick inch.

"Stop!

"Beg me to fuck you."

Yelena let out a howl instead of answering.

This time, I directed my aim to her even more vulnerable asshole. Using my two middle fingers, I gave the puckered entrance a series of harsh taps, watching as the soft pink turned a bright red. Her ass cheeks trembled as she desperately tried to clench them closed but her open, straddle position over the horse prevented her.

"Ow! Oh God! That hurts! Please stop!"

"I'm only going to ask you one more time before I get my belt. Beg me to fuck you."

"Oh God! Fuck me. Fuck me hard," she called out as she bent forward, pushing her ass into my palm.

Releasing her dress, I positioned myself behind her and unzipped my pants. I finally released my painfully erect cock. Fisting my shaft, I gave it a few pumps to relieve the building tension. With my other hand on the small of her back, I edged my hips closer. The height of the pommel horse was perfect. The brown leather covering between her legs showed a large dark wet stain from her reluctant arousal. Sliding my four fingers over her swollen and sore pussy, I coated my hand before running it down and up the length of my cock. Inching closer, I pushed the head of my cock against her asshole.

Yelena bucked. "No! Not there!"

"I don't know a better way to prove to you that your ass is literally mine," I bit back.

I shifted my hips forward, watching as the head forced its way past her clenching anus. The skin around her hole whitened and smoothed as it was forced to accept the thick intrusion.

Yelena cried out.

Undeterred, I thrust forward.

I took a sick pleasure in seeing the heavy shaft of my cock disappear into her ass. Knowing that her arousal was barely enough to slick the way. Knowing it would cause her pain that was only barely tinged by pleasure. This wasn't for her. It was for me. I needed this. I needed this ultimate possession to cool the primal rage which still coursed through my veins. Moving back, I thrust forward, pistoning in and out of her body.

Yelena groaned. Her white knuckles clutched at the metal handlebar.

I grabbed hold of her ass cheeks. The red punished skin felt hot on my palms.

Yelena hissed in pain.

Still I thrust.

Her body clenched around my shaft like a vise. I could feel every tremble, every ripple of muscle.

"Where's my cock?"

Yelena moaned.

I gave her left cheek a quick swat and gritted my teeth at the rush of sensation up my shaft as her body responded by clenching even harder.

"Where's my cock?"

"In my ass," she whimpered.

"Louder," I barked.

"In my ass," she sobbed. "Please come! Please, I can't take much more."

Taking pity on my babygirl, I reached between her legs and pushed two fingers into her cunt. I could feel the movement of my cock through the thin layer of skin that separated them. I stroked my fingers in and out in a slow rhythm. Yelena's hips raised as a low groan escaped her lips.

"That's it, baby. Come for me. Come while my cock is deep in your ass."

Yelena whimpered again as I pushed a third finger in. I knew between my cock in her ass and my fingers in her pussy, she was feeling stretched to the point of breaking. I began to thrust more violently. Her body shifted back and forth on the pommel horse as she absorbed the force.

"Oh God! Oh God!"

Her cunt spasmed around my fingers. I thrust into her several more times before releasing a thick stream of seed deep into her ass.

Yelena collapsed fully onto the horse, her arms hanging lax on the sides.

I pulled my slackening cock free, liking the sight of my seed as it dripped from her now-gaping hole. Circling around to the side of the pommel horse, I used the edge of my knuckle to raise up her chin.

"Who's my dirty babygirl?"

Yelena's lips quirked. "I really fucking hate you."

"I know, baby."

CHAPTER 37

Damien
Washington, D.C.

"You're an idiot."

"I know."

Gregor shook his head. "What were you thinking?"

I raised my glass and stared down at the amber contents for a moment before taking a sip. "Probably the same thing you were thinking before you dragged old-as-dirt Judge Matthews onto a plane to marry you and Samara."

"Fair enough."

Gregor stood and crossed to the sideboard where a tray of crystal decanters was displayed. He picked up the one which held my preferred drink of Macallan Rare scotch. Lifting it up, he turned and raised an eyebrow.

I nodded.

He crossed back to me and topped off my drink before

pouring himself another. Setting the decanter on a side table between the two of us, he sat back down across from me in the large, oxblood leather armchairs before the fire in his living room. Yelena and I had arrived a few hours earlier. The girls were upstairs in Gregor's bedroom filling each other in on the past three years.

Gregor held his glass up to the light of the fire. "This stuff isn't half bad."

My mouth quirked in a halfhearted smile. I stared past him at the red star on his yolka tree.

It was easy to imagine Yelena crouching beneath its spruce branches rifling through gold and green wrapped presents to hand one to each of our children. Her beautiful hair would be pulled back into a loose ponytail. Around her neck would be the Cartier diamond necklace I had given her the night before on Christmas Eve when the children were tucked into their beds, and we were sharing a quiet drink before the fire. It all seemed so real to me. So normal. I wanted that for my future. I wanted that life. I wanted her.

I realized now in my haste to secure her to my side, I had seriously fucked up. I had made her feel as if she and her future weren't worth any effort on my part.

"Were you really still covered in blood and mud from killing that bastard Santiago?"

I rubbed my eyes with my hand and groaned. "Yes."

"Well, what are you going to do about it?"

"Hell if I know. Any advice big brother?"

"Jewelry. Lots of expensive jewelry."

"I hope you're not implying you purchased my affections so easily?"

Both of us stood as Samara entered the room.

The change in Gregor's demeanor was startling. The energy in the room shifted. He wrapped his arm around her waist and gave her a quick kiss on the mouth. "Trust me, malýshka, there was absolutely nothing *easy* about finally making you mine."

She gave him a playful slap against his chest. Then wrapped her hand around his neck and leaned up to give him another kiss. Then she whispered against his mouth, "Yes, but I was worth it."

Gregor stroked her hair. "Yes, my love. You were definitely worth it."

The true depth of my mistake became more apparent to me. I had made Yelena feel as if she and our future weren't worth any effort on my part. No proper proposal. No ring. A half-assed shotgun wedding where I hadn't even bothered to wash the blood off my hands.

Samara cast a glance at me. "Did you tell him he's an idiot?"

Like the dutiful husband he had quickly become, Gregor nodded. "Yes, wife. Several times."

"Tell him again." She then turned to me. "It's pretty obvious to Nadia and me the way Yelena is colorfully cursing your name up there that she obviously loves you."

I started to rise. "Maybe I should go talk to her."

Samara shook her head. "I wouldn't recommend it just yet. She's still pacing back and forth and ranting. She won't stop flipping her pink stiletto knife open and closed every time she says your name."

Dammit. I knew I shouldn't have given that knife back to her.

Samara crossed over to the same sideboard and grabbed a bottle of red wine from the cabinet below. She then slipped the stems of three crystal glasses between her fingers. "I just came down to grab some wine."

Gregor cleared his throat. "Not for *all* of you?"

Samara leaned up on her toes and gave him a kiss on the cheek. "I'm having cranberry juice."

He gave her smack on the ass as she turned to walk away. "Good girl."

I raised my glass as a toast to them both. "That was fast."

Gregor returned to his chair. "It's still way too soon. We have a doctor's appointment next week. We're not telling anyone officially just yet."

I looked at him thoughtfully. "You're going to make a great father."

He swirled the contents of his glass, letting the ice cubes rattle against the crystal. "Well, our father set the bar pretty low."

"There's no reason why his or our sins should rest on your son's shoulders. We can change the future. We both have more money than God. There's no reason to continue down this path if we don't want to."

"Perhaps. And don't let Samara hear you say it's going to be a boy. She's wishing for a girl. Probably just to torture me."

I laughed. "The great Gregor Ivanov tamed by a woman and a little baby girl."

I could just imagine what a fiercely protective father he would be to his daughter. I pitied any man who came near her… let alone tried to date her.

"Don't laugh too hard. From where I'm sitting, you're in lockstep right behind me, little brother."

I raised my glass again. "To the women in our lives. May they happily torture us till our dying day."

We both drank.

Gregor rested his glass on his knee. "Speaking of the women in our lives, have you talked with Nadia yet?"

My brow furrowed. "Not yet. There hasn't been any time. Besides, when I walked through the door with Yelena, I was the last person she wanted to talk to. Those two hugged and screamed and immediately ran upstairs like two teenagers to find Samara."

"She's pissed at me. I've put her on lockdown. Won't let her go to that jewelry store of hers."

My brow furrowed. "Why?"

"I didn't want to tell you over the phone. That nastiness with Samara's parents. Before she died, her mother hinted that Egor Novikoff was going to come after Nadia after I deprived him of Samara."

I leaned back in my chair. "Fuck."

"Egor's in Russia right now, and I haven't been able to find anything to substantiate it, but I've taken some precautions just to be on the safe side."

"Like what?"

"I had Mikhail wire up some additional security cameras inside her shop," he said quickly before draining his glass. "That way we can monitor her when I finally allow her to return to it."

I whistled. He had the decency to at least look abashed. We both knew how Nadia felt about us being overprotective. She had suffered through a childhood being surrounded by bodyguards and constantly being told she couldn't do things her friends could simply because she was an Ivanov. Now that she was in her twenties and our father was dead, she liked our interference in her life even less. "And what does our illustrious Head of Security say about all this?"

"Mikhail? Hell, he wanted to do worse! He argued for me to send her away to some convent in the mountains of Switzerland until we could take care of Egor. He's pissed. He thinks I'm not taking the threat seriously enough."

The fire had started to die. I stood and lifted the iron poker near the fireplace and jabbed it into a smoldering log. Using the poker, I shifted it into a better position on top of the pile of logs where it would catch flame. "Well, he's always had a *special* interest in Nadia."

"I'm aware."

"Does he still understand it's not possible?"

Gregor nodded. "He knows this is about family honor and nothing personal."

"Maybe it's time we arranged for Nadia's marriage to someone we trust?"

"Yes, I agree. After the holidays we'll start vetting candidates."

We clinked glasses. With that settled, my mind returned to Yelena.

I sat and stared at the fire as a log popped and crackled before catching. The orange and crimson flames were reflected in the glass I was holding.

I sighed. "I'm an idiot."

Gregor just laughed.

CHAPTER 38

*Y*elena

I RETURNED to the guest bedroom where I had been staying in Gregor and Samara's house for the past week. Damien had not been pleased, but I insisted. I needed time to think… and space. When I was around him, it was hard to know my own mind. He was just so big and overwhelming and strong. The man radiated masculine energy. It was hard to resist.

On my bed was a large black box wrapped with a glittering gold ribbon.

Damien.

He had been leaving gifts for me all week. Each gift accompanied by my daily horoscope. All suspiciously pointing to a future alliance with a Scorpio mate.

Attached to the ribbon was a cream vellum tag with

gold foil. In his deeply slanted, masculine writing was today's horoscope.

The moon is in the seventh house, and Jupiter is aligned with Mars.

Now is the perfect time to align your star with Scorpio.

I'm pretty sure half of that was taken from that *Aquarius* song. Still, it was sweet.

Lifting the lid, I pushed aside the cream tissue paper and gasped. I pulled a gown out, pressed it to my chest, and twirled about the room. It was a black sheer tulle gown from Valentino's recent Spring collection. Embroidered over the long ruffled skirt and empire waist hem were incredibly elaborate zodiac signs and stars. It was perfect.

The gifts had a theme. All pointing to a future together.

First, there was the Cartier Diamond Destinee necklace. It was a stunning five carat diamond surrounded by pave diamonds on a delicate gold necklace.

Next, there were the first-class tickets to Paris just in time for the Spring shows. Included with the tickets was a letter from the head seamstress for Yves Saint Laurent agreeing to meet Damien and me for lunch to discuss a possible internship for me.

Finally, there were the two tickets for a performance of the National Symphony Orchestra for tonight. It was for a concert of Tchaikovsky's best-known works.

It would be the first time I was actually seeing him in a week.

I twirled around the room again.

* * *

I COULD HEAR his deep voice downstairs in the entryway. Despite growing up mostly in America, he still had a sexy Russian accent. I just loved the way he rolled his Rs.

He looked up as I stepped onto the landing above him.

Even from a distance, I could see his dark sapphire eyes glitter with desire as he watched me slowly descend the staircase. I swished my hips a bit so that the long ruffled skirt fanned out around me with each step.

He looked so handsome in his tuxedo. Just as I imagined he would. The perfectly tailored coat emphasized the hard planes of his chest and broad shoulders. The glimpse of his tattoos added a seductive hint of danger. Although unlike what I'd imagined all those years ago, because this time it wasn't some faceless model on his arm — it was me.

As I got closer, his expression changed. His jaw tightened as his brow furrowed.

I stopped right in front of him. Instead of telling me how beautiful I looked in the dress he'd bought me, he scowled as his gaze went from the top of my head to my toes and back, only to then settle on my breasts.

Damien stretched his arm out and pointed upstairs. "You're not going out in that. Go up and change."

Grasping the gossamer tulle fabric of my skirt I spread out my arms and twirled. "What are you talking about? I love it! It fits perfectly."

A muscle ticked in his cheek. "I mean it, Yelena. I'm ordering you to go upstairs and change."

I pointed my finger at him and jabbed it in his chest. "You're *ordering* me? *You're* the one who got me this dress!"

"Obviously"— his gaze traveled pointedly to my chest —"that was a mistake."

I looked down.

Realization dawned. The dress *was* a little see-through. Although not blatant, in the right light you could make out the outline of my breasts and just the slightest hint of nipple. I, of course, wasn't wearing a bra. The provocative glimpse of flesh was part of the haute couture allure of the dress. That is what designer fashion was about, pushing boundaries. Apparently, Damien hadn't realized this when he'd bought it for me.

I placed my fists on my hips. "I'm not changing."

He crossed his arms over his chest. "And I'm not letting another man see you in that dress."

We stood there staring each other down. Finally, Damien ran a hand through his hair and cursed low in Russian. One of these days, I was going to have to learn Russian curse words so I knew what he was always saying about me. Letting out an angry breath, he ordered, "Wait here. I'll be back."

He started to storm off and then swiftly turned. Without saying a word, he grabbed the small gold beaded clutch from my hand. Opening up the latch, he pulled the two symphony tickets out and, with a pointed look at me, he placed them in the inside jacket pocket of his tuxedo.

He then turned and left.

Angry that he had once again read my mind and deprived me of the dramatic gesture of attending the symphony without him, I stomped off to find Nadia and Samara and a glass of wine.

Thirty minutes later, Damien returned. Carrying a black garment bag into the kitchen, he tossed it onto the counter near the stool where I was sitting. He unzipped it and pulled out one of the most magnificent garments I'd ever seen.

It was a capelet, designed to delicately drape over your shoulders while not obstructing too much of your gown. This one was made entirely of glossy black feathers with the tips dipped in shimmering gold.

"Oh my God!"

Damien lifted it and placed it over my shoulders. "A feathered cape for my malen'kiy padshiy angel." He gently placed his warm palms against my neck as he lifted my curled hair out from beneath the capelet and swept it behind my shoulders.

He snapped the gold and diamond clasp closed over my breasts then took a step back. He surveyed me from head to toe then nodded his approval. He then stepped close and offered me his arm. Placing my hand in the crook of his elbow, I let him lead me out to his car.

Giving him a sidelong glance, I asked, "So how does it feel to have to compromise?"

He gave me a playful growl. "I don't like it one bit. Don't get used to it."

After taking our seats in a box at the Kennedy Center, Damien fidgeted through the entire suite from *Sleeping Beauty*.

Covering my mouth with my program, I leaned over and asked, "Are you okay?"

He ran his hands down his thighs. "Fine. I'm just sitting here thinking about you in that damn dress."

I placed my hand on his thigh. Inching it further, I could feel the hard ridge of his cock as it pressed against his tuxedo trousers. Now I was the one fidgeting and squirming in my seat. Images of him flipping up my skirt and unzipping his pants right here and now in front of all these people floated across my mind. I licked my lips.

A low growl emanated from Damien. "Dammit, woman. Don't lick your lips like that, or I swear to God I'm going to grab you by the waist and have you straddle my cock here and now."

My stomach flipped. And just because it had been a whole week since I could push his buttons, I ran the edge of my palm down his shaft.

Damien grabbed me

Pulling me onto his lap, he claimed my mouth in an act of pure possession. His tongue swept in to duel with mine the moment the symphony swelled to new heights as they played the intensely dramatic final moments of Swan Lake. My hand reached inside his jacket to caress the warm expanse of his chest through the thin silk of his shirt. His hard arousal pressed into my hip. Uncaring of the audience seated quietly below our balcony, I reached between us for the zipper of his pants.

Just as our balcony was flooded with light.

Breaking our kiss, we both turned but were blinded by the theater spotlight trained directly on us.

"Oh my God!" I buried my face against his neck.

This was beyond humiliating. I was about to be

thrown out of the Kennedy Center for a lewd act in public. I'd never be able to go to a symphony again.

Damien chuckled as he rubbed my back. "Baby, look up."

"No," I murmured, my voice muffled by his shoulder.

He placed a finger under my chin and forced my gaze to his. "I promise. It's not what you think."

Placing his hands around my waist, he lifted me off his lap and onto my feet. He then stood. Hastening a quick glance to my right, I could see countless opera glasses trained on us as a wave of hushed whispers and coughs swept through the audience.

The pianist played the dark and ominous opening cords of Rachmaninoff's Piano Concerto Number Two. The song that was playing that infamous night in Damien's car. Confused, I turned my eyes back to Damien. This was supposed to be a concert of only Tchaikovsky.

He gave me a wink and reached into his jacket pocket, pulling out a small red leather and gold embossed Cartier box just as the violins began to play in earnest.

My hands covered my mouth as he slowly lowered to one knee. He opened the ring box which had the largest, most gorgeous diamond ring I had ever seen in my life.

The breath left my body.

"Oh my God!"

He clasped my shaking left hand and placed the ring on my finger. "I know sometimes it feels like the stars are against us. But you truly are my angel. You bring light and warmth to my world, and even though you challenge my patience and my sanity at times, I know that life will never be boring with you around. I want to be there for every smile, every laugh, and every kiss. I love you, so Yelena Marie Nikitina, will you do me the honor of becoming my wife?"

"Yes! Oh my God, yes!"

I wrapped my arms around his neck and kissed him as he rose to his feet and, placing his arms tightly around my waist, lifted me off the ground.

The audience sprang to their feet and broke into applause, several even whistling and cheering. The symphony started to play the Wedding March by Wagner.

"I love you," I declared over the rousing music and applause.

He cupped my cheek. "I know… just remember who said it first."

My mouth dropped open but before I could argue with him, he started to kiss me again.

Such a Scorpio thing to do!

EPILOGUE

Mikhail

Something was wrong.

I punched in the thirteen-digit code for the surveillance system.

Working off its default protocols, the computer immediately brought up my first priority project: codename Kroshka.

As the screens glowed to life, I scanned the numerous camera angles.

Her brothers knew of my surveillance. Nadia did not. I'm sure she would be madder than hell if she knew we'd been watching over her, even after she'd left her brother's house. She had wanted her independence and having this small apartment gave her a sense of that.

But that didn't mean I stopped protecting her.

I would never stop protecting her.

Anxiously, I clicked in the command to shuffle through the various security screens. All seemed quiet. Then I saw her cellphone plugged in on the tiny shelf near the cash register. That meant, she was somewhere on property, not at her brother's house tucked safely in bed like she was supposed to be. I continued to click through the security screens searching for her. If I didn't set eyes on her, it meant she was up in her apartment, either way I was going to head over there and drag her back to her brother's.

Finally, I found her.

She was alone tinkering with something at her workbench.

I shifted to the next screen which showed the outside of her jewelry shop.

I watched as a large SUV with no plates pulled up. Three men dressed all in black got out. They had ski masks over their faces, and one of them was tucking a handgun into his waistband.

Fuck.

She was completely unaware of the coming danger.

I was down in the garage and behind the wheel of my Maserati Levante SUV in less than two minutes. It would take me three excruciating minutes to reach Nadia.

I hit the steering wheel with my fist.

Goddamn it.

I had been a bastard and a fool.

The time for just standing in the background and watching Nadia from afar was over. I was finally going to claim her as mine.

ABOUT ZOE BLAKE

USA TODAY Bestselling Author in Dark Romance
She delights in writing Dark Romance books filled with overly-possessive Billionaires, Taboo scenes and Unexpected twists. She usually spends her ill-gotten gains on martinis, travel and red lipstick. Since she can barely boil water, she's lucky enough to be married to a sexy Chef.

ALSO BY ZOE BLAKE

RUSSIAN MAFIA SERIES

SWEET CRUELTY

Dimitri & Emma's story

It was an innocent mistake.

She knocked on the wrong door.

Mine.

If I were a better man, I would've just let her go.

But I'm not.

I'm a cruel bastard.

I ruthlessly claimed her virtue for my own.

It should have been enough.

But it wasn't.

I needed more.

Craved it.

She became my obsession.

Her sweetness and purity taunted my dark soul.

The need to possess her nearly drove me mad.

A Russian arms dealer had no business pursuing a naive librarian student.

She didn't belong in my world.

I would bring her only pain.

But it was too late…

She was mine and I was keeping her.

SAVAGE VOW
Gregor & Samara's story
Ivanov Crime Family Trilogy, Book One

I took her innocence as payment.

She was far too young and naïve to be betrothed to a monster like me.

I would bring only pain and darkness into her sheltered world.

That's why she ran.

I should've just let her go…

She never asked to marry into a powerful Russian mafia family.

None of this was her choice.

Unfortunately for her, I don't care.

I own her… and after three years of searching… I've found her.

My runaway bride was about to learn disobedience has consequences… punishing ones.

Having her in my arms and under my control had become an obsession.

Nothing was going to keep me from claiming her before the eyes of God and man.

She's finally mine… and I'm never letting her go.

VICIOUS OATH
Yelena & Damien's story
Ivanov Crime Family Trilogy, Book Two

When I give an order, I expect it to be obeyed.

She's too smart for her own good, and it's going to get her killed.

Against my better judgement, I put her under the protection of my powerful Russian mafia family.

So imagine my anger when the little minx ran.

For three long years I've been on her trail, always one step behind.

Finding and claiming her had become an obsession.

It was getting harder to rein in my driving need to possess her… to own her.

But now the chase is over.

I've found her.

Soon she will be mine.

And I plan to make it official, even if I have to drag her kicking and screaming to the altar.

This time… there will be no escape from me.

BETRAYED HONOR

Mikhail & Nadia's story

Ivanov Crime Family Trilogy, Book Three

Her innocence was going to get her killed.

That was if I didn't get to her first.

She's the protected little sister of the powerful Ivanov Russian mafia family - the very definition of forbidden.

It's always been my job, as their Head of Security, to watch over her but never to touch.

That ends today.

She disobeyed me and put herself in danger.

It was time to take her in hand.

I'm the only one who can save her and I will fight anyone who tries to stop me, including her brothers.

Honor and loyalty be damned.

She's mine now.

DARK OBSESSION SERIES

WARD

Dark Obsession, Book One

It should have been a fairytale...

A Billionaire Duke sweeps a poor American actress off her feet to a romantic,

isolated English estate.

A grand love affair... except this wasn't love.

It was obsession.

He had it all planned from the beginning, before I even knew he existed. He chose me.

I'm his unwilling captive, forced to play his sadistic game.

He is playing with my mind as well as my body.

Trying to convince me it is 1895, and I'm his obedient ward, subject to his rules and discipline.

Everywhere I look it is the Victorian era.

He says that my memories of a modern life are delusions

which need to be driven from my mind through punishment.

If I don't submit, he will send me back to the asylum.

I know it's not true... any of it... at least I think it's not.

The lines between reality and this nightmare are starting to blur.

If I don't escape now, I will be lost in his world forever.

It should have been a fairytale...

GILDED CAGE

Dark Obsession, Book Two

He's controlling, manipulative, dangerous... and I'm in love with him.

Rich and powerful, Richard is used to getting whatever he wants... and he wants me.

This isn't a romance. It's a dark and twisted obsession.

A game of ever-increasingly depraved acts.

Every time I fight it, he just pulls me deeper into his deception.

The slightest disobedience to his rules brings swift punishment.

My life as I knew it is gone. He now controls everything.

I'm caught in his web, the harder I struggle, the more entangled I become.

I no longer know my own mind.

He owns my body, making me crave his painful touch.

But the worst deception of all? He's made me love him.

If I don't break free soon, there will be no escape for me.

TOXIC

Dark Obsession , Book Three

In every story there is a hero and a villain… I'm both.

I will corrupt her beautiful innocence till her soul is as dark and twisted as my own.

With every caress, every taboo touch, I will captivate and ensnare her.

She's mine and no one is going to take her from me.

No matter how many times my little bird tries to escape, I will always give chase and bring her back to where she belongs, in my arms.

Each time she defies me, the consequences become more deadly.

I may not be the hero she wanted, but I'm the man she needs.

Printed in Great Britain
by Amazon